Praise for *Welcome Home, Stranger*

"Kate Christensen's eighth novel is a brief, brilliant story of grief and love. It's Job on me⸺ ⸺ ('Wh⸺ ⸺ I still here?' but without the biblical overt⸺ ⸺ It's the novel your husband should r⸺ ⸺ enopause. It's your coolest friend's m⸺ ⸺ om page one."

—*Minneapolis Star Tribune*

"Christensen is a psychological Geiger counter, registering every particle of emotion; a wizard at dialogue and redolent settings, and an intrepid choreographer of confoundment. From gasp-inducing absurdities and betrayals to a profound sense of our paralysis in the glare of climate change to a full-on embrace of family, love, home, and decency, Christensen's whirligig tale leaves readers dizzy with fresh and provocative insights."

—*Booklist* (starred review)

"With wit and a never-ending supply of humanity, Christensen's characters navigate anger, grief, frustration, and pain like we all do: by putting one foot in front of the other. And the result is a disarmingly genuine and nuanced portrait of living." —Amazon Best of the Month Pick

"If you're looking for some dysfunctional-family schadenfreude to sweeten your holidays, look no further." —*People*

"Reading Kate Christensen's incisive eighth novel, a quote from nineteenth-century author Ivan Turgenev came to mind: 'A poet must be a psychologist.' As evidenced in her previous works, Christensen is both. Her prose glimmers and glints, more sensation than exposition, whether she's shining her light on broken family, broken dreams, or our broken Earth. In this short but mighty novel, Christensen does a psychologist's job with a poet's lyrical pen." —*San Francisco Chronicle*

"A deeply endearing story about confronting one's past and constructing a new future—under extreme duress. . . . *Welcome Home, Stranger* . . . arrives at the most lovely ending of a novel I've read all year."

—*Washington Post*

"An astute novel of grief and reconciliation. . . . One of the joys of a Kate Christensen book is her signature exuberance. No one writes about excess and appetite with such gusto, making over-the-topness a mainstay. . . . By the end, this book satisfies on a number of fronts. It's about the pull of family you thought you knew, but didn't; of long-buried resentments and freshly minted ones, as well. As a meditation on grief, it is, by turns, raucous and fiery, despairing and resolute—and wittily entertaining throughout."   —*Portland Press Herald* (South Portland, Maine)

"Few writers have a wit as razor sharp as Kate Christensen's. . . . Her new novel follows an environmental journalist as she returns to her small Maine hometown after the death of her mother, and grapples with grief, family, and aging. I would trust no less deft a hand than Christensen's to manage the balance of humor, devastation, and squabbling."

—*Literary Hub*

"Our shelves could use more women like Rachel and Sam as a counterpoint to men in midlife who've dominated fiction for decades. . . . It's exhilarating to read an uninhibited female character who is rife with contradictions. . . . Christensen also does a skillful job of animating difficult family relationships while avoiding a conventional arc of forgiveness. . . . In the end, it is surprising to see where Rachel meets herself."

—*New York Times*

"Kate Christensen's new novel, *Welcome Home, Stranger,* is a revelation, offering characters as real as your family and friends, a rich, vividly drawn setting, grab-you-by-the-throat drama and always, lurking in the shadows, a fierce authorial intelligence. What more could you ask?"

—Richard Russo, author of *Somebody's Fool*

"A fantastic study in loss—the grief kind and the yearning too, oh my god the yearning! Plus menopause. Plus Portland, Maine. I loved it."

—Catherine Newman, author of *We All Want Impossible Things*

"To the great literature of going home again we can now add Kate Christensen's superb new novel *Welcome Home, Stranger,* a triumph of intelligence and wit (which will surprise none of her many fans). The prodigal here is a brilliant journalist grieving the loss of a very difficult mother while attempting peace with those she left behind: a resentful sister and an ex-lover who can be neither trusted nor forgotten. A spellbinding book from one of our best chroniclers of the very American struggle to strive for excellence while still living in community with others."

—Ann Packer, author of *The Children's Crusade*

"Rachel Calloway is a compelling heroine for the present moment—angry, honest, independent, witty, brilliant, and in pain. She sometimes makes impulsive choices, but her integrity is always intact. This is the most contemporary novel I have ever read, and I immersed myself in Rachel's Portland, Maine, her family and friends, her knowledge of coming climate catastrophes, and her confusion about where home is for her. Then suddenly, I realized that I was reading about the entire human condition, portrayed in crystal sentences I will return to many times. *Welcome Home, Stranger* is a novel for now and for the ages."

—Alice Elliott Dark, author of *Fellowship Point* and *In the Gloaming*

"This snarky, vulnerable, complicated main character feels so real, you'll swear you actually know her."　　　　　　　　　　　　　—*Real Simple*

"In her eighth novel, Kate Christensen writes about a woman losing her mother in the context of middle age, a fifty-something who returns home after the loss and yet is contending with all the funny things in life. Vivid, real, and leaving you with a chuckle, this is an uplifting story about the inevitability of life's changes and the attitude required to get through."

—Katie Couric Media

"An intricate novel, exploring family, mothers and daughters, and the choices we make."　　　　　　　　　　　　　　　　　—Lee Woodruff

"A satisfying, intimate novel about complicated people at middle age, coming to terms with lost love, and the ghosts who shaped your life."

—*Boston Globe*

"Christensen skillfully portrays the issues at play in many families: there are deep bonds, but also deep resentments, 'volcanic' emotions, and decades-old misunderstandings. The character Lucie, an immature, thwarted tyrant, is particularly well drawn. Readers in search of an engrossing family drama will find much to like."　　　—*Publishers Weekly*

ALSO BY KATE CHRISTENSEN

Welcome Home, Stranger

A NOVEL

Kate Christensen

HARPER PERENNIAL

NEW YORK • LONDON • TORONTO • SYDNEY • NEW DELHI • AUCKLAND

HARPER PERENNIAL

A hardcover edition of this book was published in 2023 by Harper, an imprint of HarperCollins Publishers.

FIRST HARPER PERENNIAL EDITION PUBLISHED 2024.

Designed by Kyle O'Brien

The Library of Congress has catalogued the hardcover edition as follows:
Names: Christensen, Kate, author.
Title: Welcome home, stranger : a novel / Kate Christensen.
Description: First edition. | New York, NY : Harper, 2023.
Identifiers: LCCN 2023013189 | ISBN 9780063299702 (hardcover) |
ISBN 9780063299726 (ebook)
Subjects: LCGFT: Novels.
Classification: LCC PS3553.H716 W45 2023 | DDC 813/.54—
dc23/eng/20230606
LC record available at https://lccn.loc.gov/2023013189

978-0-06-329971-9 (pbk.)

24 25 26 27 28 LBC 5 4 3 2 1

For Brendan

Part I

One

My mother died two days ago. Or was it three? My sense of time has been wonky ever since I got back from the Arctic, long-term jet lag sustained by too many sixteen-hour days transcribing my notes, writing on deadline. I know she died in the evening, or maybe late afternoon, because I was still at work and the sun had just set when I got off the phone with my sister and went out into the parking lot to wander around, in shock, staring at the trees and the headlights on Annapolis Avenue beyond the fence. What do you do when your mother dies?

You get on a plane and go home.

I catch my breath as I buckle myself into my booked-last-minute middle seat, wishing I could shrinkydink myself into a pellet of inert nonsentient organic matter and roll passively around the synthetic upholstery until the ground cleaning crew plucks me up and throws me away with the rest of the flight's detritus. My head feels like it's on fire. The skin on my face is giving off enough therms to liquefy a glacier. My brain is shorting out and sparking at random. I stayed at the office all night to finish my final edits, alone in a pool of fluorescence in the wee hours, my brain lit up like a casino, with that familiar, ceaseless high crystal ringing of slot machines in my inner ear, tinnitus. I filed my piece just before eight this morning, drove my rattletrap Hyundai through rush-hour traffic from Fort Meade to my condo in Foggy Bottom to throw some things into a roller bag, and then got back into my car and crawled to Dulles, caught in a collision-caused clusterfuck of looky-loos. I arrived panting at the gate exactly in time to board my flight, not one minute to spare. My jeans are flecked with lint, my eyes are gritty, my teeth skuzzy, my hair a cloud of chaos. Even the protective glass face of my smartphone is greasy with finger-prints and smeared gunk. I look and feel exactly like what I am: a middle-aged childless recently orphaned menopausal workaholic journalist.

At least the people on either side of me seem to be minding their own business. People do, these days, these polarized days of communal dwell-ing in private virtual worlds. I dart my eyes to the aisle seat on my left and behold tattoos on plump bone-white forearms, iridescent peacock dye streaking punk-cut hair, gender not exactly indeterminate, gazing into an iPhone, plugged into earbuds. They used to call themselves baby dykes, I remember with sudden fond nostalgia for both the term and the concept. I imagine this person might find the term offensive along with all the rest of my outmoded Gen X slang, habits, and attitudes.

On my right is a late-sixtysomething lady wearing a tailored pink button-down shirt with khaki slacks. Reading glasses, short iron-gray hair, a thick paperback in her tidy trim lap. Cape Elizabeth or Falmouth, the inside of her skull like a stationery store, everything neatly in its bin, no mess, no dust. She makes me think of my fourth-grade teacher, Mrs. Marengo, who told me to stop wasting time chattering with my friends and focus more on my schoolwork. To this day, I thank her for slapping me awake at the age of nine, setting my life on its course.

A flight attendant marches down the aisle, whacking overhead bin doors shut. She doesn't tell us to put our phones in airplane mode. They don't care anymore. The phones have won. I close my eyes and lean my head back as the plane takes off, exhaling a stream of pent-up breath. I feel as if there's a wick in my scalp, sucking up oil and igniting into pure fire, lower levels of estrogen and progesterone sending my temperature-regulation systems into disarray, my hypothalamus demanding heat in a paradoxical effort to cool me down. It's the same process that's occurring on a global scale. I feel the way the planet must feel, stressed, toxic, out of control.

I turn on the overhead air nozzle and aim the hard cool stream at my scalp, cool down the poles, that's how you fix it, and slip into the human equivalent of airplane mode, a long blank time. The white roar of the engines mutes the shitshow I left behind me as well as the shitshow I'm flying toward. Eyes closed, I hang suspended in this calm, empty present, surrounded by docile strangers in a tube of metal zooming north through a clear sky.

When I open my eyes again, we're descending over thick pine forests rolling to meet the hard metallic skin of the Atlantic Ocean, glinting in the sunlight. A small, sneaky pang of emotion surges in my stomach as the plane bumps to the ground. Coming back to Maine is complicated. No one is prouder or more defensive of the place than a native daughter who went away somewhere bigger to seek her fortune. But along with my pride is something else, a small quailing dread, the knowledge that I'm an outsider here. The people I left behind, the ones who've white-knuckled it through all the winters I've missed, hacking at icy driveways and shelling out most of their income for heating oil, might think I feel superior to my own people now. And they'd be mostly right, but the rest of me feels an irrational yearning to belong here again.

In the orderly, logical sequence everyone in the world still seems to cling to even as we tumble further into chaos everywhere else, we file, seat by seat, row by row, off the plane and down the ramp with the Welcome Home sign flanked by a lobster and a moose. I pull my roller bag through the glass revolving door, and there's Celeste in her black Mercedes SUV, parked at the curb right in front. I see her tense expression through the windshield, eyes beady, neck craning in that way I know so well, preparing herself to greet me.

I wave at her, and her expression morphs instantly, a big hard smile, a zealous windshield-wiper wave back. She leaps from the car and bowls me over with the force of her hug. "You're *here*," she says on a funny breathy hiccup that catches and bursts. I can feel her skull pressed against mine. In spite of everything, I love this person with every cell in my body. We lean into each other, and I can feel her shaking with sobs as strong as hard laughter. After a moment, we pull apart. She wipes her eyes.

"Is this all?" she asks, helping me stow my bag in the wayback, tossing it as if it weighs nothing. My sister, who looks droopy and without turgor, a frail lily, has always been far stronger than I am, a stealth Amazon. "Aren't you here for two weeks?"

"This is everything," I say.

I'm an anomaly in our three-person family, now reduced to two. Our mother, Lucie Gautreau Calloway Johnson Michaud, came at life with a cosmopolitan woman-of-the-world confidence, jaunty and high-handed, whether she was tying on a gauzy, tacky Reny's scarf or professing undying admiration for a famous but mediocre artist or proudly bringing to the dinner table a deeply terrible dish. Her own devil-may-care naïveté was nothing she ever seemed to be remotely aware of. Lucie was a kook, and Celeste has always been one too, just with more self-awareness. Last time my sister came to visit me in DC, over a year ago, she brought with her, for a short weekend, an enormous squishy green behemoth of a suitcase with no wheels and a clamshell top that snapped shut with clamps. She lugged it around as if it weighed nothing, as if it were a perfectly normal thing to own.

Now, Lucie dead, Celeste and I over a half-century old, I feel queasily implicated, thinking about that green suitcase. What makes me think I'm not exactly as much of a gawky provincial kook as my mother and sister? Of course I am. The difference is that I spent my life aware of and trying to hide my own propensity for flamboyant weirdness while Lucie and Celeste happily swanned about, not caring, protected by arrogant bliss. I cultivate camouflaging drabness, not trusting myself to make good choices, given my family. I love luxurious beautiful things, but I wear almost no jewelry, no makeup, and my clothes and shoes are aggressively neutral and plain. And most of all, to counteract my mother and sister's histrionic gestures, even though my emotions often feel just as volcanic as theirs, just as outsize, terrifying in their seismic strength, I keep my tone modulated and crisp, say only things I know to be true. In other words, to avoid showing my own green suitcase, sloppy and lavish and dramatic, I squeeze myself into a small generic black roller bag. But I've never learned true moderation, only tamped-down self-abnegation, and that, more than anything else, makes me know I am exactly like my sister and mother, just nowhere near as free.

"I'm glad you're here," my sister says as she navigates us out of the Portland Jetport's system of roads. I hear a "finally" hanging in the air between us, but she lets it remain there, unsaid. "It's been crazy lately, really."

"I can imagine." It feels as inadequate as it sounds.

Celeste sobs once and stops herself, visibly holding back a tsunami of emotion. She swerves right onto Congress. An oncoming car honks at her. I'm holding onto the armrest, as if that would save me in a collision. She even drives like Lucie did.

I behold my sister with the usual bemused pleasure her appearance gives me. Even at her most melodramatic, she's dauntingly appealing to look at. Since adolescence, she's been a younger, better version of me: same thick hair, lean build, and facial bone structure, but her boobs are bigger, legs longer, cheekbones higher, lips fuller. She's the glossy, updated 2.0 me, all the bugs worked out, with better features. And even more than she resembles me, she looks like our mother, the same small jaw and wide cheekbones and deep-set slanted eyes.

"How are you?" I ask her. "Are you sleeping okay?"

"No, I'm exhausted," she says. "Mostly worried about Mallory. She's taking Mom's death hard. Her last grandparent."

"What about Jasper?"

"I don't know, stoic. I can never really tell how he feels."

"I'm sure he's sad, too."

"We all are. Since Mom died, everything feels so strange and dire. It's like the roof over our heads just blew off."

I know what she's really saying, underneath all this. She's upset that I didn't come home sooner, hurt and mad and baffled. She can't accuse me yet, and I can't explain yet, but we'll get to it, it's looming. "Me too," I manage to say, but my voice is flat. I'm smacked by the ancient familiarity of these dusty little stores along lower Congress, the hill-perching old houses, pedestrians heaving themselves through the bleak northern sunlight.

"She left you her town house," says Celeste. "In her will. She left you all her belongings."

"What did she leave you?"

"Her money. Not that there was much left. Not that I need it." She sounds brittle and hurt. "The point is, Rachel, Mom left you her place. I thought you'd like to know."

"I have no idea what to make of this fact," I say.

"Maybe she thought she was giving you a way to come home if you ever need to."

"If so, that would be the most motherly thing she ever did for me in my life. Why didn't she leave it to your kids?"

"I would say ask her that," says Celeste. "But she's gone."

Out of nowhere, I remember a phrase Celeste used to describe our mother. She was young when she said it, maybe twelve. "She has a diseased ego," she said to me after Lucie ripped all the clothes out of her bureau, threw them onto her bed, raced to her car, and drove off somewhere, leaving my sister and me alone to eat the supper we'd made, no doubt Campbell's tomato soup garnished with crumbled saltines, sitting at our Formica table in the chilly little Biddeford house. I found it a striking insight at the time, and I still do. How did Celeste know those words, that concept? It comes back to me with the force of truth. My sister always knew things about our mother somehow, in a way I couldn't. I always hoped for more from Lucie, always searched for something in her that she didn't have, that wasn't there, while my sister saw her clearly and accepted her for who she was.

Celeste steers into her garage and turns off the engine. In the sudden darkened silence, we exchange a look, our faces raw and open, and then the instant passes and we get out.

My sister lives in the West End of Portland, a grid of tree-lined streets studded with brick mansions and pocket mansions and mini-mansions and town houses, garnished with decadently ornate nineteenth-century flourishes—floor-to-ceiling bay windows, slate mansard roofs, three-story towers, glassed-in sleeping porches, turrets, and all the other opulent architectural traits of bourgeois grandiosity left over from the golden age of this little port town.

My sister's house is as grand as any of them. She and her husband, Neil, are entrenched in their middle-aged lives with teenage twins, Mallory and Jasper, and a pair of designer dogs I've only seen in Celeste's Instagram posts, cockerdoodles or cockapoos or maybe it's the same thing, Sassy and Daisy, adorable muppetlike creatures with brown button eyes, as shaggy and fluffy as a pair of Ugg boots.

The West End, as described by Celeste through the years for my amusement, is filled with other people like her and Neil, rich middle-aged couples with teenage kids and designer dogs. The women are engaged in the usual stuff of their generation, hypervigilant parenting, exercise regimens, social media, charity events, chairing boards of arts organizations, and sexual affairs with the martini-swilling hockey dads who are their friends' husbands. At the nearby expensive private academy, where their kids learn to respect ethnic and sex and religious differences and to speak Mandarin and Arabic, they are not allowed to read *Huckleberry Finn* or *Lolita*, two books I devoured at either end of adolescence and was buoyed and sustained by. Celeste loves to mock this world, even as she participates in it, the perennial outsider. Apparently, she has told me with wide, laughing eyes, amazed by this realm where she feels like Cinderella playing the part of a queen, there is a generalized parental fear of "hoboes" roaming these streets at night, looking for young white flesh to molest. So teenage kids aren't allowed to walk the few quiet leafy blocks between one another's gigantic houses. To keep their precious lily-white babies safe, she informed me, their parents actually load them into SUVs and ferry them back and forth. To augment this coddling, they are all, Mallory and Jasper included, provided with SAT tutors and language coaches, SSRIs and antidepressants and Ritalin, special meals tailored to their many allergies and intolerances.

Whenever Celeste talks about her cohort and its ways, we both laugh out loud, but we also marvel at these kids' good fortune. When we were barely older than Mallory is now, we hitchhiked from Biddeford to Old Orchard Beach on summer weekends, catching rides with skeevy older dudes we were too dumb and naive to be afraid of, and our mother certainly wasn't worried. Nor did she check on our homework, let alone hire tutors to help us with it. We both got ourselves into, and put ourselves through, college. Celeste met Neil and escaped from poverty through marrying him, and I put myself through college and grad school and never lived in Maine again. But look, we both survived. Lucie was a neglectful, problematic mother by any standards, but she also taught us certain skills, the most valuable of which might have been the ability to land on our feet.

As soon as my sister steps from the enclosed cave of her SUV, I can feel her snap back into the armor of her identity, mistress of this small fiefdom, its queen and center. I also feel her hard, brusque repudiation of me, which I deserve; the time for me to explain my absence, assuming I even could, has passed. I can feel the shift in the air between us. She doesn't have to say a word. My antennae are as hyperattuned to my sister's frequency as hers are to mine.

We cross the grass and enter the kitchen through the side door. As I greet my brother-in-law, who leaps up from a stool at the kitchen counter to give me a stiff, one-armed hug, then say hello to my niece and nephew, who burst into the kitchen and fling their adolescent bodies at me and burst right out again with my roller bag, I can feel Celeste's eyes on me, imbuing my presence in her house with all the things she most fears and wants and can't articulate. Now that I'm here among her family and possessions and life, she looks at it all through my eyes, assumes I'm judging her, and resents me for it. This entire drama takes place entirely in her head. I can do or say nothing to short-circuit it. She's uncomfortable, I imagine, because she thinks I scorn her way of life, look askance at it from the vantage point of our shared history and my own so-called professional achievements. Neil is awash in family money and calls himself a writer but has no need of a profession. Celeste has not held any sort of job since her college work-study program.

But the truth is that I'm proud of her. My little sister, the daughter of a grifter junkie deadbeat father and a criminally neglectful mentally ill mother, married a genuine Maine prince, inasmuch as such a thing can exist—not a blue-blooded Boston Brahmin, not a nouveau riche Masshole interloper—a native son, one of us. In the olden days, when abundant schools of oily little fish like herring and kippers teemed in the formerly cold, rich seas off Maine's coast, Matthew Baxter Bailey was the Canned Fish King of Maine. Everyone who grew up in coastal Maine knows the legends and jokes and stories about him. So Neil Bailey's money is old, authentic, local, and he shares it all with my little sister, his wife. And my niece and nephew are the heirs to all that money. Celeste, the younger daughter of Tommy Calloway and Lucie Gautreau, pulled that off. And she didn't have to fake anything. She genuinely loves the guy.

"You remember Molly Driscoll," Celeste is saying offhandedly. "Right?" We're on the third floor in the largest of the three guest rooms, which has its own bathroom. She's plucking the oatmeal linen and pale-green silk ornamental throw pillows from the bed and throwing them onto the equally elegant fainting couch under the dormer windows. Celeste's house is regularly redone top to bottom by professional decorators to keep up with changing styles, because my sister doesn't trust her own "tacky taste," as she puts it, in part to make me laugh, but I know she means it. She's insecure. She's Lucie's daughter. If it were up to our mother, every room would have chintz drapes and off-white wall-to-wall carpet and Lucite and chrome everywhere, our mother's unchanging ideas of classy décor that Celeste can't trust herself to transcend. I can't either, which is why my own place is all bare hardwood floors and white walls and accordion blinds and utilitarian furniture. Celeste's house is a photo-ready palace, mine is a Spartan barracks, but we're both compensating for the exact same tendencies.

"I have no idea who Molly Driscoll is."

"She married David Mansfield about two months ago."

David.

She's waiting for my reaction, but I can't answer. I've just been sucker-punched hard in the gut.

"Oh," I say, finally.

"He didn't tell you?" Her face, turning to me, is alight with avid, vindictive curiosity.

I cave in on myself like a stomped-on puffball, exhaling shocked dust. The smell of the lavender candle by the guest bed makes me light-headed. "David and I haven't been in touch in ten years."

"Oh. For some reason I just assumed you guys were still close." This sounds innocent enough on the surface but is in fact a blatant attempt to inflict a body blow, because Celeste knows perfectly well who David was to me.

I know she knows I know, and the blow has landed. I give her the point. "Who is Molly Driscoll?"

"*Molly*," says Celeste. "My best friend. Molly and David live next door. They're coming over for dinner in a little while."

"Oh," I say, hoisting my roller bag onto the trunk at the foot of the bed, busily unzipping it while I try to quell the lava eruption in my rib cage.

Celeste isn't finished yet. "She and Mom were so close at the end. In fact Molly was in the room with us when Mom died. She's been so heartbroken, she wants to be with us now."

"Okay," I say, panting gently. It's so hot up here. Sweat pools in the small of my back.

"Anyway," Celeste says, heading for the doorway, "we're all having drinks in the front parlor in about half an hour, so you have time to shower and change."

She leaves me gasping.

It's true that I haven't seen David in almost a decade. It is also true, I must admit, if only to myself and in the privacy of my own head, that I came here with the intention of seeing him—not just seeing him, having sex with him, in spite of our history and long estrangement, all the pain we inflicted on each other, if only to take temporary solace in a familiar body, get out of this hotbox of a skull I'm trapped in. David was my addiction once, and I need to relapse temporarily. But now that I know he's married, it's like learning my dealer is in prison. I'll have to find another source. I'm a little shocked by the strength of my disappointment.

I strip and get in the shower, letting the hot water stream over my head as I fixate on this Molly person, imagining the outline of a woman who resembles me, thin, dark-haired, olive-skinned. She's my body double, my replacement, she must be. I turn off the water and lean against the bathroom wall, dripping wet, hair streaming water down my back, almost blacking out with exhaustion. Swathed in one of Celeste's thick, oversize rich-person towels, I brush my teeth savagely enough to blast all the enamel off them, then brush my shoulder-length hair the same way, ripping the brush through wet skeins until my whole head tingles. I pull some clothes from my bursting suitcase: clean underwear, a charcoal-gray sweater dress that hangs on my frame like a sack, beat-up motorcycle boots. No bra. My tits are small and I don't need one and I hate wearing them. And I never use makeup because it makes me look like a drag queen; my face is too angular for it. But really, I'm dressing this way because I want Molly to see that I'm not competing with her. I can't.

As I make my way downstairs with still-wet hair, one of the fluffy yellow poodlecocks comes rushing up the stairs to sniff me.

"Hi, Sassy," I say.

"That's Daisy," says my niece, coming out of her own room and joining me on the landing. We start down the stairs together.

"Oh sorry. But they look identical."

"No, Aunt Rachel. Daisy is a puppy and Sassy is like twice as big."

Mallory's silky honey-blond hair is in a high ponytail, and she wears a pink hoodie and baggy jeans with an adorable hole in one knee. She has creamy airbrushed skin and fjord-blue eyes, a tall athletic body. I try to glimpse her through her prettiness. She's so young still, only fourteen, and there's nothing seared or etched on her yet, no evidence of the self-doubt or lifelong sense of dread I was born with. Her twin brother is the same. Jasper and Mallory, moving over the earth like Jotuns, Nordic giants. How did they both turn out so *tall*? The Gautreaus and Calloways are a bunch of stunted little shorties, and Neil's family aren't giants either. What is my sister feeding them?

"How are you doing, Mallory?"

"I'm sad about Mémé but okay actually."

Mémé is the name Celeste and Neil came up with for my mother, who despite being a Franco-American spoke no French, because the language was prohibited in Maine schools from 1919 until 1969. Anyway, this nickname isn't Celeste's way of reclaiming our stamped-out culture, she's just trying to be fancy because she has insecurity-born pretensions. The kids called their other grandmother Gam, which is pretty much the upscale

WASP version of Mémé. Meanwhile, Celeste and I called both sets of our own grandparents Grandma and Grandpa, the end.

"I'm sorry. I know you were close to her."

"Actually, Mémé didn't like me." She gives me a blunt look. "She thought I was shallow. She once told me I had no character."

I laugh. "Really?"

Mallory's full mouth quirks to one side and her thick-lashed eyes narrow, and I see something tough in her, a sense of irony, that same stubborn will-fulness I recognize in myself. "She was so mean. Like my friends' grand-mothers would all spoil them and treat them like royalty, but Lucie used to give me money and then make me pay her back. She would tell me I looked pretty and then tell me that looks don't last and vanity is a waste of a brain."

"You're not the only one she treated like that," I tell her. "Whatever she gave me, she always took away twice as much. Otherwise she felt like she'd lost. She ran a transactional economy."

"I was, like, ten," says Mallory, still laughing.

"It's the same with all mothers," I say. "We think they're uncondi-tionally generous, that's their image. But no. They're not. Otherwise, how would their children learn anything?"

At the bottom of the stairs, Mallory turns to me without warning and throws her arms around me, stooping slightly because she's a few inches taller than I am. Caught off guard, I hug her back, rubbing between her shoulder blades, giving her a kiss on her downy cheek. She smells musky and sweet, like a little kid still, with a sophisticated overlay of citrus and spice. "I'm glad you're back, Aunt Rachel," she murmurs into my ear, her breath warm and a little steamy, then just as abruptly she lets me go, peels off, and disappears into the back of the house toward the kitchen.

I pass through the French doors that lead into the front parlor. A man is sitting in a wingback chair by the fireplace. I almost don't recognize him at first, and then, in a flash, I do. He looks indrawn and hangdog. He's wearing clothes I've never seen him in before—mustard-colored cordu-roy trousers, a pea-green cardigan. His newly gray hair is cut in a weird straight line across his forehead. He looks like a lizard, a centurion, a pro-fessor emeritus—David, my wild boy, has become an old man.

Two

falter as David leaps up to greet me. The skin over his cheekbones is flushed as always, his eyes that same clear gold-brown, but there's something off in their intensity, a strange light, and his high color looks unhealthy. He takes me in his arms for a hello hug, and there is his familiar smell again, the irresistible feeling of him, his body strong and taut against mine—so briefly, and then we're apart again. My body lit up with remembered desire, I dart my gaze around, looking for Molly.

"It's good to see you, Rach." His voice sounds strained, hoarse. He has never called me Rach before, not ever. It was always Rachel. "Can it be ten years?" He studies me but doesn't exactly meet my eyes. I wonder what I look like to him, probably as hollowed-out and stringy as he looks to me. Is this what happens in middle age?

A woman comes over to stand by David's side. "You must be Rachel." She looks nothing like me, abundant red-gold hair in waves around her pleasant, snub-nosed face, clear blue eyes, genuine smile. "I'm Molly, David's wife. Wife. Wow. It's still so new, I'm not used to saying it yet."

I shake her hand, which is as warm and sure as her voice and face. She's plush, curvaceous. I feel a strange urge to hug her, to sink into her flesh, its delectable comfort.

My God, David actually married someone nice, someone young and pretty, someone who's good for him—it's clear, I see it all in a split second, with a sharp pang of loss.

My sister hovers over the coffee table, fussing with the cheese plate. Her husband turns from the bar, where he's been pouring, and hands me a bowl-size glass of red wine.

I haven't had any booze for a decade, but they always forget, which serves me right, since they hardly ever see me. I quit drinking to deny myself pleasure, because pleasure is dangerous. It leads to desire. And desire is painful for me, because it's never fulfilled.

"I don't drink," I remind Neil.

"Oops," says Neil with a grin at David. "Can't keep up with this one." He looks over at me, grin intact, but his dark eyes are dead, flat, as if there's no light on in his skull. Neil is tall and large, thick-necked, red-lipped, fat-nosed, with a black beard on his jutting chin and a big head of glossy black curls, graying now. He is not good-looking—in fact he's almost ugly, at least to me—but he presents himself as a very handsome man, inviting his viewers to perceive him that way. "Would bubbly water float your boat, sister-in-law mine?" He has always talked in the theatrical manner of some made-up version of the 1920s combined with some equally made-up hep cat lingo of an era that has never existed on earth. I know that Neil is kind, as well as thoughtful, and I suspect his affectations are due to that peculiar sense of inadequacy of people who live on piles of money they haven't earned, money they've been forced by inheritance to incorporate into their lives, money that ends up defining them. "I've got a bottle of super-primo *eau gazifiée* here in the vault."

"Oh, that would be perfect," I say with real gratitude. "Thank you."

"Here you go, stranger," he says, handing me the glass.

"Try the cheese!" shrieks Celeste, her eyes glittering with wine. "We have Humboldt Fog with fig spread and these amazing rain forest crackers!"

"Raincoast!" Neil yells festively back.

"*Raincoast*," my sister agrees with a hard exhaled laugh. Her hair looks wind-tossed, her chest is heaving. Since I quit, I can't help noticing the effect alcohol has on everyone who drinks enough of it, promising conversations devolving into blunt shouting, insistently repeated idées fixes, overblown emotions. I've been that person countless times. I know how loose and fun it feels. But I can't enjoy it sober. I wish I could. I miss it.

"The coast of rain!" Neil calls to his wife. Neil and Celeste, erstwhile theater majors and thwarted actors, have always loved to perform their marriage for any willing audience like an ongoing improvisation exercise that's entertaining to watch and seemingly genuine underneath the flourishes.

I accept the cracker from my sister. She's right; it's amazing. My stomach growls loudly as I swallow, and I realize that I haven't eaten yet today. Did I eat yesterday? I never seem to know. I treat my body like a feral stray dog, always on guard, never able to nestle or feast. Chewing gratefully, I perch on the couch next to Molly. My torso catches flame in the sudden blast of heat from the fire. My sweater dress feels like a casement of hot bricks. My face roars with flames, the top of my head vents molten air like a smokestack. I drink some cold bubbly water, which prickles my nose and bucks me up.

"Rachel," says Molly, putting a warm hand on my arm, "I'm so sad about your mother, I really loved her so much. But I hope I'm not intruding on your family time."

"Not at all," I say, meaning it.

"I told you, Molly," Celeste says, her small head quivering with feeling. "You're one of the family."

"We need all the company we can get," I can't help adding.

Molly nods. "Grief is a bitch. It takes its own path."

"Molly is a therapist," Celeste informs me.

"A clinical psychologist, actually," amends Molly.

A three-quarter-size boy appears in the doorway, his hair the same red-blond as Molly's. "*Mom*," he says with urgency. His voice cracks. He's lumpish and gangly at the same time, as miserable in his own skin as only a pubescent boy can be.

Molly gestures to this wretched creature with a hand flapping inward. "Come in, Liam, say hello."

"*Mom*"—another hoarse half whisper—"I need you *now*."

I look at David, sipping his wine, the detached new stepfather.

Wow. David has a stepson.

"Come and meet Rachel," says Molly, evidently unmoved by her son's plight, whatever it is. "Rachel, this is my son, Liam. Liam, this is Celeste's sister."

Liam fixes his mother in the tractor beam of his gaze.

"Be right back," says Molly, rolling her eyes at me. She goes out with her kid.

"How did you all meet Molly?" I ask the entire room.

"Pilates," says Celeste. "And she lives next door."

"How did you meet Molly?" I ask David directly.

His eyes are incandescent, his cheeks flushed. What is wrong with him? Is he tubercular? Addicted to speed? "She was my therapist," he says. "I saw her three times as part of my mandated treatment. Anger management. I apparently have issues." He shoots me a look. I blink peacefully at him. No longer my problem. "When that was over, I asked her to have dinner with me. . . . That was a year ago."

"How are your anger issues now?" I ask.

He gives me that complex look I know so well, limpid amusement shot through with erotic hostility. I feel a familiar prickling at the back of my neck.

"I'm perfect now," he whispers, eyes wide.

I laugh; I can't help it.

The summer after high school, David and I both worked as counselors at a summer camp near Rockland for troubled rich kids. David and I were troubled poor kids. I was a shy, serious, studious girl, and he was wild and rebellious enough for us both. He sparked something in me I hadn't even known was there. In other words, we had sex everywhere we could think of: under an upside-down canoe on the beach, behind the dining hall, in the girls' changing room during a soccer match, in the director's office in the middle of the night, on the roof of the lodge. I'm amazed the camp didn't fire us. In the thirty-five years since then, no matter how complicated things have been between us, our chemistry has never diminished. It's still there, a vibrating wire stretched between us.

"I'm going to check on dinner," says Celeste. "Pilar made Mom's favorite meal."

As Celeste bustles away, Neil, patting his breast pocket, slouches out of the room behind her with his drink, but instead of following her to the dining room, he slips out the front door. Through the window, I see him lighting a cigarette on the wraparound veranda, Molly and Liam in an intense huddle at the other end.

Alone with David, I rub the back of my neck with one hand and look into the fire.

"Hey, Rachel," he says softly. He's watching me, half tender, half sadistic. "Did they put you in the same room upstairs?"

In the past when I visited my sister, in those days before my estrangement with David, I used to leave the kitchen door unlocked for him sometimes. He would creep up to the guest room and crawl naked into bed with me, then vanish into the night afterward. Of course, he could have just slept over like an adult man, but sneaking around like teenagers felt hot and transgressive and was therefore preferable to us both.

"Congratulations on your marriage," I say as plainly as I can.

"Congratulations on your divorce," he says without missing a beat. "And condolences about your mother."

Both these statements are freighted with intimately known levels of meaning and muck from the past: he heard that my ex-husband turned out to be gay, I'm sure, and he and my mother have their own history. She flirted with him, competing with me. He flirted back with a practiced indulgence my mother interpreted as genuine and used against me in her moments of drunken sexual competitiveness when she informed me of all the things I was doing wrong, from the way I moved my mouth to the way I dressed, as was her way. "You'll never keep a man if you act like one," she said, and "Charm is a gift, and I got it, and Celeste got it, but it certainly passed you by." That bitch. It killed me when David flattered her vanity. He had no idea what he was stepping into, proving her right, annihilating me, and he didn't seem to care.

He's always getting me back somehow, righting an imbalance. That fall after our first summer together, I went away to UC Berkeley on a full scholarship. David lived at home and worked summers as a forestry intern for Weyerhauser in Bingham and graduated from the University of Maine with a degree in forest management. We both studied hard and did well, but he stayed behind, so he was the one who felt less-than. That was how it worked.

I easily hear all of these reverberations in his tone, and in the past, I would have risen to the bait, my buttons all pushed like an elevator with a six-year-old kid riding in it, and we would have gotten into something. But this time, I don't. My ability to take his provocation at face value and let it go is new for me. It's coming along with all the other, less convenient symptoms of age, as a consolation prize maybe, or a balancing side effect. As my hormones ebb, amid the turmoil, my thoughts are draining of emotion, becoming uncolored by moods. I feel as if I'm going through adolescence in reverse. Maybe I'll come out the other end of this estrogen-progesterone tunnel returned to my old eleven-year-old clarity, but with newfound perspective and autonomy. Menopause might actually be a relief. I feel its promise now, bracing me.

David is married. This has to be over.

"So where are you working these days?" I ask him, grown-up to grown-up. "Still the forestry service?"

"I took early retirement. Since then I've been teaching a course or two here and there at SMCC." He rests his foot on the opposite knee, gazes at his shoe. "My life is pretty quiet. We hike with Liam—he needs structured exercise outside. I have a weekly poker game with Neil and some other guys." His tone is defensive. He probably thinks I'll secretly mock him for this, me with my big job far away from here.

But I don't look down on one single aspect of this serene and reasonable life. I deeply envy it, in fact. To my outsider's eye, it looks like happiness. "You live next door now?"

He cocks a thumb behind him. "In that big old pile of brick, next lawn over. It's Molly's house. I moved in after we got married."

I whistle, one dirt-poor kid to another. "Good for you."

He grins at me, realizing I'm sincere. "How's everything in DC?"

"All I do is work. Luckily, I love my job."

"Same one?"

"As long as they'll have me." I can't tell him what's really going on. If he weren't married, I could blurt it all out, how freaked out I am, how fraught my situation is. Instead I tell him, "It's the most fulfilling work I've ever done."

Gratifyingly, a brief flash of something that looks like envy crosses his face. "Are you seeing anyone these days?"

"There's a guy, a climate scientist I met in the Arctic." This is a total lie, spun from a brief fling last winter that went nowhere. But I need to hold my own against his recent marriage and comfortable settled life in any way I can.

"Is he good to you?"

I can't answer this. Our gazes meet and hold, and just like that, the old flood threatens to break the dam.

"I think it's time for dinner," I say.

He smiles. "No doubt."

We both stand at the same time and manage to navigate our way out of the front parlor without touching each other. In the foyer he grasps my arm and turns me to face him. "It should have been you," he says. He looks directly into my eyes. "It's still you, Rachel, it probably always will be. But I couldn't wait forever, and I figured you'd never be back. I don't want to get old and die alone."

"You're smart," I say with some effort. I want him to believe me, because I want to mean this. "And lucky."

He looks away from my face, his eyes hooded, and motions for me to precede him into the dining room.

Three

Dinner is chaotic. The air is insanely bright, late sunlight streaming in the huge leaded windows, candles lit, the overhead chandelier blazing. A loud noise comes intermittently from the kitchen, the roar of some industrial-sounding machine. Whatever is going on with Liam, he's mad at his mother and doesn't care who knows it. "Shut *up*, Mom," he begs Molly when she tries to tell a reminiscent story about Lucie. The food is astonishing, gummy spaghetti with too-sweet tomato sauce, flat discs of charred steak, iceberg chunks submerged in lurid orange dressing, overcooked asparagus like limp green rubber pencils. I hope Pilar isn't their regular chef. Mallory and Jasper look silently at each other, some secret twin understanding whose primary underlying meaning, I fear, is unflattering to all us adults. Celeste is visibly drunk, Neil too. They slur their words, talk loudly, make odd, clumsy gestures with their forks in midair.

"Oh, I love you kids so much," says Celeste out of nowhere. She shrieks gently in the back of her throat, the sound of histrionic emotional pressure mounting like a gas.

The kids hear it too. With the same practiced preemptive fluidity I remember developing for myself with Lucie decades ago, they withdraw their attention from their mother before she explodes. It works. The drama ratchets down, the pressure leaks invisibly from Celeste's skull.

David and I sit across the table from each other, avoiding each other's eyes. But my skull is alight with the subaural radio-wave communication we can neither control nor stop. I can feel his mood, spiky and pent-up. I'm unable to turn off or even mute his signals.

"You really quit drinking?" he asks me under the general hubbub: Jasper is thumbing his phone, Mallory is leaning in, staring at the screen with her brother.

"Ten years ago."

David glances down at his full glass of red wine, then back at me. "Nothing since then?"

I shake my head. I cannot talk about the reason I quit drinking. I can't even think about it, because it's connected to the reason for our long rift. It all blooms in my skull, a messy knot of flesh and psychodrama, too painful to look at directly. I kick it safely under the surface again and look away from him.

"Aunt Jean," Jasper says to his phone, "we're all at dinner. Say hi, everyone."

A soft squawk comes from the phone as Jasper swivels it around the table, and we all wave, even me, although I have no idea what's going on. The small screen shows a kitchen sink and cupboards. No sign of Aunt Jean.

"Hi, Aunt Jean," says Mallory. "We wish you were here."

Another squawk from offscreen. A crash of something: dishes, maybe.

"Kids," says Celeste, "just prop the phone up so Aunt Jean can pretend she's eating with us."

We all look at her drab, spotless kitchen. During the winters, Jean lives in the small apartment above the family sporting-goods store in Bangor, which my grandfather, Denis Gautreau, left to his only son, my uncle Frank. If my cousin Danny hadn't killed himself, he would have inherited it. Now it's unclear what will happen to it, as well as Grandpa's hunting and fishing camp in the North Woods, Aunt Jean's inheritance. No one at this table wants either of those faraway family businesses. Danny was supposed to keep it all going. He was Uncle Frank and Aunt Debbie's only child, and Aunt Jean never married or had kids.

"We're all coming up to the camp soon, Aunt Jean," Celeste shouts at the phone. "Our mother wanted her ashes in the lake."

No response from Aunt Jean.

"Did you remember to pick up the urn, Mom?" Jasper says in what I am beginning to realize is his typical voice when addressing either of his parents, as if they're untrustworthy simpletons who have to be corralled.

"Of course I did. It's right there."

We all look at the large shiny brass thing sitting over the fireplace. It takes up most of the mantelpiece. With a shock, I realize it's Lucie. There's my mother, all that's left of her, right the fuck there. Celeste must have had her cremated the very instant she died. Not that I blame her.

"See," says Mallory to her brother. "She remembered."

I look at my sister with dread. "She wants us to throw her ashes in Gooseneck Lake?"

"I can't live with this urn for very long. We have to go up and do it before you leave."

"All the way up to the camp?" I try not to sound as horrified as I feel.

"I'm hoping Uncle Frank and Aunt Debbie will come up, too."

"I had no idea she wanted that. Why would she want that?"

Celeste goes stony, looking inward, swaying in her chair. Molly reaches over and takes her hand as Neil knocks back the rest of his wine like a cowboy doing rotgut shots in a saloon.

"Easy, Dad," says Jasper with a sidelong glance at his twin sister.

But Mallory doesn't see, because she's cooing down at her own crotch, where a little head is begging. She feeds the dog a strand of spaghetti, a chunk of steak.

"Mémé lived a big life in a small place," Neil announces to his children, who listen with suspicious wide-eyed stillness, as if they're trying not to laugh.

Molly Driscoll holds her glass up in a toast. Is she teary-eyed? "To the mother I never had."

I mutter, "To the mother *I* never had."

David catches my eye with a half smile. No one else appears to have heard me.

"She was a *force*," Celeste is saying, two fingers dangling her glass by the stem, wine sloshing to the rim. "She had a hard, hard life, and she always stayed true to herself." She leans into her arms so her layered hair falls forward, then tosses it back.

."God yes," Molly says. "A real survivor. And she lived with gusto. Even in dying, she went out with style." She turns to me. "Your mom was singing to us the day before she went. She hardly had any voice, but she got through 'Stormy Weather.' She remembered all the words. We were all crying."

I'm sitting very still. This is my family. These are my people. It's not easy to come back here, not easy to find my place again, like a book I abandoned midway through and lost the thread of.

"She would have loved this meal." My sister wipes her eyes on her napkin, takes a forkful. "She loved gloppy spaghetti like it was caviar."

"This is *delicious*, Mom," says Jasper. He grins at his mother.

Celeste smiles back at him. "Mémé's secret ingredient was a ton of sugar."

I stare at my plate, ravenous and stymied. Seeing David has made me hungry for the first time in so long, I can't remember the last time, but I can't eat any of this food. It's beyond me to contravene Wallace. I hear his horrified voice loud in my ear, my brilliant former FDA scientist ex-husband, hectoring me about the tasteless, invisible, but potentially sickening contents of every single thing on my plate: the factory-farmed antibiotic- and chemical-fed meat, the bisphenol A–tainted canned tomato sauce with glyphosate-soaked wheat pasta and pesticide-heavy asparagus and iceberg lettuce grown in phthalate-ester-mulched soil and watered with fracking byproduct. Everyone else gets to happily eat their dinners in peace and won't know what hurts them until they're diagnosed with cancer or have a heart attack or stroke. Meanwhile I sit here with my useless overload of information, sipping my glass of sparkling water, which was imported from Italy, so big carbon footprint, but it also came out of a glass bottle and is the only reasonably crap-free thing on the entire table. I feel like a veritable lunatic. I'm the woman who knows too much to eat anything, thanks to a man who never actually wanted me.

As I glance around, Molly's son, Liam, catches my gaze as it alights on him. He glares at me, instantly enraged at me just for noticing him.

His face is swollen, skin suffused with blood. His blue eyes are hot, and his red hair bristles. I notice that David is watching me watch Liam. I shoot David a look to let him know how ironic I find it that he and his stepson both have anger issues, even though they happen to live with an apparently unflappable therapist. David hardens his mouth back at me in a nonsmile. Not funny, also not his kid, so not his fault, and not his problem, either.

"To my sister," I say, raising my glass of mineral water. "For taking such good care of Mom, for dealing with everything. Thank you, Celeste, I mean it. I feel so inadequate, saying this. But it's true."

Celeste reaches across the table and clinks her wineglass against my water glass. But her eyes are slits, her voice strangled when she says, "I'll drink to that." She is so mad at me. It scares me a little.

"Rachel," says Molly, turning to me, her eyes crinkling at the edges, bright and blue, "what are some of your favorite memories of Lucie? I heard about the time she took you both to the Caribbean on her gambling winnings. Wasn't it Puerto Rico?"

My mother's absence balloons in the hot, bright air, the most real thing in the room, in the world. It feels like the inverse negative of her presence, so palpable I can hear her shouting to be heard above everyone else, her peals of oversize laughter. Her flamboyant, frank narcissism was as insuperable a fact in my life as gravity or air. If she were still alive, this whole room would be dominated by her, every sense filled by her. She'd wear a brightly patterned dress made out of something synthetic, too much perfume, a hot pink hair band framing her peroxide blonde semi-bouffant, eyes rimmed with liquid eyeliner, as if she imagined she was an actress in a campy 1960s romp playing a devil-may-care beauty born into the wrong life, the wrong time and place.

She hated it when anyone's attention wandered from her. So often when I was distracted or daydreaming, just thinking my own damn thoughts, she'd punish me. Out of the blue she'd pounce on me, "Earth to Rach," stabbing me in the forearm with a talon, rubbing the spot she'd poked, then clutching my arm as if she owned it, slyly adding a weird non sequitur half compliment—"No one can ever get one over on you, you're too *smart*."

In her voice, *smart* implied weaselly, slippery. When I rubbed the sore spot, she'd pounce again: "You're always so *sensitive*. Where's your sense of humor?" And then, my attention back on her, she'd flit on to the next subject, endlessly galvanized by her internal dramas, somehow always in control, always the center, even at her most unhinged.

Now, without her, I'm floating in a vacuum.

"Honestly," I say to Molly, determined to plant my feet on the razor's edge where hard truth meets euphemism, "I don't really have any particular favorite memory of my mother. It's all sort of one big memory of her."

I expect the conversation to bounce away, but Molly is still watching me, and the rest of the table has gone quiet.

"In other words," I add, "it's hard to talk about her."

"I get it," says Molly. But I sense that she wants something from me. Maybe she's sussing me out—maybe that's at the root of this. She shifts in her chair, gives me an encouraging smile, meant to elicit a response, the therapist's practiced goad. "I greatly admired your piece about cruise ships. I had no idea they were so bad for the environment. What are you working on next?"

The whole table is still looking at me. I passionately do not want to talk about my work right now.

"I'm about to start researching a new project on algal photosynthesis, and I just finished a series about ice," I proffer, hoping this will satisfy the collective curiosity.

Celeste toys with the stem of her wineglass, twirling her glass against the tabletop, not looking at me.

"Oh yeah!" says Jasper. "You were in Antarctica recently, right?"

Okay then. "This last winter, I spent three weeks in the Arctic on a research ship called the *North Star*." I dart a glance at my stone-faced sister. "The Antarctic was last year," I add, because my nephew is still waiting for me to go on. "I traveled with a team of research scientists, and we camped in tents on a glacier. They drilled all the way down to the rock to extract frozen rods of ice, almost two kilometers deep. Then they brought them back to a lab and melted the cylinders drop by drop. Gas bubbles trapped in the ice told them about climate conditions going back almost eight hundred thousand years. Sometimes you could even see these thin stripes of black volcanic ash in the cylinders."

"That's so cool," Jasper breathes.

"So cool," Mallory echoes. "So what did you do in the Arctic on the ship?"

"I shadowed the scientists who were taking samples from icebergs to take back to the lab so that they could study the effects of rising temperatures and test for toxins and chemicals. I hung out with them, interviewed them about their work."

"Do you ever feel freaked out?" Molly asks. "Facing the facts the way you do, with no escape?"

"All the time. Existentially, it makes my head explode. I think we all feel like that, all of us who are writing about what's happening, at least sometimes. We don't want to scare people into paralysis. But we ourselves . . . I think collectively we feel like a bunch of Cassandras, like we're saying what no one wants to hear." I look at my niece and nephew. "I think a lot about kids your age. I'm sure there's a lot of awareness and anxiety around it for you all."

"Yeah," says Jasper.

Their eyes are wide and shiny. Poor doomed children. "Are you interested in studying science?" I ask them, trying for their sake to act as if their future might be potentially bright.

"I am," says Jasper. "Specifically neuroscience."

"Good for you." I'm frankly surprised. He looks like the dreamboat male lead in a teen rom-com. I've always figured he was going to coast through life on his looks and money, if only because he can. Serves me right for judging. And underestimating.

"Yeah," he says, and ducks his head a little, I'm guessing because he's self-conscious in front of his silent father at the head of the table. "The brain is so complex, it's like there's so much we still don't know about it, it's the last undiscovered frontier in a way. Forget space, I want to explore inside our heads."

"That's fantastic," I tell him.

"Did you like it at UC Berkeley?" Jasper's voice cracks a little.

"I loved it, even though I felt like a clueless knucklehead from Maine most of the time. Everyone else was so confident and smart."

My nephew flashes a grin at me, a real one, with a glint of gratitude and fellowship. "But you obviously did okay there."

"I did fine," I say. "It was exciting and a little scary and very good for me. Anyway, back then a kid like me could get into a place like that. Nowadays I'd probably have to settle for community college."

"I doubt that. Mom told me you were always totally brilliant. Right, Mom?"

My sister stares at me, unsmiling.

I take a breath. "I'm sorry," I say to my sister. "I've been on hard deadline for this ice story. That's why I couldn't come home sooner."

"Sure," says Celeste. She clears her throat. "Of course you *could* have. But your work is more important. I get it."

My head is pounding. I'm so burned out, so bone-deep exhausted. The bright heat is making me feel like a trapped animal. My armpits are swampy. My head itches.

Across the table, David has been watching me closely. His focused attention floods my brain with a narcotic hit of serotonin.

He's married. It's still hitting me.

"I'm sorry," I say as I push my chair back and stand up, not looking at David, or Celeste, or anyone. "I need some air. Sorry, everyone."

"It's okay," Molly's voice floats after me as I leave the dining room, continuing in my disturbed wake, saying something about how everyone reacts to loss differently. Upstairs, I fetch my shoulder bag and a jacket and race back down and out the front door and down the steps to the sidewalk. Out on the quiet street in the cool blossom-softened evening, with the last of the day's sunlight filtering through new leaves, the world green and fresh, I calm down. As I walk through the West End, I suck in deep lungsful of air that I know is saturated with benzene from nearby gas stations and hazardous volatile organic compounds offgassing illegally from the oil tanks just across the Fore River estuary in South Portland. But it's a fresh spring evening, even so. I'm pretty sure I remember how to get downtown. It isn't a long walk. Nothing in Portland is.

Four

On Pine Street, I sink onto the bottom step of a brownstone stoop and look up at the empty blue sunlit sky, sober and awake this time, decades older. The rich scent of blossoms brings back a visceral memory so immediate it feels like it was five minutes ago, me at nineteen or twenty, wandering these same streets arm in arm with David after a party at someone's cousin's rich friend's house.

I was cheating on my college boyfriend with David. I always did, every summer. During the school year, far away and safe in California, I felt the weary sick relief of an addict who's only temporarily clean. My boyfriend at Berkeley, Steve Brownstein, was an astrophysicist from the San Fernando Valley who adored me. If David was my crystal meth, then Steve was my detox cleanse. He called me his "Maine shiksa." With Steve, I felt treasured and beloved and completely safe and a little bored.

When I came home for the summers, I relapsed right away. David made me feel known and scared and heartsick and zingy. And powerful too, because he wasn't as brainy as I was, and we both knew it. So I vacillated between being condescending to him, because I could be mean too, and retracting myself apologetically into a smaller mental size to soothe his ego, and both of my extremes made him have to hurt me back in any way he could. But we had so much sex, the drug we created together and became equally hooked on. It all continued while I went to grad school at

Yale and he worked for the Maine forestry service. I drove up to Maine on weekends whenever I could.

Even after I got my master's and moved to DC to work for *CORE*, David and I kept stupidly but helplessly torturing each other without resolution or clarity. It makes me shake my head to think of it now, all the internal emotional damage I was trying to mend by inflicting more on him, and vice versa, both of us serving as each other's medicine and punching bag. We were together in one way or another for twenty-five years, until I finally cut it all off, David and my mother and alcohol and my past, done, cold turkey.

I married Wallace partially as an antidote to David. His easygoing steadiness and cool remove made me feel lonely and calm instead of tormented and sexually obsessed. When I caught him in bed with Declan, his handsome young male assistant, it all suddenly made sense. In the several years since our divorce, besides a brief fling last winter, there hasn't been anyone else for me.

All along, I've subconsciously continued to believe that David and I will find each other again, even after all these years of estrangement, if only because we're too old to change the paradigm. My heart is reacting like GPS does when you make a wrong turn: David, married, too skinny, with a weird haircut, wearing a cardigan. Recalibrating.

I get up and make my way along the root-cracked brick sidewalks, leafy tunnels, to Congress Street, the main artery that runs along the peninsula's spine all the way up Munjoy Hill to the Eastern Promenade. The town has changed as much as I have. This isn't the Portland I knew. The air looks brighter somehow, everything more vivid. New people have moved here and renovated the old houses; new restaurants and stores have opened in old buildings. Twenty years ago, this town was a backwater, a little provincial northern maritime outpost, isolated and gritty and rough, out of time. Now it seems to emanate a sharp electric hum, connected to the rest of the world, plugged into the motherboard, on the same frequency as everywhere else.

Congress Street funnels me past Monument Square, and I enter a snazzy hotel restaurant. I'm seated at a two-top by the sweet young hostess, who brings me water, a menu. I look around at the zinc bar and pressed tin ceiling tiles and bright engaged faces at nearby tables, read the list of local farms the food was "sourced" from, with appropriately high prices. I could be anywhere. What happened to all those crappy, divey old joints of yesteryear, with gloppy clam chowder and limp Caesar salads and hard old gum stuck under the tabletops? Not that I miss them. Not all change is bad.

"Water is fine," I tell the waiter, a man with very dark skin and close-cropped hair. He has an elegant manner, an air of thoughtful abstraction. I try to imagine where he came from, what horrors he faced there. I have a feeling it's either South Sudan or Somalia; Maine has large refugee communities from both countries. I wonder what his profession was in his home country before he landed in this cold, foreign northern place as a new American and got this job waiting tables. Was he a professor? A doctor? He has a quiet fierceness about him, an impatient, intelligent air that brooks no trivial questions.

When he brings my plate and moves away from my table, leaving me in peaceful anticipation, I shove my food into my maw, hardly even chewing. The scallops are buttery, luscious, tender. When they're gone, I'm still hungry, so I ask the waiter for a bowl of what's described on the menu as "spring carrot and golden lentil soup with buttermilk, cilantro, and puffed wild rice." When that comes, I inhale it, too. I'm so happy to be sitting here by myself, so happy to have escaped the circle of hell that was my sister's dining table.

I catch myself watching the bartender shaking cocktails one by one, throwing all sorts of intriguing things together and pouring the frothy elixirs into beautiful glassware, garnishing them with interesting tidbits. I admit to myself for the first time that I've been craving a drink since my plane landed. I try to tell myself it's too bad, but I can't have one, but I fail; there is no actual reason I can't, it's more that I've been alcohol-free for so long that it's become a habit, a good thing I'm invested in sustaining. And I've been glad of this all along. Not drinking has sensitized me over time. I can always tell from the sharp, chemical medicinal acrid nostril-curling smell of the stuff that hits me whenever I get close enough to it—of course it pickles the liver, of course it dulls the brain, of course it makes people throw up. "What's your poison?" is an entirely real proposition.

The knowledge that my mother has left me her house is gnawing at my consciousness. My mother got it in the divorce from her third husband, so I have him to thank, obliquely. His name was Malachi Michaud, and he was a retired machinist with a mean streak. He and my mother were drinking buddies primarily, as far as I could tell. She was postmenopausal, and for a few years she carried ten or fifteen pounds of extra flesh and fat around her torso and upper arms and thighs. Malachi used to mock her for it: "Where's the girl I married?" he'd say. "Where's that supermodel? That's it, you put a ring on a girl, she gets fat, that's just the way it is." And my mother would cry privately and bitterly to Celeste and me. We told her over and over to leave him, kick him out, keep the house. And she did.

It makes me queasy, this unasked-for burden of a gift. That house was always a spiky, uncomfortable place for me, glaring and hard and exposed, an extension of my mother's psyche. Bequeathing that awful place to me wasn't generous or thoughtful at all, it was controlling and hostile. She's forcing me to face what happened there, to go back, to deal with all the shit I thought I could escape by leaving.

I need to sell it as quickly as possible and get out of here.

I fish out my phone and google the number of the one realtor I know in Maine. Before I can change my mind, I punch it in and hit dial. My call goes to voice mail, no doubt because of my unfamiliar DC cell number. "Suzanne," I blurt after the beep, "it's Rachel Calloway. I'm calling because I'm looking to sell a house here in Portland, and I'm wondering if I could list it through you. I'm up here for the next two weeks." I pause, about to sign off, then I figure what the hell. "I'm calling from the Media Hotel. I'm having dinner right now in the restaurant, if you happen to be free."

She calls me back within one minute. "Hey, Rachel," her voice bursts into my ear. "Will you still be there in half an hour?"

"I will," I say.

While I wait for Suzanne, I scroll through my news feed, the likely collapse of human civilization by 2050, the president's corrupt buffoonery, my own piece in *CORE* about the cruise ship company fined $40 million for polluting the ocean, the entire Midwest wrecked by flooding and tornadoes, dozens of migrating gray whales dying of starvation off the coast of California. My brain takes in one terrifying and sickening catastrophe at a time, and then I scroll on to the next tidbit of disaster, and it's all subsumed in the general onslaught.

Here I am in a beautiful restaurant, with a healthy body and sound mind, well fed, with a place to live, a job. This disjunction makes absolutely no sense. I have no idea how to reconcile it. No one does. But we all go on, anyway, those of us who can. It's so purely human, this cognitive dissonance, the way our brains persevere in the face of everything. It feels built into our species. It might be what got us into this mess, the fact that we can face our own extinction over a beautiful, nourishing meal, comprehend the likelihood of nuclear war or ecological breakdown in our own lifetimes as we look out at a spring evening, anticipate our own personal futures in the face of the sure knowledge that life as we know it is likely doomed. The self-generated destruction of humanity is in all our myths and prophesies; our collective imagination has always bent toward this. And yet we go on, persist in our little dramas and passions and ambitions and hopes. In spite of everything, I deeply love this about humankind.

An old Red Hot Chili Peppers song comes on the sound system, "Breaking the Girl," a funk ballad I remember from the early '90s, the singer's voice raw sex, with a bouncy bass line and a grinding guitar part and a hot drumbeat. I close my eyes and give myself over to memory, remembering how it felt to be a young woman without a past, in the grip of strong, uncontrollable emotions. I love remembering it, but I don't miss it. Whatever this phase of my life is now, that's what I'm living in, the present.

I look up as Suzanne Brown slides into the seat across from me. "Rachel," she says. "Long time."

"A very long time."

We're silent a moment, assessing each other. I zoom in on her bare left hand. I wonder whether she ever had kids. The air between us is wary and staticky for a moment, and then it smooths out, all at once, as the intervening decades assert themselves.

"Please," I say to the waiter, who has materialized again, "another seltzer with lime."

He gives me a brisk nod.

"A Stoli mule," says Suzanne as he inclines his head toward her.

I look at my old nemesis, if that's what she was, with intense interest. Her face is made up with eye shadow and a tastefully pale shade of lipstick, but I can see that her skin is deeply lined around her eyes and mouth, her fair complexion splotchy and ruddy around her nose, no doubt from all the summers on lobster boats. Her hair has been lightened, highlighted, straightened, layered, as well tended as a small purebred dog. She smells crisp and expensive and wears clunky gold earrings and a matching bracelet, a pink angora sweater over a taupe blouse, a navy linen skirt, and ballet flats.

"Well, this is unexpected," she says in her chesty smoker's voice and broad Maine accent, the same one I worked so hard to get rid of. "So how ya doing?"

"Not great," I say before I can stop myself.

She peers at me. "Why not great?"

I let it fly. What do I have to lose? "A lot of reasons."

She leans closer. "Name one."

"First of all, we've been taken over by the Death Star."

Suzanne laughs out loud, and her whole face opens up.

The waiter sets my seltzer in front of me, then delivers Suzanne's cocktail, which comes in a copper mug beaded with condensation.

"What Death Star might that be?" she asks.

"A metaphorical one. But still."

"Oh, you mean you don't like the current administration?"

"They're not exactly helping me with my work."

"Your work?"

"I'm a journalist, a staff writer at *CORE* magazine."

"Oh, okay," says Suzanne, nodding.

"I write about climate change. And they're climate change deniers."

"But you can still write what you want, last I checked."

"We stay afloat through major government funding."

"Yup," she says. "I get it. I do." We're quiet a moment, chewing on this. Then she inhales sharply. "So the way I see it, it's all a bunch of noise, it doesn't matter, it's not the point. I don't want to say fake news because that's so hot button and anyway it's all totally true, whatever you know, you're right. But yeah. It's game over. Baked in. You just have to let yourself enjoy life, that's what I do."

"Okay," I say. "Sounds great."

"I don't read the news. I know, sue me, I'm an ostrich, but it's all babble on the surface. Instead I listen to podcasts about near-death experiences where people leave their bodies and know everything and understand that it's all okay, everything happens the way it should, perfectly according to plan." She peers at me as if ascertaining my level of skepticism at all this. She finds none, because I'm listening like a kid at story hour.

Suzanne worked at the camp that summer David and I met. She was from Rockport, tough, fresh-faced, freckled, the quintessential coastal Maine girl. She was the granddaughter, niece, cousin, sister, and daughter of lobstermen. She usually worked as a sternman for one of her relatives, but that summer she took a break from the lobster traps to be the outdoor activities counselor. Suzanne Brown, the cool girl I could never be, defiantly visceral, proudly working-class, unapologetically conservative, scornful of complexity and dismissive of anything too cerebral or nuanced. "That's just weak," was her stock response. "What a load of fuzzy-headed crap."

"Go on," I say now.

"It's all true, by the way, as true as pollution and catastrophe. It's just a bigger picture, zooming out on the whole thing. All we have is this moment right now. Pain and chaos are the way of all things, they *are* life. We have to try to enjoy our time here, that's our job as living things, to find pleasure and meaning in the physical realm. What's the point of worrying about the future?"

"To take action to prevent the worst of it?"

"Yeah," she says, waving this off like a fly, "sure, but how's that working out for you?"

"I'm burned out."

She gives me an easy grin. "I recommend forgetting about it."

"It's my job not to."

"Listen, I don't see this as woo-woo, it's really the most sensible thing you could possibly do. Zoom out. Soon enough you'll rejoin the stream of energy and consciousness and be released to the universe. This is your chance to experience living inside a body in an individual consciousness. Take all the joy from that you can." She holds up her glass again. Her hands are beautifully manicured, nails painted with clear polish. "Anyway"—pragmatically dismissing the topic of global catastrophe as settled—"You married? No ring."

"And no kids either. What about you?"

"I am the cheese," she says with a grin. "I stand alone."

Neither of us looks at all sorry about it.

"I just saw David," I say, watching closely for her reaction. I used to secretly think they should have been together. When we were young, Suzanne knew everyone in Maine, meaning everyone of her own socio-economic stratum. As a member of that class myself, but a striving, uncomfortable outsider in it, I deeply envied her ease in her own skin. She inhabited her place in the world with unselfconscious straightforwardness, accepting of herself and everyone else in it. She always got along so easily with David, whereas he and I seduced each other into tormented knots. I knew that they hung out together a lot while I was away in California, but nothing ever happened between them that I was aware of. I always guessed it was because she wasn't interested.

Her eyes narrow and harden at the mention of his name. "Oh yeah? How's he doing?"

"He's married to a therapist named Molly Driscoll." I peer at her: no glimmer. "She's very nice. Also, he looks like shit."

"David was never gonna age all that well. Too bony. Unless he's fat now?"

"He's shrunk a full size." I take in the shrewd glance she gives me. I know I'm in that camp, too, the shriveled camp. I am also highly aware of my salt-and-pepper hair, which I wear chin length and trim myself, as well as my bitten cuticles and lack of any feminine self-caring gestures. I imagine Suzanne feels sorry for me, maybe just abstractly, way in the back of her mind, but still.

Or maybe not. She's shaking her head. "I haven't seen him in—Jesus, fifteen years."

"I wasn't expecting to see him. He and his new wife were over at my sister's for dinner tonight."

She's interested: a knot of gossip. "Just by chance?"

"Molly is my sister's best friend," I say. "She lives next door to my sister, now with David. And she was close to my mother, *and* she married David. I had to get out. So here I am."

"Hey, do you have a cousin named Eileen Calloway?"

I almost jump in my chair. "Yes," I say. "I haven't seen her since we were kids. Do you know her?"

"She's one of my best friends. That's wild! I'll have to tell her I saw you."

"She won't care. We're not exactly close."

"My condolences about your mother, by the way."

"Thanks. She had terrible health habits and she had cancer. We had a complicated relationship."

Suzanne gives me a sharp look. "I get it," she says. "My mother is in her eighties. It's a tightrope act to preserve her pride while she falls for ridiculous conspiracies and email scams and drives thirty-five miles an hour in the passing lane. Talk about complicated. But it's the least I can do."

"You're a better person than I am. My mother told me not to come, barked it like an order. I didn't want to, so I listened to her. Now she's gone."

Suzanne gives me another sharp look, searching and without a shred of condemnation. "You know? Mothers and daughters."

"I know."

"Good," she says. "You did what she asked."

I look searchingly back at Suzanne. "So you're still a realtor?"

"I'm officially retired, but I still have my license," she says, leaning forward. This is what she came for. The pleasantries are out of the way.

"Aren't you young to retire?"

"Oh, this town has been exploding. I landed some big-ass properties and suddenly I was absolutely stinkin' frickin' rich. By my own standards, anyway." Her eyes go wide at her own cleverness. "So I invested some and socked the rest away and retired at forty and traveled around the world by myself for a few years, then I came back here and bought a little condo on the wharf and here I am." She raises her glass again, toasting herself now with a puckish, inward grin. "You?"

"The opposite of you. I'm not rich. I work way too hard, and I live with my ex-husband."

"You were married?"

"Divorced now. He turned out to be gay. We live together in our condo with his boyfriend. The DC real estate market is a quagmire." I don't mention the ALS.

Suzanne's forehead ripples slightly, trying to express sympathy in spite of some apparent recent Botox.

"Anyway, my mother left me her house. I need to sell it as soon as possible."

Suzanne shoots me a professional, speculative look. "Where is it?"

"On Baxter Boulevard with a view of Back Cove, but the place is kind of a dump."

"You know," she says, "a view of the water? It would sell in one day for above asking."

"Really?" I look at her. "Would you handle the sale for me?"

"Of course," she says. "You know what they say, a realtor never retires till she's dead."

I never knew they said that, but I'm glad to hear it. "When can you come and take a look at it?"

"Anytime. Just give me a call. And I have to say, Rachel." She considers me frankly. "You kind of make me want to stop coloring my hair." Her expression is sincere.

"It felt like time to just let it be what it is," I say. "I'll be fifty-four next January."

"I will too, in September."

"It's a weird age, isn't it? Not old yet, not young anymore. I can feel myself becoming invisible. It's a diminishment and a superpower at the same time."

"That's why they call it middle age," says Suzanne, laughing. "The trick is to keep moving forward like a shark." She fishes her credit card out and taps its edge smartly against the table. "By the way, you don't look invisible to me."

"We can see each other," I say. "It's part of the superpower."

"I meant it as a compliment."

"My treat," I say. "Put that away."

I watch her streak out of the restaurant. Moving forward like a shark. Alone at my table again, waiting for the check, I'm aware that, in spite of everything, my body is hungry for David's, running on its own track. The last time I had sex was this past winter, with a scientist on the research ship in the Arctic, sequestered with twenty-four hours of darkness and very little distraction. Alex was cute. We slept together for a few nights. But unfortunately—since I genuinely liked him—it turned out that we had absolutely nothing to say to each other outside of work. We were two awkward, introverted professionals whose emotional growth had been stunted while we threw ourselves into realizing our aims and ambitions, compounded in my case by the details of my upbringing, and in his by what I strongly suspect was being somewhere on the autism spectrum. So our little affair fizzled out once we were back in DC with no moonlight on a frozen ocean, no world of ice aglow under a dazzling frosty starry sky.

Oh well. I've been telling myself I didn't want or expect anything more. But I know this isn't true. I'm aware that I might have revealed my starving heart during those Arctic nights in Alex's little bunk, lying sweaty and naked, sated by his body. I had not expected him to be so physically beautiful underneath all those layers of down and Gore-Tex. I hadn't expected to feel so attached to him afterward. The sudden intimacy made me vulnerable.

The truth is, I was disappointed that he didn't call me again after our one date when we were back in DC. But I didn't stop to admit this to myself. Instead, I stayed up all night transcribing the long interviews I'd done with him, and then I moved on and made myself forget about him.

I leave an enormous tip in cash on the table for my excellent waiter and walk out into the sweet chill of the spring night.

Five

After I turn off Congress Street and head into the darkness and silence of the West End, I hear rustlings in bushes. A large wildlife population lives among the mansions, I remember—raccoons and skunks, wild turkeys and foxes, opossums and chipmunks, even the occasional coyote. The air is thick with brine and oxygen and a hint of sea fog, rich with negative ions and smells of primordial life and death. A seagull shrieks from a rooftop, evidently confused by the city lights into thinking it's daytime. The old brick sidewalks heave and buckle as tree roots push inexorably and slowly upward. I smell honeysuckle and damp mulch and an occasional whiff of fresh semen from some sort of spunky tree. Streetlamps gild porticos and gingerbread trim, gables and dormers, in a Lautrec painting's absinthe haze. Bay windows shrouded in foliage and tree boughs spill mellow gold onto the leaves, offering peeks at lived-in interiors. Cigarette and pot smoke drift from invisible people on dark porches. Dogs bark. It's bracing to inhale the clean salt of the North Atlantic.

I climb the granite steps to my sister's house and let myself in. The front hall is airless and quiet. I go back into the kitchen for a glass of water to bring up to my room and see Neil sitting at a stool at the bar. The room is so bright it's like an ocular scream. All the lights—undercabinet, overhead, recessed, pendant, sconce—are at full blaze. They make the shiny pink granite counters and all-white appliances gleam so hard that they look wet. A row of glinting knives hangs on a magnetic strip. There is no food in sight, nothing edible at all. Everything is antiseptic and scrubbed.

"The kids are still out," says Neil without looking up. "Little fuckers."

I glance at the clock. It's just after ten.

"Hi, Neil," I say, taking a pint glass out of a cabinet and going to the sink to fill it.

He looks pale and shrunken in this vast kitchen, large and swarthy though he is. "Oh, it's you. I thought you were Celeste. Just out of the corner of my eye." He sounds embarrassed.

"Sorry," I say, embarrassed suddenly too, as if I've deliberately snuck up on him. "I'm just getting a glass of water."

"Okay . . ." He stares into his phone, sliding his thumb up the glass over and over.

My relationship with my brother-in-law has always been perfectly cordial, as those things go, but if I met him at a party as a stranger, I would probably keep going toward the drinks table. I suspect he feels the same neutral affability toward me, but I know this has to be tinged with Celeste's complex sisterly stew of resentment and competitive judgment, and I'm instinctively uncomfortable around people with fully formed but unspoken opinions of me that contain a grain of truth. But Neil seems lonely to me right now, sitting by himself in his too-bright kitchen, isolated in his enormous house. I badly want to climb up to my room and go to sleep, but even more than that, I feel a certain pressure to reconnect with my family.

"I walked downtown," I say. "This city has really changed."

"It really has," he says, diddling his phone screen.

I slide onto the barstool next to him. "So what's happening in the world?"

"Just checking my Twitter." His voice has an edge, as if he's used to defending himself against a woman who's trying to get him off his phone.

I think I know who that woman is. I feel a flash of sympathy for my sister, but also for Neil.

"What are you tweeting about?"

His eyebrows scrunch together. "I don't tweet, I just follow a lot of smart political thinkers. It keeps me up on what's going on. I don't like to miss anything, lest I be caught unawares."

He says "thinkers" and "unawares" with a thick tongue. His inflamed eyes are sunk into his cheeks. In front of his place at the counter is an empty glass with melting ice cubes in it. He reaches for a bottle and splashes more into his glass. He takes some whiskey into his mouth and pulls his lips hard over his teeth, then disappears for a while as I quietly drink my water.

"Oh," he says after a moment, looking surprised, as if he's briefly forgotten I'm in the room and then whooshed back again to find me there for the first time. He stares at me frankly, as he always has, as he's always looked at every woman he encounters. He's my own age, and his frank assessment of me has always registered, somewhere in the back of my mind, unconsciously but unmistakably, as the universal right of everyone to appraise women. I expect it and recognize it as the normal way of things. We're both part of a communal cultural agreement that women's looks and physical attributes are up for grabs for everyone, not just straight men but gay men and women too, to judge and value, claim ownership of and take personally. When women are being observed, we're hyperaware of it. Unconsciously or consciously, we try to please the onlooker, do our best to rise to their expectations. Our female identity is bound up in how we appear to others.

But a new thing between Neil and me, whether he knows it or not, is that my potential diminished sexual viability in his or anyone's eyes is no longer of any concern to me. And with that clarity of sight comes a new and heady kind of power. I observe that Neil looks unhappy, and that his hair is thinning on the crown of his head. He has pouches under his eyes and dried spittle in the corners of his mouth. He seems vulnerable without his lovely flibbertigibbet wife nearby to serve as a galvanizing foil. When Celeste is around, he seems saner and stronger and manlier next to her droopy, fluttering liveliness. Right now, he looks lost in his own kitchen.

I want to ask him why he isn't upstairs keeping his recently bereaved wife company, comforting her and making her laugh, but I don't know how to interfere in other people's business, even my sister's. So I don't say anything.

Neil twitches anxiously in the silence. "I like to stay abreast of what's going on," he adds after a moment.

"Yes," I say, nodding. Wallace is the same way. "That's always good."

He looks wary, as if, from the Mariana Trench of his drunkenness, he senses mockery, though I intend none. His brain seems to be calibrated with a hair-trigger alarm system, failsafe even in case of coma or paralysis. "Or maybe should I say informed," he amends.

"Being informed is important."

"Well, you're doing a lot more than that." He sounds uneasy. "You're fighting the good fight. With your warrior brain."

This unexpected kindness takes me aback for an instant. I smile at him. "I think it's time for me to put this warrior brain to sleep," I say. "May your children return home in two pieces."

"Two," he echoes in alarm.

"You have two children."

My sleepiness intensifies with each stair I climb. The air of this house smells of my sister, her aromatherapy potions, her spicy shampoo. On the spacious second-floor landing, furnished with slouchy couches and random sports equipment and bookshelves I imagine are devoid of *Huckleberry Finn*, I pause to collect myself.

"Is that you?" comes Celeste's voice. Her bedroom door is open, and the room is dark except for the telltale sharp blue glow.

"That depends on who you mean by 'you,' " I say, staring into the bedroom to my right, its floor knee-deep in clutter. It's dark, without a lit-up phone, therefore empty, so I wander in and peer around, picking out objects in the dimness, mostly enormous sneakers. This is Jasper's room. It smells of teenage boy. Top notes of sperm, pot, sweat, with the underlying wholesome scent of fresh-baked bread.

"Rachel?"

"Yes, I'm here."

"I'm still awake. Come talk to me."

I go to Celeste's doorway. She sits in her bed, propped against eight thousand pillows, staring into her phone. "Where did you go earlier?"

"I'm sorry," I say. "It was too much. I didn't know David and Molly would be here." I know I should be pissed at her for pulling this on me, but my guilt is still overriding my anger. "It all hit me at once. What did I miss?"

"Nothing." Her voice is plaintive. "The kids left right after you. David and Molly and Liam took off. Neil did the dishes. He's been so sweet since Mom died."

"Did Aunt Jean ever appear on the screen?"

"Uncle Frank and Aunt Debbie did. They sat at her table and talked to us all while she cooked and waited on them. You know Aunt Jean. She can't sit still."

"She's almost ninety. Zoom is probably not something she gets at all."

"Poor Uncle Frank," says Celeste. "He looks so much older since Danny died. They say losing a child is the worst thing that can happen. I can imagine."

The implication is that I can't possibly. Fair enough. I can't see my sister's face, but her body importunes me with its hunched isolation. I lean against the doorjamb, feeling too awkward to venture farther into the room, although I know that she yearns for me to come in and lie next to her and confide, like college roomies.

"We're orphans now," she says, her voice wet.

"I know," I say, trying to infuse my voice with the sadness she craves from me. But I can't fake it, even as I wish I could. "But we were always sort of orphans, weren't we? And at least Lucie doesn't need anything anymore."

"She was in so much pain at the end, Rach, it was horrible. I did everything for her, and she yelled at me. I annoyed her and pissed her off, because she didn't want to be old and sick and dying, but she needed me, and I couldn't abandon her, so we were both stuck. What the hell was I supposed to do?"

I know exactly what she's talking about. I had the same experience with our mother ten years ago. I nursed her through a broken leg, and instead of being grateful, she pushed me away, hard. So I went. I wish Celeste could understand why I abandoned Lucie for the last years of her life and feel no guilt or regret about it. Mostly, I wish my sister and I could be close again the way we were in childhood, back when she adored me and I protected her. But she doesn't need protecting now, and she certainly doesn't adore me anymore, not even close.

"I know," I tell her. "I'm so sorry. It was complicated for me with Mom."

"She was our *mother*."

"There are two ways to look at your family. The first way, the so-called normal way, is that you owe them everything just because you're related. But I believe that that you owe them nothing even though you're related. It's not obligatory, it's voluntary."

She's silent.

"Of course I don't feel this way about you and Neil and the kids, I love you all, but what did I owe Lucie? Who was she to me really? Everything I've done my entire life, I did for myself. She started neglecting me the minute I popped out of her. Aunt Jean fed me bottles of formula and taught me to walk. I have photos. If it hadn't been for her, I would have died before I was six months old. By the time you came along, Mom had settled down a bit, she actually managed to get sober and breastfeed you. But me? The doctor slapped me on the butt, I cried, and she went right back to drinking. Not that she quit while she was pregnant with me."

"She always swore she did. And you're not brain damaged."

"Not so sure about that. Anyway, she died surrounded by people who took care of her, you and Neil and apparently Molly. She was lucky. You were a very good daughter to her, and I wasn't, and I'll live with that forever."

Celeste sobs for a while, very quietly.

"Celeste."

"What?" Her voice is clotted, vehement.

"Lucie was always going to die someday, and now that day has come. I wish I'd been here for the end, but only to be with you, only for your sake. Not hers."

"Jesus."

"I just can't pretend," I say. Our voices are muffled by the void of semi-darkness between us, the quiet air of the house. "She commanded me to stay away, and I took her at her word. It was what she wanted. I'm so sorry I let you down."

"You stayed in DC all through the chemo and radiation and sleepless nights and morphine shots. I nursed her and went to her appointments with her and cooked special food for her and helped her shower and wiped her ass and made tea exactly the way she liked it. I moved into her hospice room for the final two weeks and left Neil to take care of everything here. It was so, so hard. She was the most difficult patient ever. I felt completely alone with it all, and she took me totally for granted."

"I did that, too, for two months, remember? I know exactly how difficult she could be."

"That was ten years ago," she says. "For a broken leg, and she got better. This was cancer. And she died. Where the fuck were you?"

"I was not here," I say, so sad I can hardly speak. "I shouldn't have listened to her. I should have helped you. I'm so, so sorry."

After a short, bleak silence, she bursts out, "She treated me like I just sat around all day eating bonbons in my privileged life. Like taking care of her was some kind of important and useful activity for me."

"Oh God," I say. I want to laugh, but it would offend my sister, so I stifle it. "She would. That sounds exactly like her. She treated me like I was on vacation, like taking care of her was a luxury cruise."

Now Celeste laughs, so I laugh along with her.

"It does occur to me that we could have hired someone, both times."

She snorts. "Come on. Like Mom would ever for one second let a stranger come near her in that state. Like you or I would ever do that."

My sister is right. When Susan Bailey was dying, Neil and his younger sister hired a stalwart Romanian nurse to care for her, and then they visited her and sat by her bedside with her polite, well-groomed grandchildren. That's how it's done in their family, their social class, because the Baileys are coastal Protestant Mainers. But we're inland Catholic Mainers, another kind of people entirely, and in the end, despite having married into money, Celeste is always going to be a Gautreau, a Calloway. We have to care for our own. It's in our DNA. And I can feel my failure and abdication now, pulsing in my blood.

"I'd better get to bed." I pause at the foot of the stairs to the third floor, trying to find a way to express the deep gratitude and tenderness I feel for this person I was inseparable from when we were kids. "Sweet dreams, little sister," is all I come up with. I hear how hollow it sounds even as I say it.

But somehow, it's the right thing to say. "Thank you," she says. "Sweet dreams to you, too."

I climb to my plush little room and close the door behind me and stand there for a moment, letting the welcome silence ring in my ears. I sense the isolated maelstroms in the lonely skulls of my sister and Neil below me, their nearly grown children out in the dangerous world to be molested by hoboes and attacked by rabid graveyard foxes. I scrabble my hands through my open suitcase, which froths with unfolded garments until it belches forth some flannel pajama bottoms and an old PJ Harvey T-shirt with a small hole in the underarm. I strip naked, throw my sweater dress on top of the open suitcase, put my pajamas on, and climb into bed. I brushed my teeth earlier. I'll wash my face tomorrow morning.

I lie in bed staring into the lamplit darkness, way up here at the top of this mansion perched on the cliff that looks out over the estuary all the way west to Mount Washington on a clear day. My body is throbbing with thwarted desire for David, and sadness, and the awful complexity of being here.

My phone explodes with Madonna singing "Don't Cry for Me, Argentina," the ringtone I assigned to Wallace for no real reason except that it makes us both laugh.

"Oh my God," I exhale into my phone. "I'm so glad it's you."

"I thought I'd better check on you. See how things are going on your first night home."

His voice is vital and immediate. This is so like Wallace, to be primarily concerned about me when his nerves are dying one by one, and his body is becoming paralyzed and weak in terrifying increments. Wallace, who for a solid decade headed up a division of the FDA and oversaw an annual budget equal to that of a Hollywood blockbuster movie, is doing nothing with the short rest of his life except preparing to die.

It's not fair. My own body isn't failing, just losing its reproductive hormones. Of course I'll die eventually too—I'm as mortal as he is. I'll just be around longer, which is a double-edged sword, because I'll have to watch my dearest friend slowly and horribly die and then somehow go on without him. I have no idea how I'll do this. Dying almost seems preferable to losing a person like Wallace; I almost envy his impending freedom, and I dread my own upcoming grief as I've never dreaded anything before in my life. Of course I keep this to myself. I'm blunt, I know, but I do try not to be cruel.

"I ran away from the dinner table and took myself out to a restaurant," I tell him.

"That bad, huh."

"I cracked."

"No, good for you, I'm sure you needed to escape. How's the little sister?"

"She thinks I'm a monster for not coming back sooner. She's right."

I hear the sucking squeak that means Wallace is smoking a cigarette, which means he's sitting out on our back deck. Since his diagnosis, he's started again. Declan made him a contraption that helps him hold the cigarettes. Why not?

"No. Your mother was a monster. Your sister is a martyr. You're a realist who hates psychodrama and bullshit obligation. Don't get sucked into her guilt trip, Ray. Let it go."

"I feel like the most terrible person who ever lived."

"Well, you're actually the best person. I would know."

I relax into my pillows, soothed as always by his calm, unvarnished clarity. It was one of the reasons I married him. "How are you, Wally?"

"Couldn't be better." He takes another lascivious drag, exhales grandly. "The stock answer for the rest of my life."

"I love you," I say, almost in tears.

"You sweet talker. So why is it so awful there? Tell me."

I can't answer.

"Rachel," he says crisply. "Hey hey. I talked to my doctor today. He told me some things."

I inhale hard to hold back an infinitude of tears. "What?"

"ALS does not affect the penis, which Declan is glad to hear. Or the brain. I might laugh and cry hysterically out of the blue a lot in the coming months, but please be assured that my mind will remain as laser sharp as ever."

"Oh, that's good," I say.

"We're talking about taking a trip, while there's still time. Maybe I could handle a cruise to Alaska to see some melting glaciers. Declan thinks it might be a good thing."

Thank God for Declan, I think. He's a tall, handsome man in his late thirties who started out as Wallace's administrative assistant back when Wallace was still in the closet, when we were still married. Declan was promoted to research fellow shortly before he and Wallace got involved and fell in love. They kept their relationship a secret, no doubt suspected by many of their coworkers, until Wallace left the FDA last year. Declan still works there, poor man, essentially a mouthpiece now for Bayer and Pfizer.

A year ago, when Wallace got his ALS diagnosis and resigned from his job at the FDA, I invited him to move in with me, back into the condo we still jointly own, along with Declan, because he'll need constant care and support for the rest of his cruelly truncated life.

"Do it," I say. "Go. Can I help pay for it?"

"My savings will last me till the end. Hold on to your money, Rachel, you're going to need it for your long and healthy life. Damn you."

"Stop. Don't. I can't take it."

"Oh, Ray. You're such a softie."

"I might be losing my job." I haven't wanted to burden him with any of this before, but it just slips out. "I think they're going to let me go, now that I took bereavement leave and got safely out of the way."

He doesn't miss a beat, which makes me suspect he already knows what's going on somehow. "We'll fight them. We'll make them sorry."

After we hang up, I put my phone facedown on the nightstand, turn out the lamp, and get under the plush comforter. Eyes shut, one hand wedged between my thighs and the other tucked under my pillow, I wait to drift into unconsciousness. But my mind continues to churn, persistently awake. Minutes pass. I urge my overactive brain to power down, shut off. It refuses. I wish I had more control over it. It occurs to me that when I trained my brain to run on its hamster wheel, I forgot to teach it to stop, get off, let go. I wish I had learned how to meditate somewhere along the line. I wish I were capable of deep breathing. I wish I had a pill to knock myself out with. Anything.

I hear a soft hushing sound that turns out to be my door being pushed open against the thick carpet. I sit upright and stare into the gloom, wondering if one of the dogs has wandered in.

A terse whisper: "Rachel."

A shape comes toward the bed. His weight compresses the mattress, and the smell and feel of him flood my senses. He stretches out alongside me, the length of his body against mine.

"David," I whisper his name through clenched teeth like a curse, urgently awake now. "How did you get in?"

"I left the back door unlocked when we left. No one noticed."

"Go away. You can't be here."

"In a minute," he whispers back, his breath sweet and boozy and so familiar. My entire body urges itself toward that smell. That was total crap, about my brain being awake because it's used to working so hard. Of course I was waiting for David to come. I knew he would.

"What are you doing?"

"I need you."

Our mouths are so close, I can feel his breath on my lips. Damn it. I'm starving for him. This is very bad in every way. I know better.

"You're *married*," I whisper, my teeth and muscles all clenched against him.

The anciently known smell of him bypasses all my defenses and I cave in, go limp. We lie together for a long, slow moment. I'm flooded with all of it, my lonely rough youth, everything I fought so hard to get away from, everything I still am, deep down. I can't fight it. I'm too tired.

To my horror, my entire body convulses as if I'm having a seizure. From deep in my underbelly come waves of silent, juddering sobs. My entire torso is shaking. My face is slick. I don't make a sound.

Sliding under the blankets, David swaddles me with his entire self, runs his hands along my arms to interlace with my fingers, presses his chest down into mine, his legs aligned with mine all the way to his feet, which capture mine by the ankles and gently swivel. He sets his forehead on top of mine and rocks my head gently from side to side. He's making a shushing noise, rhythmic and steady, as he soothes me with his whole body. I allow this to happen. Slowly I calm down, my mind gradually going blank and loose, unknotting with every heave of raw pain. Under the nape of my neck, my pillow is hot and soaked. My chest is hollowed out.

Our stomachs are still pressed together, and we're breathing in steady slow unison. I feel the old heat revving up, and David evidently isn't going to stop us. For a second, I consider letting it happen. It's just one more point of contact between us; we're already practically there, moving slowly together, hips undulating, mouths almost touching—in less than one minute, we're going to be fucking.

Just in time, I remember what happened a decade ago, too terrible to face, a bloody knot.

I scrunch myself into a ball. "Go," I whisper. "Goodbye."

He doesn't move. There's a silence while he waits. But I don't unscrunch.

He leaps in a flash from my bed and vanishes through the doorway into the darkness of my sister's house. I imagine him creeping down and out and back to his own house, barefoot over the adjoining lawns, back to his sleeping wife. Whose name is Molly. Who is lovely and kind and sane.

In the chill of his absence, a simultaneous letdown for my body and relief for my brain, I'm jarred by a piercing shriek from the landing just below me, a shrill female voice, then a brief male bark. And then the house just as abruptly stills into a shocked silence, reverberating through the dense warm air.

The surface closes over my head as I tumble through the black layers, down and slowly down to the strange, longed-for, high-pressure world of absolute, velvety, teeming, living darkness.

Part II

Six

In my dream, a giant creature is yipping at me, poking my exposed bare arm with a sharp claw. "Wake the fuck up, Rachel."

My eyes are glued shut. My mouth is thick with unbrushed tooth scum.

She won't go away. "You have to leave right this minute. Mallory just told me what happened last night. She saw David sneaking out of your room. She's devastated. She *loves* Molly. How dare you fuck my best friend's husband under my roof. My daughter is in *shock*. She's traumatized."

I pry my eyes open, sit up, and rub both palms hard over my face. "I kicked him out."

She doesn't hear me. "I called you an Uber. It'll be here in ten minutes. You're going to go stay at Mom's. Her house keys are on your suitcase."

"What time is it?"

But she's gone.

I make a dash to the bathroom, where I chug two glasses of water, pee, brush my teeth, shower, and slather expensive-feeling lavender-scented lotion on my face from the pump dispenser by the sink. I put on the same sweater dress and boots I shucked last night, zip my roller bag shut, and take my walk of shame downstairs, during which I encounter no one. I smell coffee and hear all four of their voices in the kitchen, bowls and spoons clanking, as I skulk through the foyer and out the front door and down the porch steps to the waiting car. The air is insultingly cool and fresh. The sky is as blue as a robin's egg, filled with birdsong and the smell of blossoms.

My driver is a young woman in a hijab who gives me a smile as lovely as the morning.

I hunch in the back seat and stare out the window, queasy and thirsty and in the grip of uneasy defiance. Knowing my sister, she's decided for the sake of peace and harmony that David is the innocent victim here, a poor dumb beast unable to resist my siren call, and I lured him to my bed in a crass attempt to wreck his perfect fledgling marriage. I hope she won't tell Molly. That would be flat-out cruel; David got into my bed uninvited, we didn't have sex, and then he left. For God's sake, my mother just died, my best friend is dying. Can't I get emotional and wrap myself around my old boyfriend and cry for a minute? Fuck my self-righteous prig of a sister and her precious coddled children who can't be exposed to any whiff of adult complexity. At their age, I was hitching rides to the beach from adult men, showing them my tender cleavage. So was Celeste, the hypocrite.

I watch the streets of Portland slide by out the window, all of it jarringly familiar, Congress Street to Mellon down to Deering Oaks Park. As we drive through the park, I see throngs of people standing or sitting in small groups on the grass across from the post office, listless and unkempt, an impromptu congregation of the mentally ill, drug-addicted residents of Portland's many shelters, surrounded by trash, sleeping bags, shopping carts, backpacks. A few of them slump on the curb, nodding out. Three of them hold cardboard signs at the stoplight. My driver slides through the green light and ignores them; I wonder what her story is, what country she came from, what she thinks of living here, but I'm not awake enough yet for conversation. On Baxter Boulevard she pulls the car over, and then there's nothing to do but get out and face my mother's house.

For three decades or more Lucie lived in this plain mid-twentieth-century block of vinyl-sided attached two-story "apartment townhomes" perched at the top of a sloping lawn, facing Back Cove. I take some deep breaths as I stand on the grass, looking out at the tidal flats, nakedly exposed. Canada geese paddle through faraway lapping waves as seagulls swoop in to forage. A stiff little breeze blows up from the water, carrying the intimate funk of low tide, brine, and car exhaust. Sucking this deeply familiar air into my lungs, I turn, step onto the small concrete entry stoop, and unlock the front door. I have to brace myself before I can walk in, remind myself that, improbable as it is, my mother is dead and this place is legally mine now, whether I like it or not.

As I step inside and shut the door behind me, I am instantly bathed in stale air, too warm. The heat is on, the windows sealed shut. It smells of my mother's supersize, antagonistic presence. I walk through the downstairs, looking with dread at everything. My mouth is dry. My heart is racing. The fact that this wilderness is domestic, and the stalking predator here lives only inside my skull, doesn't make any of it less frightening.

Since childhood, I've never felt comfortable in any of my mother's houses, any of the places where we lived, where I grew up. They've always been hostile environments of uncomfortable extremes, too bright and exposed in the daytime with nowhere to hide, too forebodingly dark at night with lurking unseen terrors, the furniture either too hard or too soft, the air smelling either of burned food or too much floral perfume. There's nowhere for my mind or body to settle, a lurking sense of apprehensive distress, as if the air molecules themselves carried biochemical nerve toxins.

I lug my suitcase upstairs. I plan to sleep in my mother's old bedroom. There's a second bedroom, a small room imbued with memories of private, psychic pain. Staying in my mother's room, and everything that implies, is vastly preferable to even opening the guest-room door. I walk by it fast and don't even look at it.

I stand in the front bedroom, Lucie's old room, which overlooks the water. Without her vibrant self to inhabit it, it all looks dull and sad. As in all my mother's bedrooms, the decor is Spartan, minimal—just a bed, bureau, nightstand, and chair, no pictures on the white walls, a large mirror over the dresser reflecting stark emptiness. The bed is a queen-size mattress and box spring on a metal frame with wheels that squeak when I sit down and bounce gently to test it. The mattress is so unyieldingly hard that it propels me upright again.

I embark on some nervous snooping, opening drawers, peeking inside, half expecting my mother to jump out at me and yell "Boo!"

Lucie's bureau is sparsely stocked with waist-high underwear and knee socks and flesh-tone bras, winter and summer nighties, utilitarian trousers, khaki and twill. No denim—she always hated blue jeans, never wore them. Her closet holds a row of wool sweaters and dress slacks with elasticized waistbands, outdated "fancy" party dresses I bet she didn't wear once in her last ten years, and a couple of corduroy skirts, one beige, one navy blue, both well worn.

How did these drab old-lady clothes take over my formerly glamorous mother's closet? Who was Lucie, at the end of her life?

Prickling on the surface of my skin is the creepy, irrational sense that my mother is silently watching me from some hiding place, hovering in midair over my head. I can't shake the knowledge that I'm just a tentative interloper awaiting the return of the rightful occupant. Guiltily, I close all her bureau drawers, shut her closet up tight, and go back downstairs.

In the dim little kitchen, all Formica and linoleum and scuffed laminated cupboard doors, I rummage in the fridge and pantry. The pickings are slim—no one has been here since she went to hospice two or three weeks ago, maybe even longer—but there's most of a can of Maxwell House on the counter. Once the coffee maker is gurgling, I pour a handful of bran flakes into a bowl and add a glug of room-temperature boxed milk from her cupboard.

I drink two cups of hot black coffee before I can eat, so fast I scorch the back of my throat, but I don't care, the pain feels good. While I slurp my cereal, out of childhood habit I also inhale the information on the back and sides of the cereal box. After I pour myself a second bowl, I paw through my mother's copies of *The Joy of Cooking* and Fannie Farmer, impulse buys during her extremely rare and wide-spaced fits of self-improvement and avowals to live a better life. The books are pristine. I devour their recipes as a source of vicarious warmth and cheer. They conjure an imaginary mid-twentieth-century American mother in a ruffled apron who nightly brought to the dinner table cozy, deliciously named dishes like pot roast, Irish stew, southern fried chicken, cherry pie, apple Brown Betty. She did this happily, with no other needs and desires but to nourish her husband and children. She sat quietly at the table, watching them eat with a beaming smile, selfless, loving. Sure, hot rage bubbled underneath the smile, and sure, she took God knew what pills to sustain it, but they didn't know that until later, when she ran off with her best friend to Greenwich Village and became a lesbian painter in a leotard and black cigarette pants and ballet flats.

It goes without saying that she was nothing at all like my own real-life mother.

Suddenly there I am on that day again, the afternoon when I came home from school, back in eighth grade, and walked into our shitty "snuggle-wide" house to discover my mother sprawled on the blue couch in her nightgown, stone drunk, with a nearly empty bottle of something cheap and strong on the rug next to her. My stepfather at the time, Bill Johnson, was out in the yard, installing a new gun rack on his Dodge Ram, probably in a pissed-off mood. He was a big, strapping Nam vet, a building contractor, and my mother worshipped him for reasons I will never understand. "He was a war hero," she used to tell Celeste and me. "That's the sexiest thing in the world." She was in his thrall until he left her about six years after their courthouse wedding.

"You have to wake up, Mom," I shouted into her face, slapping her cheeks with both hands just hard enough to sting. I knew from years of experience what to do with her when she was drunk, I'd been doing it all my life, but this time she seemed to be dead. A line of dried drool was pasted to her cheek. Her skin was cold to the touch. Celeste crept in, watched me try to revive her. "Get Bill," I said. Celeste ran outside, calling for him to come, something was wrong with our mother.

In the long ticking seconds it took before Bill stowed his tools and sauntered in to see what was going on this time with his shitfaced wife, before he picked Lucie up and threw her into his truck and drove her to the emergency room to have her stomach pumped and get her on IV fluids to rehydrate her, I stopped trying to wake her up and stood staring at her.

I wanted her to come to, but I also and equally wanted her to be dead, to have this over with, this misery and shame and stress and the horrible responsibility I felt, all the time, to make sure she didn't die or kill herself.

I always kept a certain distance from other kids at school, too ashamed to have anyone come over to this chaotic upside-down house where I was the responsible adult and my mother was the fucked-up problem child and

Celeste needed so much more than I could give her, and my stepfathers came and went, and my father had vanished into drugs and jail and petty crime and flophouse life.

Back then I didn't know that alcoholism was a legitimate disease, or that the stigma around mental illness was causing my mother to go undiagnosed and untreated. I'd never heard of rehab or psychiatric therapies. In other words, I didn't know that none of this was my mother's fault, I thought she was choosing to be this way. So I stood by the couch where she lay, staring down at her with heartsick despair, willing her to be dead.

And now she is.

I drown this memory like a rat in a bathtub, rinse my bowl and spoon and leave them in the dish drain, and wander out to the living room, feeling restless and itchy, unable to focus. I stand at the window, looking out at the rain squall that's just come up over the cove, blurring the small city's sort-of skyline along the gentle sweep of the peninsula. The big panes are smeared and spattered with rain. Headlights illuminate raindrops on the roadway, brake lights at the traffic signal flare through the dim downpour, reflecting in the wet black asphalt.

This morning feels interminable. It's not even nine o'clock yet. I have no idea how I'm going to get through this day. The possibilities for avoiding what needs facing are bleak and uninspiring. I could sprawl on the squooshy blue fake-velvet couch watching daytime TV, as I imagine my mother did most days. I could call Wallace. I could take a bath. I could call an Uber and get out of here. And tonight, as soon as it's plausibly bedtime, I could put on my PJs and get into my mother's bed and try to sleep in her sheets, my head on her pillows, her presence permeating my dreams.

The rain has stopped for now, so I step outside into the changeable morning with a third cup of coffee. A streaky blue sky is smudged with charcoal clouds, leftover spatterings of raindrops blowing on an almost-warm breeze, the cove roughed up and dark. Yawning, I cross Baxter Boulevard to drink my coffee on a wet bench by the running trail, watching joggers and cyclists go by, walkers with dogs on leashes. Ducks waddle around me, unsteady on their orange flippers, trolling for scraps and quacking softly at one another, but I have nothing to give them.

Spring in Maine, I remember well, is a season that stretches from the drawn-out end of the icebound, bleak winter to the galvanizing beginning of the brief blue-green-gold summer. It starts out with April, reliably cold and generally dreary, and May is just more of April with incrementally longer and warmer days, a trickster month that metes out its transition so slowly, so pinchedly, it might as well not be happening at all. In other words, spring in Maine is a nonseason, a joke that goes on much too long and whose punch line is summer, a complete failure of comic timing because it comes much too late.

I stand up and head back to my mother's house. Coffee drunk, mind clear, I can't dawdle any longer. I brace myself, push aside my revulsion, and go up to her bedroom and start going through her clothes, planning to sort them all into two piles: one to donate to the Goodwill and one to set aside in case Celeste wants to have a crack at our mother's more glamorous fripperies. But I can't imagine anyone wanting any of this stuff. I thrust things into garbage bags without really looking at them. Everything feels vaguely greasy to the touch, and in the harsh light of the suddenly fierce sun, streaming unfiltered through the naked bedroom windows, it all looks worn and cheap—her cracked hand mirror, smeared with grime, the strands of hair in the bristles of her brush, flaked with dandruff.

I don't recognize my flamboyant, vain mother in any of this. I'm looking at the wreckage of an elderly woman reduced to utilitarian necessity, unable to keep her belongings clean, unable, maybe, to recognize or notice the disintegration around her. I fill one of her old suitcases with anything remotely reusable and put it by the door to donate. In the kitchen, I pile mismatched dishes on the kitchen counters, make piles of home decorating and celebrity gossip magazines, more of her vicarious, aspirational, unfulfilled self-improvement purchases, and tie them with twine to recycle. During the course of a few hours, I fill several large trash bags and put them outside on the back porch.

While I do this blitzkrieg purging of my mother's earthly possessions, I don't go into the guest room or even open its door. I'll have to face it eventually, but it's too soon, too sudden and raw.

When I've done as much as I can in one go and am overwhelmed with dust and sadness, I stand in the middle of the living room, my brain tick-ing. I'm hungry and thirsty. For the first time, it occurs to me that maybe my mother's old car is available to me. Celeste definitely doesn't need it. It's probably sitting in the parking lot. I look out the back kitchen window and see three cars parked back there, one of which is my mother's rust-colored Subaru. I find the keys in her purse, which is dangling from a hook inside the closet by the front door, as if waiting for her to sling it over her shoulder on her way out. I wonder why she didn't bring it to hospice with her. But no doubt by then she was in no shape to ever need her keys and wallet again.

I go out the back door and lock it behind me, get into the old rattletrap and fire it up, swing onto Baxter, and drive the mile or so around the cove to Hannaford.

I've decided to make myself a cheese and mushroom omelet for supper, with steamed broccoli on the side. Back in my mother's house, with the groceries put away, I'm ironically aware that I'm mothering myself, slicing mushrooms, beating eggs, giving myself a pleasant, homey meal. I wonder if my mother ever did this for herself. What did she eat in her final decade? Did she eat any real meals these last years, or did she subsist on wine and bourbon, supplemented with saltines and Campbell's creamed soups and canned fruit cocktail and cottage cheese? I'll never know.

I take my plate out to the living room to eat at the little table by the window, perched at an angle on one of the Lucite chairs, a material far too hard for the comfort of human flesh. As I eat my solitary supper, I feel an odd pang of missing out. I think about what's probably happening at Celeste's house right now. I picture my sister coming home from Whole Foods, parking in her tidy garage, walking into her sheltering house, let-ting her son carry the groceries in for her, accepting a glass of wine from her already-shitfaced husband, bracing herself for sidelong snark from her daughter, being licked and joyously panted on by her dogs, pulling things like chicken and vegetables and butter and cream and fresh herbs from grocery bags and putting them into the well-stocked, abundant fridge. Maybe David and Molly will wander over for drinks. Maybe they're over there right now, sitting at the kitchen island, leaning chummily on their elbows, Neil's cocktails and Raincoast crackers and Humboldt Fog set in front of them.

Goddammit. That bitch. She accused me of having sex with her best friend's husband and turfed me out of bed at the crack of dawn and made me take an Uber over here. No benefit of the doubt. Not a shred of kindness.

Now I'm choking with rage, too pissed off to finish my meal.

I open the front door and go outside to stand on the lawn in the breezy spring darkness, inhaling the sweetness of wakening dirt and new grass, the brackish smells blowing up from the cove, seagrass and kelp and mud. The calm water holds pinpoint reflections of light from the city skyline rising steeply from its curve into the long double hump of the peninsula. The air is chilly, but it doesn't feel cold enough for this time of year. The Gulf of Maine is warming faster than any other body of water in the northern hemisphere, maybe the world. How long before this building is under water? I have no idea, but no matter what, it's coming.

I stare into the front picture windows of the other three units. There's nothing to see but the white glow of laptops and smartphones and flatscreens: Americans relaxing alone on a Sunday night. I feel like a grubby voyeur, watching them all, sucked into the death-ray vapor locks of their screens, as if I'm privy to something too sad to be borne. They might as well be floating in outer space in life-support pods.

The door of the town house next to my mother's opens, and someone comes out onto her own concrete stoop. I behold an old woman clutching a shawl around her. In the dim, pinkish glow of the overhead outdoor lights, she looks distraught.

"Are you Lucie's daughter?" She has a long, toothy face, wears big granny glasses. Her long, loose white hair blows in the wind off the cove. She's my height, and under the shawl her spine is straight.

"I'm Rachel," I say. "The older one."

"Well, I know Celeste, of course."

Of course.

She's still talking. "I've been away. My daughter had twins, she's a single mother, her little boy Miles is three, and there were complications, I won't bore you, so I went to Cleveland to take care of her and her babies until she got on her feet again. I just got back and heard Lucie passed. I'm so sorry I wasn't here." She sounds out of breath, which I suspect is her natural manner of speaking.

"I wasn't here either," I say bluntly. Something about this person makes me even more clipped and precise than usual. She strikes me as someone who likes to pull strangers into long, florid, hyperdramatic conversations.

"I'm so sorry." Her chest heaves. "I loved your mother very much. I'm Jenny, by the way. Jenny Baum. Have you moved into her place?"

"No, I'm just clearing it out to sell it. I live in DC."

"Lucie and I were dear friends," she goes on. "I just loved being her neighbor. She was so colorful and fun, but she struggled. She needed a lot of help and support, and I'm someone who loves to give. She always told me how much she hated being dependent on anyone. Sometimes I worried I'd overstepped."

"Actually, she loved being taken care of," I say. I can imagine this person coming into my mother's life like a godsend from right next door: chatty, caretaking, kind, a little wacky, an empathetic listener. She's Lucie's ideal friend. "I'm sure she appreciated you more than she could say."

"Thank you, dear. That means a lot, it really does."

Jenny Baum stands next to me in silence for a moment, both of us looking out over the light-streaked expanse, listening to the rushing quietude of the ebbing tide.

"Well, I'm so glad you're here," she says then, her hand resting on my arm. Her mouth is slightly open as she leans toward me. Her eyes are gaping wet holes.

I conjure up a clear image of Jenny and Lucie sitting close together on Lucie's couch, an opened bottle of something between them, Jenny making this rapaciously empathetic expression while Lucie goes on and on in her raucous voice about her various health conditions, her migraines, constipation, back pain, and of course the cancer that killed her, Jenny tearing into this emotional raw meat with her dogteeth, sucking the marrow out of it with her vampire fangs.

"It's nice to meet you," I tell her politely.

Jenny's lantern-jawed face ignites into a ferocious smile, and her voice is a rush of beseeching friendliness. "I look forward to getting to know you, dear."

"I'm leaving soon," I say, backing away. I cannot entangle myself with this person. Her loneliness is a bottomless, engulfing black pool.

From my jacket pocket, Madonna bursts into song, commanding Argentina not to cry for her. I pull out the phone, hold it up by way of excuse, and wave at Jenny Baum as I insert myself back into my mother's house, close the door behind me, and allow the prickly, supercharged air to claim me again.

Seven

"Hi, Wally," I say, leaning against the kitchen counter. "I was just about to call you."

"This is Declan."

"Did something happen?"

"Wallace fell. It was bad, but he's okay. He's in the hospital, I've been here with him, and I forgot my own phone so I'm using his."

"What happened?"

"He insisted on taking a shower by himself. He said he wasn't going to be able to ever again and it was his last chance. I let him do it. He lost control and slipped on the tiles and hit his head on the edge of the tub. He was out for a while, and they say he has a concussion. They're keeping him for observation overnight."

"Is he conscious now?"

"He was upset in the ambulance. I mean hysterical. It's a new symptom, emotional overreactions to things."

"Can he hear you right now?"

"No. I'm out in the hallway."

Declan is cool as a tulip, with waxy fresh skin and corn-silk hair and dark-blue eyes in a tender Irish face. He's devoted to my ex-husband, his former boss, mentor, lover, and now patient, a devotion that increasingly contains hints of a controlling, proprietary possessiveness. He moved into my house just over a year ago, by which I mean the duplex Wallace and I still technically, officially own together, the one we lived in as a married couple. I took over the mortgage after our divorce and had been planning to buy him out of his equity when I could, but now, of course, that's moot. I'm letting him live there with me for the rest of his life, along with Declan.

At first our cohabitation as a threesome was surprisingly harmonious and easygoing, at least for me, if only because I'm almost never home. But lately, as Wallace has weakened and become more dependent, I've been picking up hostile signals from Declan. One day about a month ago, I came home early from work with a pounding headache. *"Rachel,"* said Declan from the couch, where he was feeding Wallace his dinner. On his face was an oddly defensive pique, as if I'd walked in on them having sex in their own private bedroom without knocking rather than entering my own living room with my own key. Then he caught himself with a quick "Hey, stranger!" But it was too late; I realized, standing there with my keys in my hand, my other hand massaging my aching temple, that to Declan I had become a third wheel in our shared quarters, a regrettable inconvenience whose claim on the place by dint of ownership is all that keeps him from kicking me out. Well, it's also technically still Wallace's place, too, of course, and that gives Declan the right to live there.

Declan and I hardly know each other. We're virtual strangers bound by the punitive DC housing market and our shared love for Wallace, our mutual husband. I know he knows my history with Wallace as intimately as it can be known; he was the other party in our divorce. His affair with Wallace went on for a year before I caught them together. So he was the home-wrecker who ended our marriage, technically and literally, but I know from half-joking comments he's made that this is not how he sees it. He sees himself as Wallace's liberator, the instrument of the truth, the source of his happiness. And he sees me as the agent of that constricted, unhappy, secretive life Wallace lived before, closeted, lying to everyone, keeping his love for Declan hidden from the world.

For all these reasons and more, Declan resents me, probably competitively too, since after him, I am Wallace's closest friend. And now I know that every night when I come home and walk into their little shared world, he feels a sharp disappointment and sense of intrusion that he's usually able to conceal from me. And there's nothing I can do about this, not until Wallace dies. Declan will then, I assume, move on to wherever life takes him next, and we'll be free of each other forever.

"So I'm calling for two reasons," he's saying. "One is more immediate. You remember we talked about moving Wallace to the downstairs bedroom when things reached a certain point."

The downstairs bedroom, dim and quiet with a view of the back patio, is my bedroom, the room where I do almost nothing but lie in bed trying to sleep. It's the smaller of the two bedrooms. Wallace and Declan have the big bedroom upstairs, with a balcony and a walk-in dressing room and a large bathroom with two sinks and a soaking tub.

"So we're at that point," I say. I feel a lump in my throat, a profound sadness for Wallace, poor Wallace. And another secret, unforgivably self-ish sadness. My bedroom is the sanctuary I retreat to at the end of a long, hard day. I can't sleep there (or anywhere, let's face it), but at least I can rest my bones on my cushiony pillow-top mattress and allow my thoughts to drift in the darkness. The upstairs bedroom is too big, noisy with traffic sounds, lit by streetlamps at night and direct sunlight in the daytime. It feels bright and public. The bed, although expensive and king-size, is uncomfortable because Wallace prefers hard mattresses, and it's the bed he bought for us when we were married. When it was clear that we were not going to have a robust sex life, or really any sex life at all, I moved into the little guest room downstairs. The excuse was that I regularly came home late from work and woke up Wallace, who complained that he was chronically sleep-deprived because of my tossing and turning. But the truth was, we liked sleeping apart. I've been there ever since. And somehow I believed, childishly, that Wallace would never reach point zero.

"Okay," I say. "I'll move my stuff upstairs the instant I get home."

"Actually," Declan says, "I need to do it for you. Now. Before he comes home tomorrow. He can't climb those stairs anymore."

Even though this has been the plan all along, even though I know it's temporary, because Wallace won't live forever, this is hard for me to accept right now, standing here in my mother's dismal house, yearning to be back in my own room. It's the only place I can hide in, the one refuge I have where I'm safe and calm. This also means Wallace is that much closer to dying. I'm truly going to lose him, it's happening.

I try and fail to rise to this news with pure, instant generosity.

"Okay," I say in a pinched voice, willing the lump in my throat to melt. A tear leaks out of my eye and snail-trails its way along my cheek to the tip of my nose. I let it hang there, tickling me. "Just dump everything upstairs, I'll deal with it when I get back."

He sighs. This is a hardship for him too. He naturally prefers the larger, more luxurious bedroom. No one is happy about this, but the bedroom question is just a stand-in for our underlying grief about losing the person we both love most. This should unite us, give us empathy for each other.

"I wish I were there to help you," I say. "I'm very sorry you have to deal with this without me."

"Me too." We're quiet for a beat. He clears his throat. "So how's it going up there? How are *you* holding up?" Maybe he's spurred by a similar realization, or maybe he's suddenly remembering that I'm not exactly on a luxury vacation in Provence.

"I have to tie up some loose ends at my mother's place, figure out what to do with all her stuff."

"Well, I hope you're not planning to bring any of it down here. We have more than enough to deal with as it is."

I feel like slapping him through the phone. I try with my voice: "What's the other thing you wanted to talk about, Declan?"

"Wallace is leaving me his share of the duplex."

"What?"

"He wrote up his will yesterday."

Again: "What?"

"He's also naming me his life insurance beneficiary." I'm not imagining the sharp note of triumph in his voice, as if he's won some competition I didn't know we were having.

"Okay," I say. Of course Wallace has every right to do this. Declan is his lover, his caretaker.

Declan's voice is a filleting knife in my ear. "His idea is that I'll be able to have a place to live and a little nest egg after he dies. He wants to provide that for me."

"I see." My voice is steady, thank God. "Declan, I'm sorry, but I can't talk about this right now. My mother just died, and I'm in a world of shit. And I'm worried about Wallace and heartbroken I can't be there for him."

"Well, what would be a better time then?" He sounds snippy, the little bitch.

"I hope that Wallace will tell me himself when I get back. He and I need to have that conversation."

"I understand why you're upset, Rachel." His voice is so cold. Suddenly I am aware that he might actually hate me. "I just thought you should know as soon as possible. It's Wallace's place, too. I'm his fiancé. Husband-to-be."

"Congratulations." I poke at my phone to hang up and toss it down on the counter.

After I wash the dishes, banging pots and silverware satisfyingly around the sink, I check my phone again and find a text from Priyanka Gupta. It says, basically, the same thing as the other texts she's been sending me since I left the office to fly up here: "FaceTime me as soon as you can."

Something's going on at *CORE*. I don't want to know what it is; I don't want to be involved with it in any way. And I profoundly do not want to FaceTime with Priyanka right now, much as I like her, much as I trust and respect her judgment. But I have to assume it's urgent, or she, of all people, wouldn't be hounding me. So either our funding has been pulled or they're pursuing a big story so exciting I have to hear about it right away. I'm guessing it's not the latter, pretty sure it's not good news at all. There's rarely any good news anymore.

I lower myself onto my mother's blue couch, which is so spongy it's like a carnivorous plant whose petals close around me, dissolving me to jelly as it absorbs my life force. It's covered in a bright-blue fabric as slick and soft as oil. I don't know where it originally came from or when my mother got it, but this is the same couch she got drunk and passed out on in all our houses throughout my childhood. When she moved into this house in the early 1990s with Malachi, her third husband, this damn couch came with her, and here it still is.

I stash my legs under my butt and surrender myself to the cushions as I call Priyanka.

Her face fills the screen right away: horn-rimmed glasses framing long-lashed brown eyes, full mouth compressed, a deep furrow between her young brows, rich brown skin turned sallow and dull by the harsh fluorescent lights. I can see from the background that she's in the conference room, surrounded by people. It's after eight on a Sunday, but of course they're all at the office. The issue has to be put to bed by tomorrow morning.

"Rachel, there you are," she says. Her voice echoes metallically, as if she's submerged in a galvanized water tank. "Hold on just a minute, I'm going into the hallway. It's Rachel," she says to someone offscreen, already on the move. Then I see the dull beige paint of the hallway behind her. "Okay, I have to talk fast. He's announced some deep budget cuts. I think he's gunning for you."

"Okay," I say. "Thank you for the heads-up."

Priyanka huffs. "I can't believe that pissant is doing this now, while you're on bereavement leave."

"He's clearly gone on the offensive. If he wants me out, I'm out."

"He" is Martin Gold, our evil little lickspittle rodent of a newly appointed editor in chief, even younger than Priyanka.

"You don't know that for sure," says Priyanka. She sounds like she's pleading with me to make this true. "Maybe you should get in touch with Edison soon and make sure he goes to bat for you." Edison Fellows is my longtime mentor and our project director, a seasoned warhorse approaching seventy.

"It's very clear how this is going to go," I tell her. "Edison's days are numbered, because apparently they're trying to force him to take early retirement, and I'm probably headed down the chute right behind him."

"Well, that pretty much means the end of all of us," says Priyanka. "So I'm right behind you. Prep for slaughter."

"Moo," I say.

She laughs. I laugh too, through a jolt of anger. Priyanka is so brilliant, so well-educated and hardworking, I wish I could offer her the career I found at her age, a whole exciting rich field just waiting for me. But those days were already long gone by the time she came to the magazine two years ago with a freshly minted journalism degree from Northwestern and a raft of good ideas.

She and I work well together. I know she's bucking for my job when I leave, and she'll probably get it. Our friendship is both limited and bolstered by our age difference and the fact that she needs me to move on, step aside, vanish. Every mentor-protégé relationship has this tension. Ours has worked better than most.

"I have to go back to the meeting," she tells me. "Let me know what Edison says when you talk to him?"

"Of course."

We say goodbye and my phone's screen blips to the FaceTime app logo.

No matter what, I'll have a big fight on my hands when I get back, probably a fruitless and quixotic one, but I can't give up this easily. I can't let a smug, pink-faced little douchenozzle like Martin Gold win so easily, not after everything I've put into getting approval for my two most recent projects. One is an already-funded series about algal photosynthesis, which I'm planning to start researching as soon as I get home. The other is a proposal for a three-part exposé of geoengineering, which I submitted to Edison two weeks ago and still haven't heard back from him about. It's been nagging at me. I need to know right now whether or not it's going to fly. I need this to cheer me up, the comforting, concrete sense of the next six months of my work life.

I'm afraid that without my job, I won't fully exist. My work is all I have, my whole life. Without it, who am I?

I send Edison a quick email, a gentle nudge, asking for an update.

This day is finally over.

Eight

I lie awake for hours in my mother's rock-hard bed. My entire body is rigid, restless, finding no cushioning to sink into. Her pillows smell of her. Her sheets smell of her. I should have changed them earlier, should have put clean linen on her bed, but too late. I lie there awash in her dead skin cells, the residue of her hair oils, the history of her body in this bed.

The place behind my eyes is concentrated into a strong, slow throb. God, I hate this house. Being here makes my brain itch, burns my skin with an invisible, potent rash. Hatred of a place isn't like any other kind of hate. It's specific, location-based, and easy to avoid: the obvious solution and instant cure is to just leave.

I fight a strong urge to get the first flight out to DC early tomorrow morning. I imagine leaning back in my seat as the plane takes off, watching Maine recede and blur and vanish. It gives me a small, mean pleasure to imagine Declan's pissy expression when I walk in, unexpected, to find him mid-move with an armload of my clothes.

But I'm not finished here.

Agitated, I turn on the bedside light. On my mother's nightstand is a beat-up copy of *The Birds of New England* by Lucy Chappell. I know this book. I remember it well from my grandfather's old camp up in the north woods. My mother probably stole it from the lodge bookshelves. I used to leaf through its pages as a kid instead of venturing outside to actually identify any real birds. I was just happy with the book itself.

I flip through it until I find the drawing of the Atlantic puffin, my favorite from childhood. The bird is nobly comical, with a geometric head and white belly, black widow's-peak cap and cape, orange beak and feet. I check the copyright page and with a pang of sadness note the publication date: 1945. The once "near-ubiquitous" puffin is threatened now. With a voluptuous nostalgia I stroke the pages of the book, loving all over again the rich, glossy old-timey paper, the entertainingly written captions, cozy and comforting in their chatty, informative precision. These relics of the last century, so certain of the permanence of its taxonomies and publishing standards.

Finally I turn off the light again and lie with my eyes shut, awake but a little calmer. I feel my mother in this room. Not her, but some other part of her that lingers on after her death and cremation. I know it's my own brain, manufacturing this feeling, a projection of my memories of her, but she's here, floating in the air above the bed.

When I fall into a kind of half sleep, the memories I've been actively suppressing finally rise up through my weakened consciousness, whole, unblunted by time. My brain's projector replays the two months when I took care of my mother: flying up to Maine, arriving at the hospital as she woke up from the first surgery, taking her home to await her second one for three nightmarish days.

Ten years ago, she fell down the porch stairs of the inn where she was having dinner. I assume she was drunk, although of course she would never admit it. The man she'd been having dinner with called an ambulance. Celeste called me from the ER of Maine Medical to inform me that our mother had broken her tibia in two places and would have to undergo two surgeries, followed by rehab and a lengthy recovery.

Unthinkable as it seems now, and only because in those days Celeste was swamped with two small kids at home and couldn't do it herself, I took a family-illness leave, flew up to Maine, and stayed here in this house with Lucie for two entire months, helping her on and off the toilet, driving her to and from physical therapy, managing her meds, cooking for her, waiting on her and nursing her until she could live alone again.

And somehow, throughout this entire time, she remained under the staggering delusion that I was there for my own enjoyment, as a sort of vacation from my stressful job, as if this were some sort of honor for me, and the pleasure of her company was its own reward.

"My goodness," I can still hear her saying in a high, sniffy voice, "I'm not a helpless old lady, stop being such a *bully.*"

She was a terrible patient, imperious and needy, demanding and high-handed, histrionic and obtuse. She had a horrible little bell she rang to summon me. Trapped and bound to do her bidding because of blood, by the end I found myself repulsed by the very heat of her body in its thin nightgown, crushed by her importunately demanding presence, the inside of my head one long silent wordless shriek. The entire experience was as close to hell as anything has ever been in my life.

Asleep in bed in her guest room on that first night, I was awakened in the wee hours out of a rare deep sleep by my mother's plaintive voice, calling me to open her bedroom window because she "couldn't breathe" for lack of fresh air. It was already open. I informed her of this, went back to bed, and lay fuming, awake, flailing in the too-soft guest bed, for the rest of the night.

The following day, starting just after dawn, she called me to her bedside table to whisk things away and bring her others as her requirements changed: first, her comb and hairpins and makeup bag and toothbrush, toothpaste, a glass of water, then her reading glasses, glossy magazines, an array of pills, a small glass of prune juice. Delirious from lack of sleep, I called her doctor to ask about upping her pain meds, fetched more pillows, lowered the blinds to block the harsh morning sunlight.

After the second surgery she went to rehab for ten days, but this was no respite for me, because the entire time she was there, she hounded me to bring her home-cooked food every evening, since the rehab food was "inedible," as if she ever actually cared about food. Meanwhile I had to get the house ready for her return, which meant buying and installing wheelchair ramps and shower bars and toilet safety rails, dealing with an unreliable handyman who overcharged me, trapped me with hours-long monologues about the memoir he was planning to write, and took forever to get the plywood ramps "up to code." I ended up painting them myself, just to get rid of him.

Lucie was a frantic, fretful toddler by the time she got back from rehab. Her leg was encased in a cast, and she had a wheelchair and crutches and a heap of exercises to do. Her primary activity was punishing me for my own relative youth and mobility. First thing in the morning, I forced her to do her exercises by doing them with her. Then she picked at her oatmeal and told me the tea was too weak, so I whisked the offending dishes away, helped her to and from the toilet, then installed her back on the blue couch.

The mornings ground on, inexorable and glacial. I repeatedly adjusted the volume of her radio news station, since she couldn't be bothered to do it herself. She had a chill, so I turned up the heat. Then the house was stuffy, so I cracked a window. Then she was chilly again, so I shut the window, and the radio was giving her a headache, so I turned it off, and she was thirsty for ginger ale, but when I brought it, she said no, not with ice, so I brought it without ice, and then she wanted her neck pillow from upstairs.

Then it was time for lunch. I brought her a bowl of Campbell's cream of asparagus soup, her favorite, with a plateful of saltines and a bowl of salty black olives, which she said she was craving. She ate slowly, so slowly, while I hovered, yawning with desperate fatigue and intense boredom, waiting for the command to whisk the dishes away.

Finally, when the dishes were washed, she fell asleep under her afghan, so I snuck upstairs and lay fretting and tossing in my bed. Just as I sank down into sleep, she tinkled her little bell. When I ran downstairs to find out what she needed, she couldn't remember. So I went into the kitchen to think about what the hell to make for supper. The fridge and cupboards, well stocked by Celeste when I arrived, were sparse now.

"I'm going to run to Hannaford," I told her, putting on my coat.

With a piteous cry she said, "Don't go, I can't be alone, what if I fall? Call Celeste, ask her to shop!"

"She's giving the kids their supper now, and then she's putting them to bed. I'll just be gone twenty minutes."

"We can order in Chinese."

I was desperate to get away. I couldn't sit in this too-hot, too-bright room with my mother and wait for the food to be delivered, trapped, envying the delivery person his freedom to leave. I needed a change of scene, even if it was just other people buying cornflakes and ice cream, normal life. I needed a brief jaunt of freedom, briny air blowing through the open car window as I drove the short distance to and from the supermarket.

So I went upstairs and closed the door to the guest room and called David, heaving with a fuming teary hatred I would have given anything on earth not to feel.

"I'll come right over," he said. "I'll keep her company and stay for dinner and help you cook, if you want."

The instant David walked through the door, my mother turned her charm machine back on. I saw it happen. One second before, she had been a droopy, frail, unpleasant elderly woman. The arrival of a handsome man made her sparkle, dimpling and fluttering her eyelashes, all prettified and alluring. "Oh, thank goodness you're here," she cooed to him. "I've been cooped up with Nurse Ratched for days on end! Come and sit by me and tell me all about what's happening in the world. You'll stay for dinner, won't you? Rachel, bring our guest a glass of wine and get me one, too, while you're at it!"

While Nurse Ratched fetched them glasses of wine and drove to Hannaford and shopped and came back and put the groceries away and cooked supper, Lucie entrapped David on the couch next to her, pawing at his arm and leaning in to whisper playful nothings, asking provocative questions and laughing at everything he said with a demented, breathy cackle.

I remember exactly what I made, because rage-cooking sears itself on the memory: pork chops with applesauce alongside, buttered egg noodles, and peas.

I loaded up two plates and carted them out to Lucie and David, set them on the coffee table, returned with cutlery, napkins, and more wine, and then came back with my own food and wine to sit at the little table by the window. I was glad my mother had David to talk to, so grateful to him for entertaining her just to give me some quiet in the privacy of my own head to think my thoughts and gather my strength for the drudgery and tantrums that awaited me after he went home.

The two of them flirted away all through dinner. I remember opening a second bottle of wine, and then, after I'd cleared the plates and washed the dishes, a third. I was drunk too, hoping to lure David to the guest room after I put Lucie to bed. Sex with him would help me so much, give me something of my own in the face of this ordeal. At the time, David and I were both technically single but still connected to each other in the same complex subterranean way we'd always been.

She stayed up past midnight, throwing pointed glances at me. I sat in the armchair, and David was pinned on the couch next to my mother. He and I exchanged looks as the evening wore on, mine frantic and apologetic, his resigned, sheepish, acquiescing. In my mother's eyes, David was probably just an ex-boyfriend from my youth. She may not have realized, giving her the benefit of the doubt, that he was still very much my lover, at least when I was home.

Finally she snapped, "Oh, just go to bed, Rachel. Stop sitting there and spoiling my fun."

I looked at David, waiting for him to set things straight. He was nodding at me. "Go ahead," he said to me. "I know you're tired. It's okay."

I stared at them both, my mother kittenish and slitty-eyed, David passive and smirking. "Well then," I said slowly. A cold gel gripped my scalp. "Good night."

I went up the stairs, and they stayed on the couch. He must have helped put her to bed. Beyond that, I did not want to think. If my mother seduced David, I didn't want to know. The fact that this was even a possibility in my head told me everything about both of them.

The next morning, I heard her little bell tinkling. I stayed in bed, ignoring it. Eventually the ringing stopped. I got up when I was good and ready and heard my mother calling me from the couch as I passed through the living room on my way to the kitchen.

I skipped her exercises. I was done being her coach. If she didn't want to do them, she could just be a damn cripple for the rest of her life.

I took my sweet time making her breakfast tray. I brought it to her, set it next to her on the couch,, and turned to go without a word. Although I didn't look at her, I could feel her vibrating with excitement.

"My, that was a fun night!" she said brightly to my retreating back.

I turned and looked her in the eye. "No," I said. "That was not a fun night."

"You're such a spoilsport. Do you think David just sees me as an old lady? I've been told I look very young for my age."

"I have no idea," I said. "You'll have to ask him."

"Well, that did me good. It's not healthy for me to be cooped up all the time. I'm a good-time girl, I need to have some fun. I'm not all nose to the grindstone like you."

Ignoring the dig, I had to ask. "Did David put you to bed?"

"Oh yes, he did, and he was a perfect gentleman about it."

Thank God, I thought.

"And he gave me the nicest kiss good night."

"What do you mean?"

"He leaned right over me and kissed me like he meant it."

He had flirted with her all night, sent me to bed, and stroked her ego. He had sold me out, let my mother annihilate me sexually, as she had been trying to do since I was twelve. Lucie had won, had vanquished me, and she needed me to know it. And David had given her this, *my* David.

Now, as I lie in her bed, replaying it all, I remember seeing my mother in that moment as a terrified, mortal, aging, weak, selfish old woman, all her charm stripped away. Looking down at her, awash in the knowledge of betrayal, I knew with a brutal and final certainty that I didn't exist for her at all and never had, except as a projection of her own needs and fears. To Lucie, it was always either *her or me*. Those were the terms she had set up, the lines she'd drawn. Of course she chose herself. I understood my mother so well, maybe better than anyone else ever had or would. I empathized with her horror of getting old, her terror of her own mortality and frailty. But that didn't mean I had to take her shit or see her ever again as long as I lived.

The instant she was given the all-clear by her doctor and pronounced able to get around by herself and drive again, I flew home to DC and went on with the rest of my life.

She never made the slightest effort to win me back: no hint of apology, no recognition of what I'd done for her, just twice-yearly birthday and Christmas emails. And I replied in kind. It was clear to me that we were both relieved to be rid of each other. For the first time in my life, despite all the residual sadness and anger, I was free. This was nothing I could ever begin to try to explain to my sister, who wouldn't understand. And so the wedge grew between Celeste and me, which was also what our mother had always wanted, to come between us, to reign supreme.

The following year, I met Wallace at a garden party. I liked him immediately. He was appealing and wry and soft-spoken, elegant and understated. He asked me to dinner. We had a second date. Our sex life was initiated by us both after our fifth date, right on schedule, and was always pleasant but infrequent and polite and effortful. He asked for little, appreciated my ambition instead of being threatened by it, and was refreshingly, subversively funny. I felt completely safe with him. We never met each other's families; we were both estranged from them. Two islands in a stream, we called ourselves.

We were married by a justice of the peace on a weekday afternoon, bought our small Foggy Bottom duplex together, and set up house, working insane hours and seeing each other rarely. Years passed. Then I came home unexpectedly early one fine spring evening to find my husband in bed with Declan. The divorce was swift and clean. He moved out of our condo into an apartment, and I took over the mortgage, and that was that. We didn't speak for almost a year. One day he called me and asked me to lunch, and I went. He apologized, I forgave him, and we allowed our mutual fondness and respect to turn into a real friendship, the loving, true friendship that had been buried under our fake coupledom. I agreed to be properly introduced to Declan. The three of us went out to dinner together a few times. I saw how much they loved each other, and so I decided to befriend Declan to the extent that, when Wallace was diagnosed with

ALS just over a year ago, our three-way cohabitation felt like a natural, practical arrangement.

During all that time, ten years, I never contacted David. I never came back to Portland or saw my mother again. Maine faded in my mind to a terrible faraway place that existed only in the past, a dark northern blot on the map I did my best to forget.

Nine

The next morning, cup of coffee in hand like a shield, I hit Celeste's number and wait through five rings, imagining her looking at her phone, trying to decide whether or not to answer. "Pick up, you asshole," I say through gritted teeth.

The sixth ring is cut short, just before it rolls to voicemail. Her voice is clipped. "Hi, Rachel."

"I didn't fuck David."

"What?"

"You heard me. How dare you judge me? Throwing me out like that. Jesus."

"Mallory saw him leaving your room. She's still upset."

"For God's sake, Celeste, she's a teenager, she'll survive. And that was completely on David. He snuck in. I kicked him out."

"He's married!"

"Do you think I don't know that, Celeste?"

There's a hot silence between us. We're both breathing a little hard, as if we'd been physically fighting.

I ratchet down the offensive, realizing one of us has to if we're going to get anywhere. "Just talk to me. Can we go do something? Take a walk? Drive to Two Lights and get lobster rolls?"

She huffs. I feel her resisting this olive branch to punish me. She has a busy day of yoga, social-media scrolling, and online shopping ahead of her.

Maybe a meeting with her decorator. Maybe a consultation with Pilar, if Pilar is their regular cook.

"We're going for a drive," I bark, pulling rank. I'm the older sister. "We need to clear the air. Right now."

It works like a magic spell. "Fine." She sighs, put-upon, but she's caved. "I'll pick you up in ten minutes."

I go outside and wait, staring hard at the flat, shimmering cove through narrowed eyes, the blood pounding in my head, watching seabirds swoop down, talons outstretched. When Celeste pulls up to the curb at the bottom of the lawn, I circle her car and slide into the passenger seat, and we're off without a word. She heads us toward I-295 and takes the southbound on-ramp.

I dive straight in. "Why are you so angry at me?"

"What do you mean?"

"All the time, Celeste. I constantly offend you and hurt your feelings and piss you off."

She flicks her gaze at me, an arrow with a poisoned tip. "Why did you leave the table the other night? In the middle of Mom's special meal?"

"This is exactly what I'm talking about. You're the victim and I'm in the wrong, no matter what I do or don't do."

She cuts her slitty eyes at me again. This isn't what she wants to hear, any expression of my own feelings in all of this. She wants us to focus on her aggrieved sense of betrayal. Nothing else will meet this moment.

"It's true, though," I go on. "I feel like a monster, blundering around. I have to be so careful with you all the time so you won't blow up at me."

"I never blow up at you."

This is true, technically. "But I feel it there, all the time, brewing. You attack me indirectly. Don't think I'm not fully aware of what you're doing. Pretending you didn't know that David and I were together for our entire adult lives. Inviting him and Molly over my first night back. Punishing me in that passive-aggressive way, and taking everything I do or don't do so personally. Sometimes you're as self-involved and victimized as Mom."

Now I've gone too far. It feels incredibly relieving to say all of this because it's true and I'm on the defensive, but I shouldn't have said one word comparing her to our mother, a fatal mistake, because all it's done is to open the gates of permission for her to strike back at me as hard as she wants.

"Oh, wow." Celeste's mouth hangs open for a second. "I'm like Mom? Me? The one who stayed and took care of her when she never, ever took care of us? I'm a good mother—of course I'm not perfect, but I'm *devoted* to my kids. I've stayed with my husband, and that's not perfect either by any means, but I'm still there, I stayed in Maine, I made a stable structured life for me and my family. So I'm self-involved? I'm victimized? How *dare* you."

Angry tears are coursing down her cheeks. She hasn't looked at me once through any of this. She's staring grimly ahead at the interstate, hunched over the wheel, gunning the SUV as fast as she can make it go.

Her words keep shooting out. "You're the one who's like Mom, selfish and never thinking about anyone else besides yourself. You're the one who disappears when anyone needs you. You're the one who doesn't care about family."

"Oh," I say. I'm interested to hear that her marriage isn't perfect, and I want very badly to ask her about that, but I'm too caught up in this fight, or whatever it is. "That's right, I'm selfish for leaving Maine. I'm not thinking about anyone else because I had the nerve to be ambitious and pursue an actual career. And I had a husband, too, you know. It's not my fault Wallace is gay, but now he's dying and living with me again because for better or worse means something to me too, so fuck you. Anyway, marrying a multimillionaire and giving birth and keeping your mansion clean does not make you a paragon of angelhood, I'm sorry, you can't throw that in my face. Having kids is nothing special or worthy of a gold star. From my point of view, it's the most selfish thing you can do, put more humans on this overcrowded planet."

"Oh my God," she mutters.

"Also," I say, bulldozing right over her, "Mom pushed me away. She made it clear she didn't want me around ever again. Meanwhile, you *chose* to take care of her. And good for you, but no one forced you."

"She was our mother."

"She would have hated it if I'd flown up here to wipe her ass. It was the last thing she wanted."

"You're wrong." Her voice is soft, sad. It makes me want to slug her. "So wrong."

"You want me to feel guilty? Tough shit. I owed that crazy bitch *nothing*. Nothing."

"Do you even have any friends down there in DC?"

I have to think for a minute. I'm used to talking about my work. Not my personal life. But screw Celeste for treating me like some introverted antisocial freak. "Of course I do. I have my colleagues, the people in my office. I live with Wallace and Declan."

"People in your office." She blinks. "Your ex-husband and his boyfriend."

I'm not sure, from her tone, whether she's judging me, or where this line of inquiry is going, or why we're talking about this at all. I fight a rising defensiveness.

I don't have any female friends because I've never trusted women enough to let down my guard with them. Celeste is the only woman I'm remotely close to, this is true, and everything is fraught between us because she had the same mother I did and we're each wrestling with our own different demons in the fallout. But I can't say any of this to her right now.

"You are so alone," says Celeste.

"I'm free."

"You're trapped in anger."

"Anger isn't a trap."

Abruptly, we both go quiet, and the interior of the SUV rings with the force of the things we've both just said and can't unsay. I feel a little limp with relief, or just exhaustion. She takes the exit for Biddeford and slows down on the off-ramp. A few miles of settled woods and marshland flash by.

I'm so thirsty. "Do you have a bottle of water anywhere in here?"

Celeste snorts. "Do you think all moms who drive SUVs are just equipped like that? Snacks, water, gum, lip balm?" I can plainly hear a thrumming thread of tension in her voice. So far, I've had the last word in this particular battle. I stumped her with "Anger isn't a trap," but I can hear her brain clicking away, looking for a rational way to inform me that anger is indeed a trap, and I'm caught in it, and I only think I'm free because I'm too alone to know what freedom is. She can't figure out how to say all this without sounding childish, so she says nothing, but her stymied silence is only temporary.

We're flying along again. She's speeding, but the road is empty, and I don't see any cops lurking in the underbrush, so I don't say anything. I can feel her anxiety, as palpable as the high ringing tinnitus in my ears. If she needs to go seventy in a fifty-mile-an-hour zone, so be it.

I turn to her, pretending I'm Molly, my voice as rich with concern and interest as I can make it. "What did you mean when you said your marriage isn't perfect? Is everything okay with you and Neil?"

Just like that, her face opens up, softens. "Oh God," she says with a brittle laugh that ends in a small sob, an inhaled hiccup, and I feel a pang of genuine empathy for my sister. "We're fine, I guess, on the surface, but we have some issues—well, who doesn't after thirty years."

"Thirty," I repeat wonderingly, feeling like we're about to have a real conversation, finally. "I imagine you would, then."

"It's mostly just one thing."

I have always found it touching that Celeste shifts gears so easily from wanting to disembowel me with a sharp stick to earnestly confiding her secrets to me. She can't hold a grudge—she doesn't have the attention span, which says something about her character, how fundamentally self-involved she is, of course, but also how willing she is to forgive and move on. Her default mode seems to be an eager hunger for positive attention in any form—advice, compliments, reassurance, affection, she needs those things more than she needs to be right, or to win, or to prove anything. It's adorable. It makes me love her all over again.

"What is it?"

"He drinks way too much. I'm sure you noticed. Everyone does, I know, but he *really* does. He kind of disappears. Every night. The kids can tell. It bothers them. I drink too, mostly to keep him company. I want so badly to say something to him about it."

"Why can't you say something? Like, 'Neil, I think we're both drinking too much, would you be willing to give it up with me?' "

"Can you imagine his reaction?" Her voice goes nasal and deep. " 'Wife of mine, you're free to teetotal to your heart's delight, but I'll never forsake my nightly glut of spirits.' " She glances at me to make sure I appreciate this spot-on mimicry of her husband. When she sees me grinning, she gives a twisted half smile back. "He has no idea how much he actually puts away every night. He drinks whiskey till one or two in the morning, then he comes to bed and thrashes around and snores and wakes me up. I'm so tired all the time. And lonely. I really miss him."

"That's a form of spousal abuse," I say, half serious. "Alcohol-related neglect. Inflicting sleep deprivation."

"It's not funny. I worry about his long-term health. Early dementia. Cancer. Liver disease. The effect this is having on the kids."

"I was only half joking," I say. "Trying to cheer you up, that's all. You're right, it's a serious problem."

"It's been going on for years. I think he needs a job. He spends the day in his study with the door shut. He says he's working on a play. He says it's going well. He's been saying that for five years. But as far as I know, he has nothing to show for it. I suspect he has a bottle of something in his desk drawer, but I'm not a snoop, so I haven't actually looked. It reminds me of how Mom talked about Dad's addiction, how she tried not to go around looking for used needles, packets of drugs."

"Mom was one to talk about addiction."

"Well, Dad's killed him."

"What do you remember about him?"

"He was a junkie. He died."

"He was our father," I say. "I know, Mom taught us to hate him, but do you ever wonder about all those Calloways, all those people we're related to?"

She doesn't answer. But I know what she's thinking. My mother used to call the Calloways white trash, back when people used that term freely. Apparently, according to Lucie, the corrupting influence of our father's extended family was irresistible and permanent, and she repeatedly told her daughters to stay the hell away from them all.

"I just wonder," I say. "We have all these aunts and uncles and cousins."

"Since when do you care about family?"

"It's more that they're a mystery that's never been solved for me."

We reach the end of the winding road, and suddenly there's the ocean. Celeste pulls into the gravel lot and parks and we get out and climb the stone steps to the seafood shack, perched above the rocky shoreline. We get in line behind a small crowd, not too bad this early in the season. Waves explode in white foam against flat shingled rocks. The ionized air glints with salt crystals. Seagulls lurk around the red picnic tables, eyeing scraps on the patio's broad concrete apron. A chilly wind whips the umbrellas, flapping the canvas. Out on the ocean, a container ship slides over the gray-green surface.

Celeste treats me to a lobster roll, fries, and a blueberry soda.

"I'm just so worried about Molly," she says as she deposits the tray on our table and slides onto the bench across from me.

"Why?"

"Now that you're back, David seems different with her. They came over last night, and he hardly looked at her. Have you been in touch with him?"

So we're at war again. I try to keep up. "No," I say, looking her straight in the eye. "I have not texted, phoned, messaged, seen, or fucked him."

"Not funny." She gives me a sharp look. Here it comes. "I don't want you to crash her honeymoon glow with David. They're so blissful. Until you came back, it's been perfect."

"It can't be perfect." I can't help it. I'm an asshole. "She's married to David, remember?"

"He's changed, Rach. I've gotten to know him really well."

"No, he hasn't."

"You might want to think he hasn't."

I give her an expressionless sidelong look, and then I stare out at the container ship, which has advanced about an inch along the horizon.

Of course she takes my silence for encouragement. "She makes him happy. Maybe you two never brought out the best in each other, but they really do."

And now she's got me. I cannot stop myself. "You threw him and his marriage in my face. He sneaked up to my room—what did you expect?"

"I did it so you could see that he was happily married and get over it. That's on you for not being an adult about it."

"He got into bed with me, I kicked him out. Where do you get off? I thought everyone had affairs in the West End."

"All I know is that having you under my roof is nothing but trouble."

Even for Celeste, this is astonishing bitchery. I'm so shocked, I choke on my soda and can't talk for a while. And when I do regain the power of speech, I realize I have nothing to say to her. She evidently feels the same way about me, because we sit, staring ahead in stony silence, until we've finished our food. And we're silent on the entire drive back to Portland. Celeste stops at the bottom of the lawn in front of our mother's house and barely waits for me to get out before she guns the engine and drives away.

Ten

Edison's response to my email arrives late that afternoon as I'm standing at the window, looking out at the light draining from the sky. I read it fast, anticipating a generally positive go-ahead, but in fact, he writes that my new idea has potential, it's got my trademark forward thinking, but it's not fleshed out enough yet, and he's not sure yet why he should care about the dubious pros and frightening cons of climate geoengineering, why it's worthwhile to investigate the various hypothetical technological methods of fighting climate change. He doesn't buy my hunch that weather modification and solar radiation management are about to be hot-button topics.

"I took the liberty of passing your proposal along to Melissa Johnson," he adds at the end. "I've attached her response, which as you'll see dovetails with mine."

I've never worked with Melissa before. She's a young editor, a recent hire, but from her cogent, articulate email, I can see that she knows what she's doing. Her sharp assessment of my proposal instantly makes me want to revise it, fine-tune it, show more clearly what I'm thinking. Her ideas are sound, and her tone is respectful and engaged.

In fact, I feel a yearning to work with her instead of Edison, who can be both condescending and short on helpful revision ideas. Admittedly, my proposals and first drafts are often rough, written in a kind of easy shorthand, but only because I tend to assume Edison will get it, since we've worked together for so long. But instead of giving me guidance or structural feedback, he generally just tells me to go and make them better. Isn't he my editor? Isn't it his job to edit me? Instead I get vague marching orders from him, and off I go like a good little chipmunk to spin straw into gold, every time.

Okay, fair enough. I need to up my game.

But there's more, another chunk of text, underneath Melissa's email, so I scroll down. I'm not sure what I'm reading at first, and then I get it: it's the email Edison wrote to Melissa along with my proposal. As I read, I see that it's a blunt assessment of not only me as a writer but my entire career.

I'm pretty sure he didn't mean for me to see it; he surely sent it by accident, or rather, forgot it was underneath her email when he forwarded it to me.

Phrases explode in my eyes with little shocks: "I confess that I am a fan of Rachel's voice on the page, and her work is feminine in the best way, but nothing she's done has really worked since her tour-de-force Big Organic series twelve years ago," and "I'm hoping you can give me some ideas to generate the tough love she needs at this stage, because she needs a mid- to late-career hit to energize things," and "Rachel's long-ago prizewinning story about the recycling business was a mess at first, but she buckled down and pulled it off, so we live in hope."

This is all plausibly true, I guess, but it feels like a stab in the chest. Feminine in the best way? Tough love? Buckle down? We live in hope? I wonder whether Edison, my erstwhile mentor and (I thought) true-blue champion, would have said such things about any of our male colleagues. I can't imagine for one minute that he would have.

The truth is that, time after time, I took my rough first drafts and made them into structured, polished pieces without any editorial help. And instead of recognizing that this was a strength of mine and giving me credit, or at least the benefit of the doubt, Edison instead opted to lecture me about "the journalistic process" as if I were a twenty-four-year-old kid just out of J-school.

Not that any of this matters now, since he's leaving. There's no point letting him know I even saw his email. I write back two lines promising him a revised proposal, as professional and thorough as I'm capable of being. I'll talk to him in person when I'm back, and our conversation will be brief and bitter and laden with unspoken undercurrents.

So I try to let it go, rise above it, but this humiliating, casual dismissal keeps sucker-punching me. So he thinks I've gone downhill, he thinks I haven't delivered on my early promise, all these years when I thought I was doing good honest hard work, earning my paycheck, writing stories that needed to be told. I can't help feeling that he's considered me a charity case all along, a misguided, temperamental diva who has to be handled so gingerly that he feels the need to ask a younger colleague to tell him how best to take me to task.

All right then. Point taken.

I collapse onto the blue couch and close my eyes, worn out from this whole stupid day.

But evidently this stupid day isn't done with me yet. The air erupts with a sharp blat. It takes a second for me to recognize it as the doorbell. I leap up and open the door, and there's David, hunched in a jacket, looking furtively over his shoulder, his cheekbones protruding blades, his eyes hollow. The sight of him is like doing a little bump of a drug I kicked long ago but never fully recovered from, an acrid trickle in my throat, a fizz through my veins.

"David." My voice is filled with everything that name means to me. I'm too caught off guard to hide anything.

"Rachel." His amber eyes cast their liquid light on me, and I lean into his warmth.

Within the space of a few hard heartbeats, he's sinking into the blue couch, looking into the wineglass I just fetched for him and filled from an opened bottle of red in my mother's cupboard. I sit next to him, gaze at him, drink him in. David's youthful beauty was rock-solid, sculptural, irrefutable. Even now, he's hard to look away from. Through the scrim of memory, his current face dissolves into his young one before my eyes, along with the visceral but very distant recollection of excruciating intertwined pain and passion. Maybe we'll always see our young selves when we see each other; maybe we're permanently mutually eighteen or twenty years old, imprinted on each other the way long-married couples seem to be, so we'll be beautiful to each other when we're senile, toothless ninety-eight-year-old wrecks. It's inescapable. I'm glad to know I might always be beautiful to one person, even if that person is married to another woman and everything is history between us now.

"Goddammit," he's saying to me, reading my mind. "You're more beautiful than ever. It's not fair."

I flash on that night with my mother, ten years ago. I wonder what he remembers. Thinking of Molly, I try to derail this train. "It's the magic of menopause," I tell him.

He goes blank. The word *menopause* tends to have this effect on middle-aged men, as if the word itself smelled of mothballs and musty undergarments. And so I think I've succeeded in ratcheting down the intensity between us.

I see his glass is empty and get up and open another bottle and bring it into the living room, where I fill his glass and leave the bottle on the floor by him for easy access.

"So why are you here, David?"

His face blazes white. It's strange to see him on this couch, in this house again. Like a temporal shift. "I need to ask you something."

"Out with it. You have nothing to lose."

"I need to know. And I still don't know." He's staring at our reflections in the big front window. "Why didn't things work out between you and I? Why did you leave?"

You and *me*, I correct him silently. I need to be moving around right now—I can't sit on this life-sapping couch another second. I get up and start pacing in front of the couch. "I had to, David."

"What do you mean, you had to?" He gets up and stands in my way and forces me to meet his eyes. "Was there a gun to your head?"

I move backward, and he advances. He's keeping in step with me, as if we're dancing. "Not literally."

"Was I that bad?" he asks in a warm, beseeching rush.

Laughing in spite of myself, I stop in my tracks and keep him at arm's length with an extended hand. "Yeah, David, you were fucking terrible."

I put my head down and turn away, as if obeying blocking directions from a pretentious European movie director. I walk to the window, in need of a distancing view, but of course all I see is my own damn self.

"I lied about my job the other night," I tell him. "I lied about my entire life in DC."

"What do you mean?"

"It's hell," I say. "My life down there is hell."

He looks skeptical. "Hell, like challenging and important?"

"Hell, like literally hellish. They're pushing me out of my job. My editor is being forced into retirement, and he just dissed me to his replacement in an email I wasn't supposed to see."

He raises his eyebrows. He didn't expect this. "So leave."

I stare at him. He makes it sound so simple.

"Move back here. It's changed a lot since we were kids."

For a brief few seconds, I entertain the idea of walking away from all the roadblocks and internal strife. I think of Martin Gold, young and ruthless, gunning for me, and I know he's going to succeed in pushing me out. It's inevitable as I get older, which is happening now.

"I can't," I say. I look at the shelf by the door, at Lucie's collection of small ceramic figurines, the ones that used to come in every box of Red Rose tea, cheap relics of a bygone era. The sight of them makes me want to weep. "Well, I technically could, I guess, but I can't let the bastards win. It would be admitting defeat."

"I get that, Rachel, but why not just let yourself enjoy life sometimes?" He takes a meaty gulp of wine.

I look into my glass of lime seltzer, wishing it held straight vodka, or laudanum. David has always made me want to dive headfirst into the darkness and drown in it. "I can't give up."

"I thought they were pushing you out."

"They are."

"You poor doll," he says, his voice so gentle it makes my innards liquefy. Our gazes meet and hold.

"Oh no," I say, crisp, deflecting. "Don't waste time worrying about me."

"You can't tell me what to think." He grins at me. I know that grin. "Although I always loved it when you did. Your sharp brain, slice-and-dicing me."

"I thought you felt like I was being condescending."

His eyes glint. "God, no. I've always loved that you're smarter than me. I love the challenge of keeping up with you. It's exciting."

"I thought—"

"A massive, huge turn-on."

He takes my hand and pulls me down onto the couch with him. We're sitting so close together I can smell the sweet warmth of his skin, so familiar.

"There's something else," I tell him. "I'm not really seeing anyone. I had a short fling with a scientist in the Arctic, but it's over."

"You're such a liar." His voice crackles. He's laughing at me.

"And by the way, what happened the other night was wrong." It comes out as vehemently as I intend it to. "You should not have come up to my room, David."

"Rachel." My name in his mouth has always sounded like a smoochy, full-lipped kiss. "Nothing happened."

"You tried."

He rolls his eyes and says nothing.

"David, this is serious. I'm afraid Celeste is going to tell Molly."

"Oh, she told Molly all right."

I can't breathe. I hate my sister with the force of a Mack truck doing eighty on a straightaway. I put a hand over my eyes, then over my mouth, staring at him. "What happened?"

"Nothing. Molly already knew."

"She caught you coming home?"

"No, I told her." His eyes are round and innocent on mine.

I exhale with sharp amazement. "What did she say?"

"She was upset."

"So why did you tell her?"

"It's the one condition of our marriage. No lying."

"*When* did you tell her?"

"The next morning, as soon as she woke up."

"Okay," I say. "Wow. And you're still married?"

"Rachel." And there's the warm kiss of my name again. "I would never have left you. I would have gone to DC with you. Or anywhere. I loved you."

"That's not what I meant."

"I would have followed you wherever you asked me to go. I wasn't trying to keep you here. You wouldn't have been stuck here. I just wanted to be with you. It's all I ever wanted."

"Well, now you have Molly. And a stepson. You have a whole new life, David, it's a really good life, you should be proud of yourself."

He's not listening. "I understand that you had to leave Maine, your mother, I get that. But why did you have to lump me in with everything else?" His voice is warm and urgent. His face is wide open. He's holding nothing back from me, he's splayed out and completely vulnerable, his entire physical being trembling, taut with focus on me, alight with specific desire for me and only me, a desire whose force envelops me in an erotic spell so powerful nothing else exists. This is the David I loved.

"Where does Molly think you are right now?" My voice is unsteady.

He barely misses a beat. "She took Liam to her mother's for the night. In Boston."

I give him a significant, skeptical, sidelong look. "Are you going to tell her you were here?"

He presses his warm palm against mine and interlaces our fingers. I should pull my hand away and tell him to go home. He takes my seltzer glass and sets it on the floor, cups the back of my head, and tilts my face toward his. I should not let him kiss me. His mouth tastes like wine. He feels like home.

I get up and close the curtains. We shuck our clothes and sink back onto the couch. Naked, he's David again, my David, mine again. He knows his way around my body just like I know my way around his. I skim the backs of my fingers up his inner arms, burrow my face into the tender side of his neck, breathe softly into his ear. He looks deeply into my eyes, his hands interlacing with mine and holding me down with his whole body. I gaze up at the rich amber light of his eyes and the planes of his cheekbones and his beautiful mouth. He kisses me slowly. I feel my entire self respond, every part of me.

No one else has ever done this to me, made me feel this way. My college boyfriend Steve was eager and clumsy and too gentle, an ardent boy. Wallace's desire for me was artificial and sporadic and willed from a reluctant aversion, desperate to prove to us both that he was straight. And my recent fling Alex Wang was remote and cerebral and strangely rough. No one else has ever known to slide his fingers into me with just that pressure, right there, so softly, then a little bit harder, not too fast, the heel of his hand bearing down just right, his breaths riding my breaths, his eyes watching my face as my eyes flutter and my mouth goes soft. His body and mine come together so easily, like interlocking halves of a whole, skin and muscle sliding together in synchronous motion like an oiled machine, our stomachs pressed flat together, our bodies in undulating unison, our mouths easy and still and open to each other, our hands firm and possessive and assured. Our bodies generate a dynamic heat, electricity whipping between us, back and forth.

But even so, even now, no matter how connected we are physically, my mind stays separate, fulminating, distanced. It's always been this way, since the very beginning. Of course even now, even as I hear myself give a small gasp, as David's expert fingers tease me, as I open up to them, I'm thinking about Molly, his wife, trusting, out of town; she hasn't left my mind for even a second. I'm doing this, with David, with the full knowledge that she exists, letting this happen with absolute cognizance of my own wrongness and selfishness in giving myself something I want and need, taking it from her, and I know also that this is one of the worst things I've ever done. And the thought of Molly all by itself would and should be enough to make me detach from this pleasure that I should not be taking. The thought of Molly should make me push him away and shove him out the door.

But there's another woman here, too, besides Molly, and she's been here all along, all my life. And I have something to prove to her right now.

There's something I need to do, to understand and experience, and I can only do this with David, like this, right now, on this couch. I need to right an age-old wrong and set something straight for myself. And that is why I'm letting this happen. I have to. I feel like I can't live without it. Just once, and then it will all be over.

My mother watches me with David, coldly, like a crow from her perch inside my head, clinging to my brain folds with her talons, cawing plainly in my inner ear, "You're doing it wrong, you have no idea how to be seductive, no clue about what men want from a woman, he would rather be with me, I know how to please a man." Her voice blots out my own thoughts and cancels them. Her words burrow into my own body's movements and sensations to contort them, mock them. She's appropriating my own pleasure to prove her superior sexual prowess, a form of psychic bodysnatching.

And so, as always during sex with David, to shield myself from her, I empathetically attach myself to his desire and abdicate my own. I take shelter in him from my mother's twisting words.

It's so fucked up. I never fully realized it until now. I never truly understood my mother's occupation of me, the way her existence has canceled mine out, the way her needs always superseded mine. She appropriated me from birth, earmarked me as the custodian and caretaker of her own lifelong unmet emotional needs. Even when I was a young child, she made it clear that my job was to bolster and nurture her, and I wasn't allowed to express any needs of my own. But her real campaign was waged as soon as my sexuality started to burgeon. Then my mother's destructive competitiveness was unleashed on me.

"Come back," David whispers, giving me a little shake. "Where did you go?"

"I'm right here," I whisper back. We're not fucking yet, just hotly bound, skin to skin and limb to limb. He's hard and wet and gliding over me. My thighs are open, ready to take him inside me, but I stall us, keep him idling, cradle his body with mine in a small rocking undulation that maintains our connection but doesn't increase the charge between us. I want to fuck him. I want it so badly. But my workaday brain is trained to seek and find the truth at any cost. And I am in pursuit of a fundamental truth, and this is the only way to find it. It all happened right here, the night I knew I had to leave forever, all of it clotted into one terrible knot of David, my mother, Maine, the past.

When Celeste and I blossomed into lithe, nubile young gazelles, it was terrible for our mother's ego. She blatantly considered Celeste and me, from adolescence onward, competitive sexual threats to be schooled and shamed and put in our place. She annihilated us unerringly, pretending to be motherly with cloyingly caustic swipes. To anyone within earshot, our stepfathers, her friends, she shot her mock-playful scorn at our budding curves and breasts ("They're busting out of their clothes!"), our puppyish attempts at sexiness ("Oh, honey, go fix your hair, you look like a little poodle"), our anxious preening adolescent self regard ("I never had pimples like that when I was your age"). Our adolescence was pure fuel for her jealous narcissism.

At least Celeste, to her advantage, was fun and insouciant and bubbly like Lucie. I was serious, shy, and hypersensitive, and my mother's domination of me in particular, the way she twisted my youthful sexuality to serve her own need for supremacy, was a noxious smoke that choked my secret desire and stunted my nascent pleasure.

I've never had an orgasm with another person. No man can make me come. Even David. When I get close, her voice squawks in my head, mocking the way my breasts slide to the sides of my rib cage as my body arches toward its own heedless pleasure, my ugly facial expressions as I lose control, and it's gone. Every time. Even masturbating, she's there to tell me I'm doing it wrong, but when I'm alone, I can crowd her out with the right fantasies. A man in real life is too much catnip for Lucie to resist. She can't let go; I can't dislodge her.

So it's always been so much easier to leave my own mind and morph with David's and enter his brain and body to become fused with his desire for me. I seek completion in his own pleasure and forget about my own. This is the only way I've ever found to shut Lucie up.

It's happening again now. My mother is here, right above us, looking down at us. I can feel myself escaping from her voice into David's desire for me, being aroused by his own arousal. But I hold back this time. I force myself to allow the three of us to exist separately, me, and David, and Lucie, willing myself with effort to stay in my own body and its sensations. I float in myself, taking stock.

Of course that's it, that's the reason I'm alone. I have never dealt with my mother's sexual appropriation of me.

I lift my hips, and he enters me, finally, and we both gasp into each other's mouths. He starts to move inside me, and to my total shock, a searing pain rips through me. Every thrust is like being penetrated with a knife.

"Stop," I say. "Stop."

He pulls back to look into my face. "What?"

I lift his hips with my hands and pull him out of me. "It hurts so much," I say.

He stares at me. "Molly is pregnant."

At first, I think I've misheard. "What?"

"She's going to have a baby."

Horrified, jolted out of my head, I shove him off me, hard. "Oh my God, David. What?"

"I'm going to be a father."

He's looking pointedly at my C-section scar, just a faint pink line now. In my mid-thirties, I underwent surgery to remove three large flesh balls, benign fibroid tumors on the outside of my uterus, the size of a cantaloupe, an orange, and a lime. Afterward, I was put on the maternity ward with the new mothers, who all went home with babies. All I got was this thick, pink scar. David knows this, and he also knows how hard that was for me at the time.

My brain clicks: he's punishing me for pushing him away. He doesn't care that sex with him was hurting me. He's taking it personally.

"Get out, David. I mean it. Get dressed. Go home."

He gives me a wide-eyed look that tells me how spooked and freaked out he is by all of this. "It's not easy being married to someone so good, you have no idea. I can't be that guy she thinks I am. I'm playing a role. How am I going to act like a dad?"

Am I even in the room?

David looks like an aged boy, aging from stasis rather than evolution, an unnatural preservation. There is no hard-won depth of character in his face, no earned weight of gravitas, no wry spark of self-awareness. He knows nothing beyond himself, his fears and insecurities and diminishing powers.

I can't believe how heartsick I was for years over this putz, how ardently I used to want to drown myself in his cruel beauty. I blame hormones for that, the blinding, binding scourge of womanhood. Now, as the sharp, sane, ice-hot clarity of my new hormone-free brain asserts itself and slaps me out of this stupid residual David-induced fog once and for all, I look at him clearly for the first time in my life.

"So that's why you're still married? Why she forgave you for the other night? Because she's pregnant?" As I talk, I'm disentangling from him, heaving myself up from the couch, finding my clothes, pulling them on as fast as I can.

"It's the reason we're married at all."

"Don't you love her?"

He hesitates, then scrambles into his pants, buttons his shirt, and pulls on his shoes. "I love you," he says. His voice is breathy, wheedling. "I always have and always will."

I watch him, silently urging him to go faster. "You know why it didn't work out between you and me?"

He stops zipping up his jacket and squints at me. "Why?"

"Ten years ago, you let my mother seduce you."

His face is bewildered and weak. "I did what?"

"You and my mother. That night."

Then I see it: a quick flash, unmistakable. So my mother wasn't lying.

"Rachel, Jesus, no, I swear I have no memory of——"

"Liar. You kissed my mother on the mouth."

"She needed to feel young again."

I hear something terrible in his voice. "Oh my God. Did you have *sex* with my mother?"

"No! Not that night!"

"*Another* night?"

His face blanches with naked shock. I remember David's catlike, languid sexiness, back when we were twenty and Lucie was still young and beautiful, determined to steal any attention she could from him. The fact that this even strikes me as a potential truth is enough. I don't ever want to talk or think about it again.

"Never mind," I say. "You married someone good, a real grown-up."

"I know." He groans in anguish.

"David, I mean it, do not fuck this up. Don't tell her this happened, don't tell her you were even here. That would be purely selfish. Don't open your mouth, and it won't be a lie." I frog-march him to the front door and push him firmly out onto the concrete stoop and into the night. "You need to face yourself. This is your one chance."

The knucklehead actually tries to kiss me.

I give him another shove. "Goodbye, David, for real."

After I close the door behind him, I stand silently for a moment. I realize I'm grinning at nothing. Weird laughter is bubbling in my chest. Loopy, buzzing, I pick up the wine bottle and dance with it, clicking my heels together in midair in a manic jig. I dance into the kitchen and pour the rest of the wine down the drain, because if I don't, I know I'm going to guzzle all of it, straight from the bottle.

Part III

Eleven

Celeste was right: I am so alone.

I wake up early in the morning with a hollow feeling of dread that gets worse when Martin Gold calls me.

"I was sorry to hear about your mother," he says in his clipped, anal-retentive vocal fry. He sounds exactly like what he is, a former C-student frat boy with big ideas for himself, a ferociously ambitious striver who's trying to appear meek and harmless, playing it safe because he's a coward and he doesn't want the real killers to smell his blood and come after him. "My condolences. I'm afraid I'm not calling with good news."

I lean wearily against the counter as fresh coffee drips through the filter. "Spit it out, then."

"You know we've been up against deep budget cuts. I know it was approved, but the funding for your algal photosynthesis project has been withdrawn. As a result, your position has been eliminated."

"I see," I say. I expected this after my conversation with Priyanka, so I'm able to sound cool and detached, thank God, because I refuse to let this rat-faced sociopathic little fuckweasel have the satisfaction of hearing my voice tremble and break. "So I no longer have a job."

"That's right," he says.

While he informs me that I will of course receive a severance package and eligibility to pay "out of pocket" for a full year of health insurance coverage, the terms of which an HR person will inform me about at my convenience, I'm perversely grateful that at least he's affording me the dignity of not pretending to be sorry.

"I understand," I say with a thread of steel in my voice. "Goodbye, Martin."

And just like that, it's over, my entire career, built painstakingly over the course of three decades, ended with a two-minute phone call. *Sic transit gloria mundi.*

My phone chimes with an incoming text from Suzanne Brown: "Just wondering whether you're still thinking of selling your mother's place."

She picks up after one ring.

"Suzanne, thanks for checking in. I am absolutely still thinking of selling. When can you come take a look?"

"I'm at the salon. Give me an hour."

After I text her the address, I get dressed and bolt some coffee and go out into the bright, sparkling day, stomping around the cove toward the peninsula. The chilly bright sunlight tingles on my face. Ducks and geese ride the high-tide saltwater swells close to shore, paddling through the brown tips of sea grasses. I walk briskly, inhaling the salt wind off the marshes.

It's bracing to walk around this small, almost-familiar city, seeing the world at eye level and foot speed, hearing the crunch of my own shoes. The rhythm of my head bobbing up and down alters my apprehension like a heartbeat in motion. I'm used to glimpsing life through my car's windshield, all of it a blip out of the corner of my eye as I drive headlong to or from work. I work out in an indoor pool, inhaling chlorine and keeping to my lane. I've lived at a remove, through screens, through other people's lives and work, through professional language and journalistic principles. Walking makes my brain go quiet and calm and empty, lulls me into a state of curiosity and pleasure.

I watch three seagulls swaggering around the grass with fierce eyes, beaks jutting, ready to defend their territory, and pass a small, short-legged dog trotting along on its leash, looking up at its person with what I could swear is a smile. Two young women in jogging clothes run slowly around me, one of them talking heatedly, the other punctuating it with encouragement. They recede ahead of me until I can't hear them anymore.

I feel a deep nostalgic craving to get back out into the wilderness. My series on algae was going to take me to sea again on a research ship, out into the expanse, so different from this tame urban parklike trail. I'm almost looking forward to going up to the camp in a few days, to the uninhabited quiet of Gooseneck Lake, my old childhood summer escape from the humdrum squalor of the rest of the year. Much as I dread seeing my elderly relatives, I'm looking forward to being in the northern woods again.

As I climb Preble Street up toward Congress, passing a shelter, I notice that some of the people hanging out smoking on the sidewalk in front have dogs. I have never in my life paid much attention to dogs, but I feel sudden little sparks of envy, watching these displaced, rough-living outcasts as they talk to their little companions, ruffle their fur, feed them treats. Every person-and-dog duo seems to glow a little, encased in a warm bubble of mutual love. These dogs are clearly far better fed and emotionally well-balanced than their people, who seem to bestow upon their animal companions all the love and nurturing they themselves lack in the world, reaping in return a steady stream of grounding affirmation.

My eye is caught by a guy sitting at a picnic table with a few other men. A dog lies at his feet. He looks uncannily like my dead cousin Danny, same age, same general demeanor. I stop and stare at him for a moment, unable to look away. Like Danny, he's swarthy, muscular, with a shaved head and full beard. To be fair, there are a lot of men in Maine who strongly resemble my cousin. He was a certain type of Franco-American dude, and I've seen more than a few of his doppelgängers around town. But there's something particular about the way this guy is inclining his head, something unmistakable about the shape of the dome of his skull. And he's dressed in head-to-toe camo, which my cousin always wore after he got back from Afghanistan, and which he was no doubt wearing a few months later when he went out to our grandfather's old hunting cabin in the woods near the camp at Gooseneck Lake and blew his own brains out with his handgun.

Danny was the late baby of older parents, the miracle night-train child for Lucie's older brother Frank and his wife, my aunt Debbie. He was ten years younger than me. He grew up coming to the camp, too. I remember him as a dark, skinny boy building a lonely fort down by the lake, too young for Celeste and me to take any interest in, a moody, awkward kid who seemed most comfortable alone. It was Aunt Jean who called to tell me of Danny's suicide. My mother always despised him, for reasons I never understood.

The guy catches me staring at him, and I look away and accidentally meet the eye of a woman I guess to be about my age, early fifties, thin and olive-skinned like me. She stares back at me pugnaciously. An old, dignified dog with pricked ears and a gray muzzle sits by her feet.

"Your dog is beautiful," I tell her, feeling compelled to say something nice. "What's her name?"

The woman exhales cigarette smoke. Her face is gaunt and deeply lined, her voice hoarse. "Trixie," she says angrily. "I got her because she looks just like Stella. The love of my life, she died fifteen years ago. I thought this was Stella, reincarnated. But come to find out she's totally different. Not Stella at all, are you, Trixie?"

From the sidewalk, Trixie meets my gaze. She seems to understand that she's a disappointing, unsatisfactory nonreplacement, and is bearing the sorrow of the situation for her human with the utmost grace.

"She's a good dog," I say. "Stella or no Stella, you're lucky to have her."

The woman and Trixie both regard me with pity for my obvious incomprehension of the entire foundation of their alliance.

As I walk back down the hill through the industrial and commercial zone, under the interstate overpass, to the trail around the cove, I call Wallace, hoping he's in possession of his phone and that his gatekeeper Declan is nowhere within earshot of our conversation. To my relief, he answers just as I'm gearing up to leave a voice mail, sounding like himself. "Hey, Ray," he says. "I heard you talked to Declan last night."

I skitter around the topic. "How are you, Wally? Are you home from the hospital?"

"Oh, I'm peachy. Little bump on the head. We just got home, it's good to be back on the couch. How's everything up there?"

"I don't even know where to start," I say. "That fuckwit teenage overlord Martin Gold just fired me. It's over."

"Oh my lord. Oh Ray, I'm so sorry."

"I have no idea what I'm going to do now. And it's Peyton Place up here."

He chuckles. My heart hurts. "Do tell," he says.

For Wallace's amusement, I dance around the rim of the ravine I'm trying not to fall back into. "Celeste is still convinced that I fucked David under her roof, which I didn't, but she's furious at me. Although to be fair, I actually did fuck him last night, so she's not wrong. It was a colossal mistake. His wife is pregnant. I feel like a villain. And I'm planning to sell my dead mother's house. So that's the local gossip."

"Oh honey. At least you got to fuck David."

"Anyway," I say. "I hear you're moving downstairs. I'm so sorry I'm not there to help."

"We're fine," he says. "I'm just worried about you. When can you get out of that rat's nest of a snake pit?"

"As soon as I sell my mother's house." Oh, what the hell, why not rip the Band-Aid off? "I can use the money from the sale to buy Declan out of our duplex when the time comes, which I hope it never does."

"Ray," he says, his voice contrite, "I'm so sorry you had to hear it from him. I should have been the one to tell you. He sprang it on you. We actually need to have a whole conversation about it."

"Too late, cat's out of the bag. It's okay, Wally. Well, nothing is okay about you having ALS, that's not what I meant, and I wish I could wave a magic wand. But I see why you're doing this, I get it." I remember then that Declan called himself Wallace's fiancé. "So you're getting married! Are you planning a wedding?"

"City Hall, weekday."

"Just like we did."

"That's right." His voice is tender, sorrowful.

"Congratulations," I say. "The second time's the charm."

"This will be an even shorter marriage than ours was."

I sigh. It's so sad I can't bear it. "So how the hell did you fall?"

"I didn't mean to."

"Of course you didn't mean to."

"This sneaky disease progresses in cliffs and plateaus, and after a long plateau, I fell off a cliff. My left leg was fine, I thought, but as I was getting out of the shower, it suddenly got too weak to hold me up, so down I went like a cut tree, boom."

"Oh, Wally."

"I know. It's a terrible thing. But I'm still here."

"Are you guys going on the Alaska cruise for your honeymoon?"

"You know we are. Thank you for giving me your blessing, even though we both know that cruise ships are the worst pollution machines on earth. We're sailing from Seattle in mid-June for two weeks, and then Declan thinks it might be nice to take a land cruise, rent an RV, and explore the California coast while we're out west. We're planning to be gone for a while, maybe the whole summer. Maybe we'll never come back."

"Wow, that's so great," I say. There's a lump in my throat. The ocean wind is blowing hard against my face now. "I'll miss you. It's so good to hear your voice, Wally. You sound just fine. No residual effects from the concussion that I can hear."

"Oh my lord, I hope not. Here's Declan, time to burst into action. I'll call you again soon to check up on you."

"I'll call *you* again soon to check up on you."

I walk the last mile or so in silence under a big streaky pale-blue sky clotted with percussive clouds, inhaling the fresh stink of the outgoing tide.

When I get back to the house, Suzanne Brown is already waiting in her idling car, wedged illegally into a corner of my mother's building's little parking lot. She rolls down the window when she sees me, and as she waves, new-agey music chimes forth, a low voice chanting over bells and synth chords that abruptly die as she gets out, slams her door, and chirps it locked with her fob. I can see that she looks different. Is it her hair? Is it darker? I can never tell these things.

"I am beyond excited to get a look inside the place. I've been wanting to get my hands on one of these townhomes for years." She talks fast, rat-tat-tat. Yes, her hair is a sort of honey-caramel blond now, and shorter, more shaped around her head. She looks good. "They never come on the market. Does everyone just leave them to their adult kids when they die, like your mother did?"

I lead her around to the front door, and we burst into the house together. Suzanne looks around with raw curiosity.

"Coffee or tea?" I ask, heading to the kitchen, leaving her gawping at the picture window with its view over the cove to the low city skyline, the sweep of the church spires on Mellen Street all the way east to Tukey's Bridge. The view is the best thing about my mother's house. It's a remarkable view. Who wouldn't buy this place? Seeing it through Suzanne's eyes, I'm freshly aware of its charms.

I make coffee while Suzanne explores, and then we settle together onto the couch with our mugs. For a queasy second, I flash on the memory of having sex with David on this same couch, right where Suzanne is sitting now.

"Let's cut to the chase," she says. She takes a sip of hot coffee and looks straight at me. "What a view, but the place itself is a little run-down—it needs some TLC, some sprucing up. Even though the market is hot right now for two-bedrooms with water views—I mean, I could sell it tomorrow, I'd list it at maybe four twenty-five and we'd get over asking—but what's the rush, am I right? I think with some fresh paint and good staging, we could goose it up easily fifty thousand. We could even ask five."

"No rush," I say.

Suzanne settles deeper into the couch. She looks more at home here than I've ever felt. "Do you have a good contractor? I bet there are hardwood floors under this carpet, you could refinish them, replace the kitchen cabinet doors, that's cheap and fast, paint everything white, and the whole place will feel more awake. A two-bedroom with water views and downstairs half bath, yeah, it won't take long. Might even be a same day over asking. When the time comes, we'll hire a stager to zhuzh it up. I know the best one in town, Michelle, she's a genius."

"You really think it'll sell that fast and easily?"

"Well, it seems like everyone wants to move up here right now."

"I can probably do a lot of that work, myself."

"You'll probably have to—the market's so insane, no one is available on short notice. Contractors and workmen are all booked out a year, sometimes even more. Do you have time to take this on?"

"Could be," I say. "I don't actually know what my plans are. I just lost my job."

She looks genuinely distressed. "Oh no! What happened?"

My gut tells me that I like this person, and I can trust her. I tell her about Martin Gold, how he was appointed, essentially, to neutralize and erase my work. I tell her about Edison's dismissive appraisal of me as he handed me off to his successor.

Her eyes narrow, and she listens with rapt calculating attention. "Men can't deal with us," she says. "At this age. We're neither fish nor fowl to them. We're too strong and set in our ways. And we're not impressed by them, we see them for who they are. They hate that."

"I trusted all along that Edison knew my worth and respected me. I deserved that. I worked so hard, and I wrote so well, for years and years. I know I did."

"You're a brilliant journalist! You'll get snapped up in a hot minute."

"I'm fifty-three. Also, print journalism is dying. There are no jobs for me, even if I were hirable."

"Do you have a pension? Savings or investments? Maybe you can retire."

"Every cent I have is tied up in my DC condo. Nothing liquid, no portfolio. I lived paycheck to paycheck. I'm flat busted."

Suzanne is quivering like a rat terrier, her brain all fired up. "I'll think of something. I will."

"Keep moving forward like a shark," I say.

"That's right."

I lean into the relief of having a woman my age to talk to who isn't my sister, but someone I've known forever. "I have a personal question. About sex."

"Not that I have a whole lot of it, but shoot."

"It hurts all of a sudden. Like a sharp knife."

She winces. "You know, there's a cream for that. My friend Liz swears by it. I'll get the name from her and text it to you."

"Thanks," I say. "Do you know everything?"

"Just about." Suzanne is done here, on the move. "Call me as soon as you're ready to show this place, I'll get my stager in, and we're off to market."

With a wave, she's gone. I see her bustling past the window, punching something into her phone, her new hairdo bouncing in the sunlight.

The house subsides into torpid quietude in her wake. Alone again, nervous and agitated, I pace around, making figure eights from kitchen to living room and back again, circling the perimeter of each room, a caged animal in motion, eyeing the horrible wall-to-wall carpet, the dingy walls, the dilapidated kitchen cabinets, feeling my mother's presence all around me, watching me. It almost feels as if she's goading me.

Suzanne is right, everything does look run-down and shabby. The kitchen cabinet doors are ugly old fake-wood veneer brown. The walls, upstairs and down, were all painted a drab greige sometime back in the last century. I picture the carpet gone, wood floors stripped and sanded and gleaming. Cosmetic improvements will make a huge difference, and I need something do to right now that's mindless and physical with fast, tangible results. I'm pretty sure I can manage this. My first stepfather was a building contractor, and when I needed a job the summer after eleventh grade, he hired me to help out and taught me the basics. Whatever else I need, I can find on YouTube. Home renovation is not rocket science, or even climate science.

I bend down and scrabble my fingers at the edges of the powder-blue living room carpet until I get my nails dug in, and then I pull hard and steadily until it starts to come up, staples and glue popping loose. Underneath, below a layer of tar paper, there are oak floorboards, tongue-and-groove. I'll need to rent a floor sander, buy some polyurethane. But first I have to take the suitcases and bags of clothes to Goodwill, then donate all the furniture and kitchen stuff to the Habitat for Humanity ReStore, call a portable rent-a-dumpster company for the demo, and after this place is stripped empty, go to Home Depot, the hardware store, the paint store, make it all airy and bright and shipshape and modern.

Holy mackerel, as Aunt Jean would say, that's a lot of work. Can I really do it all by myself? Maybe I should just sell it as is, take the hit, get out of here, and never come back.

I miss my job. There's an empty ache in my chest, a sudden sharp yearning for the Arctic, a memory from back in February, one early morning when I walked out onto the top deck of the *North Star*, climbed the metal staircase, and emerged into the dark air, where the bitter cold stunned me breathless. I stood at the railing, looking out at the sea ice the ship had been deliberately frozen into for a year, the ship's bright lights splashing the slick reflective surface of the ice with artificial daylight, this frozen slab thick enough to land supply planes on. The roaring of the generators sounded like a city on trash day. Snow was falling. I slipped off one glove and put out my bare hand, palm up, and watched particles gather on my warm skin, pure white snowflakes from the sky and black sooty flakes from the ship, melting and running together on my open palm. The sun-bright electric lights shot beams into the vast polar blackness at the top of the planet, as the ship's puny human sounds were swallowed by the great silence stretching far beyond us.

I lived for these research expeditions, the concrete satisfaction of the work, the immediacy of science I was there to observe, and the scientists themselves, professionally removed from everything but their own brains and data. I loved the truncated interactions with climate scientists, my fellow obsessive indoor people, their skin as sallow and pasty as mine was, no matter what race or age they were. I loved their fierce obsessiveness, their rootedness in observable phenomena. And I loved being somewhere so remote and beautiful. When my time was up, I never wanted to leave.

But that's all over now; my job is gone forever. The final installment of my ice series is slated to come out in August, which is sure to be the hottest month of the hottest year on record, very timely. And with that last essay put to bed, I had planned to spend the rest of May and part of June interviewing marine biologists and biotechnologists at the forefront of research into algae, which are basically solar-driven carbon-fixing cell factories that account for half of the photosynthesis on the planet. The field is new and incredibly exciting, and I've been itching to finish up with ice so I can jump into the world of aquatic photosynthetic organisms.

I loved my job so much. I loved everything about it, from generating ideas to the final copyedits, every step of the way I was passionately and fully engaged. I gave it everything I had, every bit of myself.

What the hell will I do now?

This question is far too large and terrifying to grapple with, so my mind returns to Edison's condescending assessment of my life's work. In some ways, it hurts much more than Martin's cold dismissal of me. Then again, Edison has been dismissed, too, another old white whale in a changing world. And his email says more about him, I think, than it does about me. Contained in his phrasing, which is seared in memory, is the reason he's been forcibly retired. Ultimately, I can't take this personally.

I realize I'm stroking the oily, slick blue couch material, almost caressing it. The only power I have right now, the only scrap of agency, is in moving on, adapting, and surmounting my own sudden irrelevance. I'm still alive. And I come from generations of stoic, flinty Mainers whose mettle was tested much more than mine will ever be.

I push myself off the cushions, launch myself upward, toward what, I don't know. The whole point is getting the hell off this couch.

Twelve

Just after six, as I'm putting a weird sort of casserole I just invented into the oven, my sister bursts in the front door. Under her leather jacket, she's wearing a gauzy little hippie blouse over a tight white tank top and low-slung skinny jeans. Her face is tense and wild-eyed. She's carrying a plastic grocery bag.

"Celeste," I say, "are you okay?"

She sinks onto the couch and runs her hands through her hair, kicking off her stiletto-heeled ankle boots and stretching her bare feet onto the coffee table. She looks at her toenails as if they hold the answer, reaches into the plastic bag, pulls out a bag of Humpty Dumpty potato chips, sour cream and clam flavored, and plunks it with a six-pack next to her feet on the table.

"Dinner's just about ready," I say. "Are you hungry?"

"Starving." She rips open the bag, pulls a can from the six-pack, and cracks it. Humpty Dumpty chips! Things are dire indeed.

"What are you drinking?"

"Spiked seltzer," says Celeste. "It's like a wine cooler, remember those? But better. Want one?"

"No, thanks," I say, although I'm feeling tempted. I have to admit, if only to myself, that it's getting harder by the hour to justify my self-imposed sobriety. While "No thanks" has been my reflex for years, whatever foundation it was built on has evidently eroded over the past few days, until there's barely anything undergirding it anymore. I'm not an alcoholic like my mother was. I wasn't even a problem drinker. I've always been able to stop after one or two drinks and call it a night. There's never been any urgent reason not to drink, except that I didn't want to give myself the pleasure, open myself to other yearnings.

Celeste collapses into the oil puddle of the couch's back. "I don't want Neil and the kids to come up to the camp with us. I've already told them."

"Okay," I say. "It's your decision. But you might regret it."

"I never regret anything, Rachel. I hated it up there. I don't want to expose my kids to that place. And Neil, he'll just make everything worse. He can't understand. His family was always so perfect."

She seems to be waiting for me to ask her something, or to respond in some specific way, as if there's something I should know here, but I have no clue what that is. So I say, "Okay, it's entirely your decision," and she sighs, stares at me with evident disappointment, and shoves another handful of chips into her mouth.

For a few minutes she crunches away as we look out the window together. I figure she'll tell me what's going on when she's good and ready, so I'm quiet, giving her room. She takes a swig of hard seltzer, burps loudly, and wipes her mouth on the back of her hand.

"I confronted Neil about his drinking." Her voice is high and sharp.

I'm genuinely startled. This wasn't at all what I expected. "What did you say?"

"That I really love him, but it's like he's checked out all the time. I can't take the loneliness anymore." She stares at me with glittering eyes, shoves another handful of chips into her mouth, crushes them to dust with her molars, swills more spiked seltzer.

"What did he say?"

"He laughed at me. Laughed!" She dashes at her cheek with the back of the hand that's holding the can. "He said he's not going to change, he's fine the way he is, but I'm welcome to find my own happiness however I need to."

"Well, it's good you said something."

"For all the good it did."

"I'm sorry."

"He doesn't even know I left the house." She looks bleakly at me. "I wonder when he'll realize. Would he care? He doesn't even see me. I don't want to go back to that house. It's like being buried alive." She nestles herself deeper into the couch and takes a shuddering breath. "No one needs me anymore."

"Your kids need you."

"They mock every word I say." Her voice is a wail. "They call me a basic bougie bitch. Right now they're both out. Who knows where they are? I'm sure they lie to me constantly. They could be in a crack house for all I know, or OD'ing in a gutter." Her eyes are pinpoints on my face. "You know what Mom would be saying right now?"

As a matter of fact, I do. "Tell me."

"She would tell me to go out and have some fun. She would tell me Neil's asking for it, and I should go find my own happiness. And above all, she would *drink* with me." Celeste detaches a second can from the six-pack and thrusts it at me. "Come on, Rach, it's just a seltzer."

"You definitely need to have some fun," I say, ignoring the can she's waggling at me. "You do deserve it."

"You know what?" She gives an angry half laugh, gives up on corrupting me. "I'm craving a cheeseburger. And a cocktail." Her voice is defiant, as if Neil has single-handedly deprived her of meat and booze all these years, which I know is far from the case.

"I made baked cheesy cauliflower," I say.

"Let's go out!" she says with hectic gaiety. "My treat."

I turn off the oven, leave everything where it is, and get my jacket. We climb into the big dark plush cave of Celeste's SUV with its tinted windows and leather seats and dashboard screen as complex and vital as the control panel of a jumbo jet. Tapping her thumbs against the steering wheel, flooding the cabin with lush female synth-pop from her Bluetooth system, Celeste drives us onto the peninsula and parks on a side street, sliding the enormous behemoth into a space that seems much too small for it, of course effortlessly, because Celeste is the best parallel parker I've ever known. If it were an Olympic sport, she'd be the gold medalist every time.

"Congress Bar and Grill?" she says.

This tells me more about Celeste's current mood than anything she's said so far. It's an old beloved hangout from our decadent youth. I'm sure neither of us has been back in decades.

"Of course," I say. "I should have guessed."

Once we're facing each other across a cramped two-top, Celeste looks around the bar, takes a sip of water, checks her phone, shakes her head so her hair falls just so, fiddles with her fork.

"I have to tell you something," I say. "Two things, actually."

Instantly, she's motionless. It's like one of those old slumber-party games where everyone is dancing frenziedly and has to freeze when the music is randomly turned off. "Okay."

"I got shitcanned."

She gasps theatrically. "What? Are you kidding? Why?"

"Internal politics. My funding was cut. They're getting rid of everyone over forty-five."

"So what are you going to do?"

"I don't know yet," I say. "Go back to DC and fight them, maybe? For all the good it will do."

"You can find another job in a second. You're such a good writer, who wouldn't hire you? Or maybe this is a good chance for you to do something else. A silver lining. You could come back here."

"Also," I tell my sister, "I'm putting Mom's house on the market. I talked to a realtor today."

Her eyes narrow. "Already?"

"Yes."

"I mean, she hasn't even been dead for a week."

"I know."

She stares at me. "What do you want me to say here?"

"Nothing. I'm just wondering if you want to keep anything of hers. I'm in the process of emptying the place out, and it occurred to me that maybe there are some things you want."

"I don't know!" She sounds anguished. "It's so fast."

"That's right. I'm not wasting any time. I took some bags of clothes to the Goodwill. A truck is coming from ReStore to pick up the furniture. I'm boxing up the kitchen. So if there's anything you want me to put aside, let me know."

I wait. She shoots her gaze across the room. "Why did you stay away for so long? *Really*, why?"

"Because I couldn't tolerate Mom one more minute." I'm too surprised to blunt the truth. "Remember when I nursed her through her leg break ten years ago? Some shit happened. I stayed away to protect myself from her craziness. Her darkness."

Celeste leans back in her chair. "You hated her that much?"

"I didn't hate her," I say, feeling my way into the words. "I just couldn't stand her. She was toxic to me. And I think it was mutual."

Celeste gives me a look of abrupt naked heartsickness. "Oh Rachie," she says. "I don't want to leave my husband. I want to stay in my marriage and my house and my life, it's all so comfortable and safe and familiar. But right now I feel like I can't."

So she doesn't care if I sell the place; her consternation was just for show. Okay then, good. I'm as relieved as she is to abandon the topic of our mother's house, as well as perfectly happy to help her prop up her marriage. I can't imagine my sister's life without Neil. What would she do? They've been together since they fell in love as eighteen-year-old freshmen at Colby College. They both majored in theater, Celeste with the idea that she was going to be a star, because she was easily beautiful enough, and Neil because theater was fun, and he would never need a job as long as he lived. Right from the beginning, I looked to Celeste and Neil as a functional, golden antidote to the messy stew of David and me. To my knowledge, they had only one hitch in all their years of happiness, during their junior year, when my sister called me tearfully and told me that Neil had cheated on her, a drunken one-night stand with her roommate that he swore wouldn't happen again and didn't mean anything. After a few weeks of ignoring his increasingly frantic pleas and apologies, she forgave him, because Celeste is not and has never been a fool. After graduation, they moved to Hollywood together to try to break into the movie business. When that didn't work out, they moved back to the East Coast and tried their luck with the theatrical world of New York. Through mutual professional disappointment, they stayed happily together, at least partly because, let's be honest, they didn't have to struggle. They were free of those stressors; they always had money, no matter what happened or didn't happen. Eventually, inevitably, Neil proposed, and then they caved to inevitability and reality and moved back home to Maine, announcing that it was time to "settle down and start a family." Ever since, their family life has served as my model of grown-up stability.

"You don't have to leave," I tell my sister now. "Why not change some things instead? Do some soul-searching. Ask your husband to go to therapy with you. Make your life what you need it to be. It'll take some hard work, but you can do it."

But she's not really listening. She's on her own trajectory. "I've diminished myself down to nothing. Such a big house, and I'm a tiny little pebble rolling around in it. All I do is take care of them. And they all despise me. I feel like the maid."

"So change! Declare your independence! Don't retreat. Don't cast yourself out and screw yourself over. Make them adapt."

She shakes her head. "That house sometimes feels like a low-security super deluxurious prison." She swigs her drink, grins at me. "I've busted out tonight. I'm on the lam."

Our food arrives, and as one, united in hunger, we attack the greasy, savory cheeseburgers and fries with our hands, shoving everything into our mouths, dousing everything in ketchup, not speaking. We order another round, a tequila gimlet for her and ginger beer with lime for me, and we drink those too.

"I'm dying for a cigarette," my sister says as we're waiting for the check.

I stare at her. After our semiwild youth, hers maybe even wilder than mine, as soon as the twins were born Celeste morphed and became aggressively fervent, militantly pure except for her daily dose of wine, which is evidently cultural and social and therefore doesn't count. Just a year ago, when she caught thirteen-year-old Mallory vaping, she had a "total helicopter freakout meltdown," according to my niece, who called me right afterward, the one and only time we've ever spoken on the phone, and then she sent her precious daughter to a therapist and tracked her every move for weeks. Celeste has always been a person of extremes, either rigidly ascetic or aggressively hedonistic, and she's clearly snapped back into the second mode. My only acceptable role here is evidently to cheer her on her as she rebels against her self-imposed constraints.

"Maybe you should bum one," is all I say. "I'll get the check and meet you outside."

She shoves her credit card at me.

By the time I pay the check, put on my coat and scarf, pocket my stuff, and get outside, Celeste is puffing away on the sidewalk with a young guy who was evidently happy to supply her with a cigarette. Celeste is talking fast, gesturing with her cigarette. He's listening, leaning toward her. They're slouched side by side against the brick wall, both of them feline and lean and beautiful, like two actors in a movie.

"This is Fred," she says when she sees me. "He's cheering me up. Fred, this is my sister Rachel."

"Hi," Fred and I say to each other.

Celeste exhales grandly. "Everything is fucked. We might as well go get drunk."

"You should go to the Painted Circus," says Fred, pointing across the street. "It's a speakeasy—you've probably walked right by it and never known it was there. It will make you forget the fuckery."

"I love that place, and you're coming with us," says Celeste. "I like your lack of bullshit. The West End is so full of bullshit. So superficial."

"Welcome to the real Maine," says Fred, grinding his butt underfoot.

"Oh," says Celeste, "I'm *from* the real Maine."

"Well, if you ever want to move *back* to the real Maine, I just lost my roommate. So there's a nice room for rent, right near here, in East Bayside."

"East Bayside is no more the real Maine than the West End," says Celeste. "It's all hipsters now. Breweries and gastropubs. Kombucha tasting rooms." She laughs.

Fred eyes her with speculative combativeness. Is he trying to get her to move in with him? "The rent is only eight hundred a month."

She gleams with triumph. "For a bedroom in a crappy neighborhood? I think I've made my point."

"It sounds like a great deal to me," I say, because apparently I'm the yenta at this mating dance. "But I live in DC."

Celeste shoots me a look. "So are we getting a nightcap, Rach?"

Before I answer, my sister takes me by the arm and commandeers me across the street. Fred seems very happy to come along with us without persuasion.

We push our way through the heavy velvet curtain into the bar. It's still early, but it feels like 3:00 a.m. in here. The place is dark and glittery. Electronic music pulses the air. Flickering low candles cast underwater shadows on walls festooned with sea fans and candelabras and vintage lace. The bartender's eyelids are shellacked in luminescent gold, a tattoo of a purple tulip on one forearm, muscular biceps exposed in a black tank top.

"Oh my God, they have a cocktail with absinthe in it," says Celeste.

"Get out," says Fred with a cocked eyebrow.

They both go for the absinthe. I order a mocktail called the Shirley Temple Black, ginger beer with a shot of black currant syrup instead of grenadine. We carry our drinks upstairs to the small mezzanine lounge, where I perch on a club chair while Fred and Celeste sink side by side onto a fainting couch under fringed lampshades.

The corporate pop songlet that was playing on the bar's sound system gives way to Roxy Music's "If There Was Something," with its sexy, slow build to Bryan Ferry's coked-up tremolo, lush chords, the feeling of endless nights, being young and in love, heedless and euphoric. I'm impervious to it. Whatever we did last night, David is out of my system now. Even so, part of me envies my sister's ability to get drunk and hit on a man at least twenty years her junior. Of course, in theory anyway, I could do the same thing if I wanted to. But that's the thing: I don't want to. What I want is to go home to bed like a boring adult.

As the song ends, I finish my drink and stand up, sliding into my jacket. "I'm off," I say. "I'll call an Uber. Nice to meet you, Fred. Good night, Cellie."

They look up at me, startled out of their warming cloud of chatty mutual attraction, and before they can pretend to try to convince me to stay, I'm on my way down the stairs. I push through the heavy curtains and out the door, my phone to my ear.

Early the next morning, as I go downstairs in my pajamas and walk through the living room, I see to my mild surprise that Fred is asleep on the couch, his bare feet sticking out from my mother's crocheted afghan, his body deeply sunk into the blue goo. I make myself some coffee and toast with marmalade and carry my breakfast back upstairs. The guest room door is closed, but I assume my sister is in there. I shower, put on jeans and a pullover, and comb my hair, then go down to get myself another cup of coffee and see what the hell is going on.

The couch is empty. Celeste is standing wrapped in the afghan by the front window, looking out, as if she's watching Fred leave. As far as I can tell, she's wearing just her panties underneath. Her wild hair snakes freely around her head, riding currents of static electricity and magic. I take in her extraordinary leggy olive-skinned beauty as I always have, with a half-detached envy that borders on aesthetic but is much more visceral, that feels akin to lust.

"Good morning." Her voice is a honey-thick purr.

"I imagine you want coffee," I say, as always impressed by my sister's sangfroid in any situation, as well as her eternal ability to look like this after a night of drinking and smoking and misbehaving. She's fifty-one freaking years old.

"I gave up caffeine." She quirks her mouth at me, self-aware, amused at herself. "But okay, maybe a little, just for my hangover."

She follows me to the kitchen, where I hand her a big-ass cup of coffee richly lightened with half-and-half. She stirs in a heaping teaspoon of sugar, yawns, and stretches with self-mocking ostentation. "I am so tired," she says. Last night, she was emotional and volatile. Today she's a purring Cleopatra.

I resist an urge to ask if she had sex with Fred. It's none of my business, or rather, I don't need to ask; of course she did. I give her a sidelong look. "I bet you are," I say, laughing. I have no right to judge. We're the adulterous Calloway sisters.

"I know, I know," she says, "I'm acting like a teenager right now. I was so bad last night."

A question hangs in the air between us. I hear it ringing loud and clear.

"Of course I won't tell anyone," I tell her. "I promise. I'm also not judging you for one second."

She's visibly relieved. "Oh, thank you. I needed that. I don't know why. It was crazy of me. But I feel better now."

"Well, you know that Mom would approve," I say. "She believed in getting what she needed at any cost."

"Do you think this is hormonal? Like a midlife crisis?"

"Just about everything turns out to be hormonal when you have hormones," I tell her. "Do you still get periods?"

"Do I ever," she says. "Every three weeks, a hemorrhage. Wicked mood swings along with them. Like I'm thirteen again."

"I haven't had one in about nine months," I say. "Yeah, it's like a second adolescence in reverse. But the mood swings are going away."

"So none of this is permanent?"

"I promise, there's calm at the end of this typhoon."

"Meanwhile," she says. "Last night was the first time I've had sex in . . . God, I don't even want to say. Such a long time. I needed it."

"You mean you want to, and Neil doesn't?"

"Let me put it this way," she says. "I feel like a houseplant."

"Listen, Celeste," I tell her, my voice strong and hard. "Neil has to wake up and stop getting shitfaced every night and put his phone down and actually look at you once in a while."

"In theory, yes." She's snuggled into the afghan with her mug at her chin, leaning against the counter. "But he's never going to change."

"What about couples' therapy? I know, I sound like a broken record. Or AA?"

"Ha," she says. "You know him, the life he was born into. He's never had to do anything in his entire life that he didn't want to do. He is who he is. I have to take him or leave him."

"If you want to stay here for a while just to take some time for yourself, feel free. It's your place too."

"Oh no," she says. "I hate cramping your style."

"I have no style. I mean it. I'd love the company. It's weird and lonely here."

Celeste inhales deeply, as if she's bucking herself up. "No," she says in a decisive burst. "I'm really okay now. And it's time for me to go home and turn back into a grown-up."

I search her face for any sign of the anguish she was feeling when she burst in last night. "This has to be the shortest midlife crisis in human history."

"You remember when Neil slept with my college roommate?"

"Over thirty years ago."

"Now we're even."

"It can't be that simple."

She holds out her coffee cup with a self-mocking puppy-eyed expression, and I refill it. "Don't judge me, Rachie."

I laugh. "Who am I to judge you?"

She looks at me seriously, as if she's waiting for me to say something.

"You know," I say, feeling my way into it, "I've been realizing how Mom played us against each other all our lives. Maybe on purpose, to keep us at odds, so she'd have both of us to herself."

"Of course." Celeste squints at me. "She always had to be the center of attention."

"You were fun and sexy, I was the serious one."

She takes a sip of coffee and holds it in her mouth with ruminative deliberation. She has done this all her life, suspended a bit of food or drink on her tongue as a sort of thinking aid, a simple, dramatic device to sustain the attention of her listener while she figures something out. She swallows. "You were smart and ambitious. I was superficial and boring."

"You were beautiful and funny. I was uptight and bossy." We're talking in past tense, because Lucie is gone.

Celeste is smiling. She's enjoying this. "You got away, and I stayed behind."

"You had kids and a husband," I say. "I was a sterile old maid."

"You had a big important career; I did nothing with myself."

We grin at each other in silence as a few seconds tick by.

"Those are all completely fake differences," I say. "The way she made us compete with each other, so we'd hate each other under the skin. She engineered that."

"I never hated you."

I don't bother refuting this obvious lie.

"Mom was so damaged," I say.

"Seriously." Slouching against the counter, wrapped in the crocheted blanket, she could be two years old again, or eight, or fifteen. I put my arms around her and give her a squeeze. She knocks her head against mine. "Listen," she says. "You're the only person I ever act out with. The only one I trust with all my darkest feelings. I don't show any of my craziness to anyone else. Just you."

"Lucky me," I say, and we both laugh. For the first time since before we were teenagers, the air between us feels neutral, even warm, as if by saying these things out loud, we've stripped our rivalry of its lethal charge, erased the battle lines our mother drew between us in her decades-long campaign to turn us against each other so she could dominate the no-man's-land in between. There is no tension between us in this moment, our détente ballooning like a fragile, shining bubble, sure to pop any second.

"Want some breakfast?" I say.

"No, what I need is a shower."

She climbs the stairs languidly but hurriedly, an oxymoronic combination only my sister is capable of executing. "Don't forget," she calls down from the landing. "We're driving Mom's ashes up to the camp next weekend. I want to leave early Saturday morning. I told Aunt Jean we're spending two nights up there. Uncle Frank and Aunt Debbie are coming."

"Stay for breakfast, I'm going to get some groceries," I call after her, noticing the empty Humpty Dumpty chips bag crumpled on the floor. I imagine Fred finishing them in a fit of post-coital hunger before crashing on the couch, where I further imagine Celeste told him to sleep to preserve appearances, even if it's only for the likes of me, the recent wanton seductress of her best friend's husband.

Half an hour later, carrying a grocery bag full of bacon, eggs, jam, bread, and orange juice, I come back into the house and hear low voices. The TV is on, Drew Barrymore's face with its long patrician chin and doe eyes in some 1990s rom-com. The house is otherwise empty, with a light haze of shower steam, a brief smell of shampoo. Celeste evidently took off in the middle of the movie and left it running.

Disappointed that my sister's gone, I turn the TV off. As I put the groceries away and look around me at everything I need to do, the morning's unexpected pleasures evaporate into a funk of angry unease. Nothing is solved. My life is as fucked up as ever.

I can feel the house mocking me, and I'm overcome with a powerful urge to strip it, tear it apart until there isn't a single trace of my mother left, until she is fully, and finally, erased from the face of the earth, so help me God.

Part IV

Thirteen

I start in the bedroom. Lucie's top bureau drawers are a ferment of costume jewelry, scarves, old cast-off makeup, cheap broken watches, boxes of buttons, and bright magpie trinkets, none of which I recognize. I shove it all into a contractor-size garbage bag and move on to the closet. A box falls on me from the overhead shelf, and I shriek, as if my mother had pushed it on me, as gaudy hats, feathered and plumed, leap out like uncaged parrots. Into the garbage bag they go. Likewise the contents of her bathroom medicine cabinet, which is crammed full of expired over-the-counter drugs and a vast array of perfume bottles and makeup and toiletries.

Bedroom and bathroom done, I take a deep breath and swashbuckle my way into the guest room, methodically working through the boxes stacked in the closet, the clothes hanging there, the particleboard bookshelf full of mass-market paperbacks, all the random crap in the bureau drawers. This room is a repository of my mother's past selves through the decades, a sort of personal museum. I recognize a bright orange one-piece bathing suit, the sea-green chiffon mermaid dress she wore to Celeste and Neil's wedding, the gauzy scarves she loved to throw over her shoulders on summer evenings, theatrically, as if they were the finest silk shawls and she Audrey Hepburn. With a frisson of horror, I find the crutches she used after rehab when I stayed here to take care of her. I can't bring myself to touch them. I kick them downstairs, childishly, and watch as they land on the carpeting below with a creepy clatter of voodoo bones.

I pad downstairs and kick the terrible crutches into the corner by the front door.

When I look up, there are those little Red Rose Tea figurines arrayed on the shelf, those talismans of my mother's occasional attempts to quit drinking. I don't know why, but I find it heartbreaking that she kept them all these years by her front door, household gods to greet her when she came home to her solitary life. I peer closely at all the tiny hand-painted ceramic animals: walrus, buffalo, orangutan, fox, bear, giraffe, kangaroo, koala, lion, gorilla, rhino, tiger, two or three or even four of each, carefully arranged.

During her self-imposed episodes of sobriety, she'd drink endless cups of tea with milk and sugar, sucking them down as if she were the queen of England herself. "It's so much better to drink tea!" she'd trill with desperate joy. "More refined." During these sober interludes, she used to take Celeste and me on spur-of-the-moment sprees and adventures in her old Chevy station wagon, to the aquarium in Boston, up to Damariscotta to eat oysters, once as far as the Berkshires for a weekend at the Stockbridge Red Lion Inn, where Lucie sat on the front porch in a rocker and drank Earl Grey out of an antique teapot with matching sugar bowl and creamer, her pinkie extended as she sipped from the little china cup and set it ever so delicately on its saucer. I could feel how much she wanted to appear high-class to the staff there, a real lady, cultured and knowledgeable. "Now, do you think this is a genuine Edwardian piece? It is? Oh, how lovely! What a wonderful place this is."

Celeste and I loved these sober interludes. But they never lasted long. Eventually Lucie would start drinking again, and always at the moment when we actually started to believe with naive and irrational hope that maybe this time it would stick. Then we'd come home from school to find her sprawled on the blue couch with a bottle half empty on the floor, snoring, her carefully curated array of Red Rose figurines looking as sad and abandoned as we felt.

My mother had the absolute wrong personality for a working-class provincial Maine girl, the wrong aspirations and affectations. She was too lazy, too invested in glamour and decadence, for her station. If only she had been a blue-blooded Boston Brahmin heiress who grew up in a Back Bay mansion, went to Radcliffe to study art history in a genteel fashion, then married a rich Harvard boy of an equally good pedigree, her hard drinking and penchant for fripperies and general wackiness would have been absorbed by her milieu. Beautiful and pampered and safe in her moneyed life, she could have bought all the antique teapots and elegant scarves she wanted, indulged all her desires.

Instead, her life was poor and isolated. She was stuck marrying plain-spoken working-class men who couldn't possibly understand her, relegated to living in double-wide trailers and crappy apartments, forced to make do with polyester and cheap knockoffs. But it's to my mother's credit that she never apologized for her inborn desire for nice things, never once capitulated to the female drudgery and stoicism she was born to bear. Looking at these crude little figurines, I know she would have preferred to collect Hummels, but this was the best she could do, so she loved and treasured them. Likewise, drinking must have been her only means of lifting herself out of the truth, blunting its edges. Drunk, she could swan about in the pearly light of fantasy. Of course sobriety was impossible for her to sustain. Without alcohol, she eventually had to face who she was. No amount of tea could hide the truth from her forever.

Unfortunately for us both, I, her firstborn daughter, was obsessed with truth. Analytical and realistic, of course I saw my mother as weak. And of course she hated me for seeing her so clearly and judging her, instead of participating in her delusions about herself and dutifully reflecting them back to her, shoring her up with the reassuring compliments she craved like air or water.

But at the same time, she was proud of my differences from her, my ability to work hard, to succeed in a tough field. Yes, she competed with me sexually, but never professionally, not once. She didn't understand what I did, but she was never anything but fiercely supportive of my ambition. If she were here now to know I'd been fired, she would erupt with hot, loyal indignation. "They can't fire you! Who works harder? Your recycling piece was famous, for God's sake! You won a flipping Pulitzer Prize!" She was so proud of my accomplishments, so sure I'd succeed even when I was young.

She was thrilled when I told her I was going to college in Berkeley, California, all the way across the continent, on a full scholarship. "Of course they'd be idiots not to take you," she said. Then when I got my graduate degree, she threw a party for me at which she got so drunk, she fell over onto Aunt Jean, who'd driven down from Bangor for the occasion and was sitting perched on an uncomfortable chair with a can of beer. Aunt Jean patted her sister's shoulder with tentative disapproval and looked at me as if this were all my fault.

Lucie may not have read everything I wrote, or even anything at all, but she knew what it meant in the world, that it was important, and she was proud of me. She also told Celeste she was beautiful and charming enough to be a movie star, to marry a rich prince, to have whatever she wanted in life. To my mother's credit, she encouraged us to live the lives she wanted and couldn't have. Maybe it was her insistence that these things were possible for us that enabled us both to fulfill her expectations, to have the guts and sense of self-worth to go for it.

And maybe I haven't wanted to remember any of this because it complicates my internal story about my mother and kind of breaks my heart. But it's true.

By now I'm done packing up the kitchen, all of its ancient appliances, cracked dishes, and cheap aluminum pots. After three trips to the Goodwill and another to the dump, I call Habitat for Humanity and arrange for their truck to come first thing tomorrow morning to pick up all the downstairs furniture, the squishy blue couch, armchair, coffee table, and Lucite dining table and chairs. By now it's dark. Exhausted, I make myself a turkey sandwich, take a shower, and fall into bed. I sleep badly.

The Habitat ReStore truck comes just as I'm drinking my second cup of coffee, two beefy Maine guys with tattoos, no-nonsense and sweetly taciturn. I feel almost ecstatic watching them carry my mother's furniture away, culminating with the oily blue couch, on which so much of my emotional life has taken place. Getting rid of it feels almost like a ceremony, a triumphant cleansing celebration, albeit private. "Goodbye, cruel and evil couch," I say out loud to the little Red Rose Tea figurines as the truck drives away. They're the only things of my mother's besides the coffeemaker that remain downstairs; I've decided to keep them for symbolic reasons, at least for now.

I spend the entire day scrubbing and cleaning every square inch I can reach, until the whole place gleams. As I wander around my mother's spotless, echoing house, the evening an empty void stretching in front of me, it finally occurs to me to wonder what's going on with my sister. I haven't heard from her since she went home yesterday morning. I picture her sliding guiltily back into her wife-and-mother role at home, picking up where she left off, nothing solved, nothing improved, no questions asked, everything left bubbling under the surface, as always.

I'm sure I'm right, because even if he did suspect that she'd had a one-night stand, Neil is too much of a tamped-down, genteel WASP to instigate any kind of confrontation. And my sister is too much of a people pleaser to make a scene, as I know now, with anyone but me. I'm sure that she's still as lonely and frustrated as ever, only now she feels guilty about sleeping with Fred on top of everything else, so she's even more stuck than she was before.

It has certainly never been my habit to interfere in Celeste's life, and my sister is no helpless victim. She can fend for herself perfectly well. It's not in my nature to meddle where I'm not asked. Even so, I'm itching to go over to her house. All I want to do is make sure everything's okay with her, I tell myself as I get into my mother's car and aim it at the West End. I also need to tell Celeste that all our mother's stuff is gone now, even though I asked her the other night what she wanted, and she ignored the question. Knowing Celeste, she'll change her mind out of the blue, and then it will be my fault that I didn't read it correctly.

Anyway, as it happens, I have a perfectly good excuse for dropping by. I need to borrow some tools. So I park on the street in front of my sister's house and let myself in the side kitchen door. Neil, Jasper, and Mallory are all sitting in a row at the counter, eating meatloaf, wooden salad bowl and serving dish of mashed potatoes and ketchup bottle strewn across the granite acreage. All three of them have their phones directly in front of them, next to their plates. Neil clutches the stem of a wineglass, the bottle in front of him. Mallory is sneaking a tidbit to one of the fluffy dogs. Jasper's long, skinny bare legs are splayed in baggy cargo shorts, his feet in enormous puffy sneakers lolling on their sides. When he sees me, he gets up for a brief, polite hug. His face bristles with new growth.

"Sorry to just drop in like this," I say. "I didn't mean to interrupt your supper."

"Aunt Rachel!" Mallory leaps from her stool and throws her arms around me. Apparently she's recovered from the shock of seeing David outside her bedroom the other night. Or maybe, and more likely, Celeste wildly exaggerated it. Accepting my niece's affection at face value, I hug her tightly and kiss her cheek.

Celeste breezes through the garage door into the kitchen, dressed entirely in white cotton, yoga mat tucked under her arm, hair tied back. She looks startled to see me. I can't tell if I'm welcome or not.

"I just came to see if I could borrow some tools," I say.

"Sure," she says. "Whatever you need. In fact, I'll get a glass of wine and take you out to the garage." She smiles tightly at me as she takes a wineglass from the dish drainer and plucks the bottle up from in front of her husband.

Jasper and Mallory mill around her, their big ungainly adolescent bodies nudging and bouncing off their mother as if they crave physical contact with her.

"Hello, Rachel," Neil says.

"How's summer vacation going?" I ask the kids, ignoring him. "Are you guys having fun?"

Jasper grunts something, not in the mood for conversation.

"I start work soon," says Mallory brightly. "For my college application essay, I'm interning with a professional person working in the field I hope to enter."

"Okay," I say. She's only fourteen. College already? "What's your chosen field?"

She looks mildly offended, as if I really should know that. "I'm going to be an eco-chef."

"I have no idea what that is," I say, "but it sounds impressive."

As Celeste pours herself a glass of wine, Neil thrusts his wineglass in his wife's direction without making eye contact or saying a word.

Celeste holds the bottle in midair and considers him for a moment, then cocks her head at me. We stare at each other without breaking eye contact.

"You see what I'm dealing with here?" Celeste says to me.

Neil looks up at her in mild bemusement.

I narrow my eyes, feeling the inside of my skull glowing white with protective ire. "My God, Neil. You could at least ask your wife directly instead of shoving your glass out without even looking at her."

Neil's head snaps erect between his stooped shoulders. I sense both kids in the periphery, shocked into attention.

I leap into the silence. "She's waiting on you hand and foot. All of you." I gesture theatrically so he can't ignore me. "Do you not see that?"

Neil glances at his empty glass. Apparently no one has ever said boo to this man in his life. "Well," he says. "She's holding the bottle. How much trouble is it to pour a little more?"

Celeste is quiet, but she isn't making any move to pour.

I inhale sharply. "You obviously have no clue how lucky you are to have my sister. You kids, too."

"We know," says Mallory. There's a cold glint in her voice.

I have no interest in mollifying or even countenancing my niece's resistance to what I'm about to say. She has to shut up and listen right now. I take another deep inhale, enough air to contain the words I need these people to hear. "My sister has devoted her entire life, all her beauty and grace and charm, to the well-being of you three lucky people. But you need to understand something. No one taught her how to do this. She had to do it all from scratch. She came from the most neglected, deprived childhood you can imagine. Trust me, I know. We had none of this growing up." I'm an erupting volcano. I've never let this happen before in my life. So this was how Lucie felt all the time, letting fly with any little thought or feeling she wanted to express. It feels amazing to let this all burst out of my mouth. It feels decadent and freeing and powerful, as good as an orgasm, maybe better. "She could just as easily have turned out like Lucie, living in a cloud of chaos and not caring how much it fucked you kids up, not caring about anything or anyone but herself. But instead, she turned this big old pile of bricks into a cozy, beautiful house where you're all fed and loved and surrounded by every comfort imaginable.".

"We know," says Mallory again. But the coldness in her voice is gone. She sounds sad.

For their parts, Neil and Jasper are staring at me like primitives watching a solar eclipse. I have their full attention, and possibly their fear. I'm not looking at my sister. If she's pissed at me for exploding like this, I'll deal with that later.

"Do you? Then you should show some appreciation instead of treating her like your servant and mocking her." I look all three of them in the eye, one by one. Jesus. These people aren't even moving. Their lives are so cushioned and abstracted, any dose of truth makes them freeze. They can't cope. "How did it feel to have Celeste gone for a whole night last week?"

They all look baffled. Clearly, no one has talked about this yet. Celeste must have come back to a house of silent recrimination and unspoken questions and gone right back to her usual defensive, lonesome life. I'm not surprised, but I'm saddened on her behalf.

"We were worried," says Mallory.

"Do you know where she went?" Neil asks.

"Yeah," says Jasper. "We still don't know."

I glance at my sister. Celeste's eyes are vapor-locked on my face.

"As a matter of fact"—I give her a quick nod—"she was with me."

Neil looks smug. "I thought so."

"She came over to talk to me because apparently she can't talk to you. She told me she feels invisible and taken for granted. She thinks you don't care about her. She's fed up."

Jasper's eyes go to his mother. "Mom," he says. His voice cracks a little. "Is that true?" Good boy.

Celeste says nothing. She doesn't take her eyes off me.

So I answer for her. "Of course it's true. I don't care what happens here, I just want my sister to be happy. She could walk out of here right now, whenever she wants, and leave you all to fend for yourselves. It's her choice. I told her she could come and live with me, anytime, for as long as she wants."

"We've been married almost twenty-eight years," says Neil, as if this were any kind of argument.

"So what?" I snap at him. "Who says marriage has to last forever? And you kids are teenagers, you'll leave home in a few years. She told me you treat her like she's stupid. I've seen you do it myself, so don't deny it."

"No, Mom!" says Mallory, with earnest desperation. "That's so not true. We love you and we need you!"

Neil looks at his empty glass again. His expression is not hard to read. He wants me to shut my trap and go far, far away, but he's too well bred to say it.

"She needs connection," I tell him. "She needs a real marriage."

He gives a petulant huff that makes me want to smack him hard. "Oh, please." Hanging in the air around his head, I see the words "You're divorced and childless, what the hell do you know?" as clear as skywriting.

"Listen, Neil, you're blitzed out of your mind every single night. You might as well be on Pluto." There is a soft gasp from both kids. "Your alcoholism is at the root of most of the problems in this house, and no one can say it, no one else can tell you, but I can, because I don't give a shit if you never speak to me again. Here's the truth. Nothing will be solved until you deal with your drinking. You are keeping your entire family stuck in it with you. Is that what you want your kids to remember about you? He was drunk every night? We hardly knew him?"

"This is quite frankly none of your business." Neil's voice sounds faint. Here he is, lord of his demesne, keeper of his inherited crystal and silver and vases and paintings and antiques.

"Aunt Rachel's right, Dad," says Mallory. Good girl. "I've been worried about you. You really do drink way too much. Alcohol is so bad for you. It's a powerful carcinogen."

My work is done here. I've shot my wad. "I have to get going," I say. "I can find the tools, Celeste."

"No, I'll come with you," she says. Sparks are shooting off her.

I turn and walk out of the kitchen, and my sister follows closely behind, leaving them all in the cooling lava flow. In the garage, she points me to the shelves full of tools and hardware.

I pluck tools from the shelves—a belt sander, an electric drill in its case, a set of screwdrivers, a wrench to fix the leaking kitchen faucet—and put them into the canvas tote my sister handed me. She stands in the doorway, watching me.

"Wow," I say, gathering the tools, half laughing. "I thought for a second I was going to sock your husband in the face."

"Well, thank you very much for not doing that."

There's an edge to her voice that makes me stop what I'm doing and turn to her. "Wait, are you mad?"

"You need to mind your own business."

"I'm sorry," I say. "I thought telling the truth would help. Honestly."

"You're such a mess. You make such a mess. Just take the tools and go."

She turns and goes back into her house. I have to take a couple of deep breaths to stave off my dizziness.

Carrying and dragging the tools down the driveway to my car, I glance up and see Molly and David in their garden next door, kneeling next to each other, wielding trowels. They're both dressed in pullovers and jeans. They look like a glamorous but ordinary middle-aged couple in an advertisement for erectile dysfunction drugs or an active-living community.

When they catch sight of me, both of them stand up and wave, in tandem. "Hello, Rachel," Molly calls. Her voice is flat, impersonal. I see now that what I mistook for curvaceous plushness is her pregnant belly, protruding slightly under her sweater. Her original warmth is gone, and I'm pretty sure I know why.

As for David, we lock eyes for one split second, and I catch a flash of something in his face. And just as quickly we look away, and then we both go on, I guess, with the rest of our lives.

Fourteen

Sitting in the usual long line of cars at the red light by Deering Oaks Park, I find myself staring at the people thronging the shadowy, wooded lawn between High Street and Forest Avenue. I realize I'm looking for that guy I saw a couple of days ago, the one who reminds me of my cousin Danny, but I don't see him. There are three or four women in the crowd, but the rest are men. Most of them look beaten down. A few are energetically talking, either to themselves or to one another, but their energy glitters with the sad menace of mental illness and drugs. A shambolic man hectors a skinny, potbellied woman with a skewed face. All the women appear to be connected to one or more men and not at all to each other. Homeless women rarely seem to band together, at least not visibly, publicly.

When the light turns, an old reckless, self-destructive urge makes me drive past my mother's house and head out to Deering instead. I'm pointing myself at the Alley Kat, a bar I used to go to with David back when we were young.

It's still there. I park in back, walk into the long, dim room, exactly the same as it used to be, and take a seat at the bar.

"Hey," says the bartender, a sweet young thing with a lip ring and a punk haircut. "What can I get you?"

"Hendrick's martini, very dry, straight up, with a twist," I hear myself say.

My brain idling in an anticipatory hum, I watch the bartender upend the gin bottle into an ice-filled shaker, wave the vermouth over it, give the shaker a maraca solo's worth of action, and pour.

My martini is set before me, shining in its chalice, clear and oily and icy, with a curved skin of lemon twisting in it. I raise the glass to my lips, wet my mouth with gin, then lap steadily at my glass of straight cold liquor and smile at nothing. Or maybe I'm smiling at the irony of having just lectured my brother-in-law about his drinking problem, then promptly driving to the nearest bar to perform a spectacular swan-diving face plant off the proverbial wagon. But I don't care. Optimism floods my veins. My anxiety dissolves along with stress and despair. I can't remember why I stopped drinking for all those years. I could have had this feeling all along. So alcohol is poisonous and carcinogenic and bad for every cell of my body and brain. What does it matter? In the face of things, what?

Just like that, my glass is empty.

"Please," I say to the bartender when I catch her attention, "could I have another one?"

She swipes my glass up by the stem and gives me a brisk nod, then goes over to attend to the solitary man on the other side of the bar who just flicked his finger in the air to catch her eye. He holds his smartphone in his splayed-open palm, resting on his two middle fingers like a miniature artist's easel, and he wears the big, dark-rimmed glasses that are trendy now but used to be popular mainly with dentists and orthodontists. He deliberates over the beer list for a while. The bartender advises him with the patience of an animal trainer.

When my second martini arrives, I drink it slowly, attentively, and then I pay the check and drive very carefully back to my mother's house and go upstairs and fall into bed, fully clothed, to lie on my back like a flounder on the sea floor.

Why is the bed so hard? How could she sleep here night after night? The stained off-white ceiling wavers in and out of focus. I'm visited by thirst, an itch on my nose, an itch in the middle of my back between my shoulder blades, the urge to weep, a sense of shame as strong as a physical pain, pressure on my bladder.

It all passes through me. My brain lies in its casement of bone, on a low simmer. I know I should get up and brush my teeth and get into pajamas, but the ongoing care and upkeep of my body is so much trouble, all that repetitive eating and voiding and breathing and washing and dressing, over and over and over. And for what?

I fantasize about ribbons of algae undulating in the sunlit ocean, photosynthesizing away. Until it was pulled, I had the funding to travel to the experts where they are, in London and Belgium and Canada and California. I anticipated heading back to my own office with a sheaf of sound files and a notebook of jotted notes. And then would come the really fun part, transcribing and synthesizing and shaping and boiling down all the information, making all of the data and scientific language and concepts accessible and cogent. At my age, my level of jaundiced realism, any fantasy I might have entertained of winning another Pulitzer wasn't nearly as urgent as the impetus to bury my despair in something all-consuming and important and germane. And now I have nowhere to put it.

Meanwhile, I have $3,875 in my bank account, at last count, and less than $10,000 of savings. My condo mortgage payment of $3,250 is due on the first of June. My severance will last a few months if I'm careful, and then it's over. I'll be dead broke. Who wants to hire a worn-out, irrelevant, expensive fifty-three-year-old white woman when there's a vast pool of cheap, sparky, bright young chipmunks to choose from?

Also, does anyone really need another article identifying the degree to which we're fucked and proposing solutions that will come too late? By now, anyone who's paying attention knows exactly what's going on. It's too late for algae; ice analysis is only confirming the presence of a terminal disease; and geoengineering is insane, desperate, and dangerous. It's too late to do anything with all of this information scientists have been gathering and analyzing, information that feckless journalists like me have been doggedly translating for the world. Who needs to be told? What use is it? I am obsolete, and my work is pointless.

Time elapses. More time elapses. My mind is a fierce blank, baffled by this titanic shift in my circumstances. Its screen is gray, shot through with glinting darts of random light. Nothing in my past connects me to this moment right now, and the future is a blank wall. I'm suspended in some sort of neutral fluid that's devoid of life and free of interference from the world. It's a strange new state, one I have never experienced before, a nullity, an erasure, in which I am pinned and immobilized. It's a truly curious experience for me. I explore its boundaries like a solitary paramecium in a petri dish of distilled water, flagellating without purpose or growth.

Glancing over at the window, I see that it's daylight—morning. The night has passed somehow. Feeling creaky and fuzzy-headed, hung over for the first time in ten years, I get up. Downstairs, I make a pot of coffee. As I suck down my first cup, the habitual musculature of my work habits lifts my new flab of despair. This is my work now, the only work I have. I need to get this done, get my money, and get the hell out of Maine before I completely lose my shit. Setting my second cup of coffee on the windowsill, I begin to attack the edge of the living room carpet, pulling it up bit by bit, scraping my knuckles repeatedly on the multitude of nails until I've released a whole corner's worth.

After a while I stand up slowly, unfolding myself to give my middle-aged back and knees a break, suck on a torn bleeding cuticle, survey what I've done so far. I gulp down the now-cool coffee. Then I get back to it. After I've ripped the whole damn carpet up, pulled out all the tacks, and swept the scuffed but viable wood floor clean of threads and stray nails, I shove all the detritus into the back of the Subaru and drive it to Riverside Recycling. I head to Home Depot, where I rent a floor sander and buy a Shop-Vac. I muscle them into the house, heaving them one by one out of the car and bumping them over the doorsill and dragging them into the living room. I spend the next day sanding off the top layer of wood, vacuuming the fresh oak boards clean, and finally rubbing the whole floor with a chamois cloth on hands and knees until every molecule of dust has been picked up. I feel my muscles spasming and contracting, my lungs heaving with effort. My mouth goes dry, and I chug cold water. My lower back aches, and I do stretches to ease it—whatever it takes to get my machine of a body to do the tasks at hand. I spend the following two days with a respirator strapped to my face, polyurethaning the naked floor with a little foam brush, waiting overnight, sanding again, hitting the edges with

Celeste's belt sander, vacuuming again, picking up any dust residue again with a chamois cloth, polyurethaning again. When the second coat is on, it's nine at night, and I've poly'd myself onto the bottom stair.

I go upstairs, where I've stashed supplies. Earlier, at Hannaford, my basket filled with the groceries I'd come for, I stood in the wine aisle, clicking my tongue against my upper teeth, pondering the implications of what I was about to do before I added a couple of bottles of Rioja to my haul. Now I slam two peanut butter sandwiches into my maw, pour myself a big fat fucking glass of wine, fill the tub with hot water, strip off my clothes, and climb in with a gasp of surprised pleasure. Once I'm settled, I hit Wallace's phone number and wait for it to ring. But it goes straight to voice mail, so I hang up without leaving a message. I drink the glass of wine, pour myself another glass, and drink that, too. When the water cools, I get out, dry myself off, and get into bed, windows wide open, door shut.

The next morning I wake up feeling shaky, as if I've emerged from a high fever that had me in the grip of hallucinations and chills and night sweats. I'm hung over again. It's a breezy, sparkling-fresh blue-green-gold morning, a Maine maritime almost-summer day. I left the windows open all night to let fresh air pour in and blow the polyurethane fumes out. While coffee brews, I wander barefoot through the downstairs, my brain ticking with all the work I need to do. The kitchen cabinets are in terrible shape, warped and cracked from years of Lucie slamming and kicking and punching them in her moods. I need to replace them. I have to primer and paint the entire place. God, what a lot of work there is still to do. My muscles are already sore from refinishing the floors.

With a cup of coffee, I sit on the living room floor and google a list of local professional painters. But after the eleventh painter gives me a flat, weary no, I realize that Suzanne was right. Everyone is booked solid, backed up for months. I call several general contractors and get the same answer. Workers are in short supply in this town, even at the best of times, and there's a building boom on. No one has time, and no one can recommend anyone who might. There is evidently no way to hire someone last-minute in this town for any job at all. Okay then. Time to head back to Home Depot, return the floor sander, and buy some paint and supplies.

On the way back to my mother's with a car full of paint cans, I sit idling in a long line of cars at the red light by Deering Oaks Park. My car creeps forward, then stops again. This must be the longest red light in town, and the shortest green. I imagine lugging all these cans of paint from the car into the house, then stirring primer, pouring it into a tray, cutting in, rolling out, painting trim, walls, ceilings, doorways, window frames. When I'm done with the primer, I'll have to do two coats of paint, both upstairs and down, both bedrooms, the hall, the bathroom, the stairwell, the living room and kitchen.

It's too much. I'm not afraid of hard work, but the thought of all that painting paralyzes me.

I glance over at the people sitting in the grass under the trees. And there's the guy who looks like Danny, listening to the hectoring, insistent dude next to him. I see him duck his head. Danny used to do that when he was shy or uncomfortable. My mother liked to come at him with aggressively mocking curiosity: "What little project have you got now?" or "What the heck are you doing, you funny kid?" and he'd look up at her from the shattered privacy of his G.I. Joe action figures or Lego buildings, ducking his head with that same sidelong, desperate hunch.

I pull off into the Enterprise lot, find an empty spot facing the park, and turn off my car. I hesitate, for good reason—the thing I'm about to do is insane. It's an all-around bad idea. This guy is not my sweet cousin Danny. He's a stranger who, I assume, is sleeping in the park and doing street drugs. His mental health is no doubt fragile, his life unstable. He might be violent. There's nothing for me here but a lot of potential trouble.

Maybe drinking again is causing me to make terrible decisions. There's a reason they call it liquid confidence. But before I can talk myself out it, I'm already out of my car and crossing Forest Avenue on foot. As I approach the small group huddled in the grass, I realize I've just entered the sacred space of the outliers, crossed the Rubicon into their shadowy pocket of life. I inhale a miasmic funk of cigarette smoke and sweat and old dried piss.

The Danny lookalike still hasn't seen me. He's still in thrall to the burly guy with a ponytail, who is shouting into his face. It's not too late. I could turn around, walk back to my car, and drive away.

But my feet are propelling me forward, awkward but determined, across the grass. I see the group notice me, and then I'm looking down at them all, and it's on.

I start talking before I can think. "Is anyone interested in a job?"

There's some surprised muttering, a hostile wisecrack or two—*I'm busy, You look like my ex-wife.*

My target looks up at me, cocks his head, squints. "What kind of job?" His face is narrower than my cousin's, nose beakier. But he has a small gap between his two front teeth, like Danny did.

"I'm looking to hire someone to help me paint the interior of a house."

"When and how much?"

"Starting right now, if you're available. I can pay you ten bucks an hour."

"Ten? I could make more panhandling."

"All right, fifteen," I say.

"Got a place for me to crash?"

This is madness. "I guess so."

"My dog comes too."

Even crazier. "Fine. But you have to pick up its shit," I tell him.

"Come on, Wanda," he says to the dog lying in the shade nearby. He stands unsteadily, swaying a bit, gets his bearings. Hoisting a backpack, he waves to his friends, who are watching us, all of them silent since our negotiation began. The dog trots along next to him as he follows me back to my car. He lets her up onto the backseat and climbs into the passenger seat, sets the pack on his knees, and leans his head back against the headrest. As we pull out, he closes his eyes, his head bobbing with a gentle rhythm.

I glance over at him. So opiates, heroin, something in that general direction.

"I'm not high," he announces, his eyes still closed, as if reading my mind. "I'm just fucking exhausted. I haven't slept in days. Gotta stay awake and guard my shit."

"Isn't that your dog's job?"

"She sleeps. And eats, even if I don't."

"Nice for her," I say. "I'm Rachel Calloway, by the way."

"Jesse. Jesse Fecteau."

So I was right, he's a Franco. It makes me hope his work ethic will match mine. Also, for no reason except primitive superstition, it makes me hope I can trust him not to rip me off or murder me in cold blood. Up close, even with his eyes closed, his body gives off an electrical charge, like the threatening zing in the air right before a storm. I can't tell if the strong gamy smell is him or the dog, or both of them. But I'm not afraid of him. I know his type. I grew up with guys like him. While he may not actually be my cousin Danny, that little pipsqueak with big ears in flood Wranglers and no-brand high-top sneakers off by himself playing with sticks and rocks, he's familiar. He could easily be a distant cousin on my mother's side, a fact which I admit is both comforting and terrifying in equal measure.

Fifteen

I park in the usual space. Jesse shoulders his pack and lets the dog out as I open the back of the car and pull out the box of paint cans, balancing it on one raised knee while I sling the bag full of paintbrushes and trays and rollers over my wrist. Jesse takes the heavy box from me and carries it without being asked. I unlock the door and lead him inside. The dog comes along behind us.

Jesse and his dog prowl through the empty downstairs, the stripped-bare kitchen, the echoing living room with its freshly poly'd floor. Nervous, unsettled, I drop the bag on top of the cloth tarp puddled in one corner and motion for him to set the box there.

Here inside the house, he seems smaller somehow, diminished by the low ceilings, the domestic air we're breathing. Outside, he looked tough and menacing, but now his neck looks like it's retracting, disappearing into his olive-green shirt. Maybe it's my imagination. Maybe it's the fact that he's about my same height, broad chest and shoulders, long torso, short bandy legs, like the Gautreau men, my relatives. The Acadian male physique is pretty consistent.

"So what's the deal?" he says. "This is your house?"

"My mother left it to me—she died last week. I have no use for it. I live in DC. I'm going to sell it as soon as I can."

"Let me guess," he says. "You couldn't find anyone else in the entire state of Maine to hire."

I grin at him. "So I forgot to ask, do you have experience with this kind of work?"

Jesse laughs, a real laugh, hearty and amused. "You could say that. Many years, working construction."

"That's a crazy in-demand skill right now. You could be raking it in."

"I used to work for a roofing company, about ten years. Then I fell off a roof one day and broke my friggin' back. I was out for a year. No worker's comp, nothing. Hospital took everything I had and got me hooked on oxy. So now I spend my disability checks on pills and live in the park. The American dream, right?"

"Jesus. I'm sorry."

"It's fine. The park's as good as anywhere else."

"I can pay you in cash."

His eyes glint. "I have a bank account. A check is fine."

I hear a growling sound and look down at the dog, sitting, ears pricked and alert, watching me.

"Is your dog going to attack me?"

"Wanda," he says to the dog. "Be cool with the lady."

She gives a quick, squeaky yawn that ends in a half growl and eyes me warily.

"So can I check out that place to crash? I'll stash my gear there."

"Upstairs," I say. "Door on the right." I realize I haven't bothered to change the sheets since Celeste slept in them with her boy toy. Somehow I don't think Jesse will notice.

He plods up the stairs with his backpack, Wanda at his heels, disappears into the guest room, and reappears a moment later, the dog right behind him. "Should I start cutting in primer?"

"Sure," I say. "I'm ready if you are."

As we get to work, I'm acutely aware of his presence. The air in here feels different, disturbed, its flow interrupted by the presence of another human, along with a dog. But gradually, as Jesse works in the living room and I work in the kitchen, the dog lying in the doorway between the two rooms, I almost forget he's there. I've noticed all my life about working with people that bodies tend to fall into rhythmic sync, just by virtue of proximity and a shared activity. It's no different with Jesse. After an hour or two I feel the static electricity in the air dissipate, replaced by a confluence of purpose and movement and breath, like an unchoreographed, improvised, but coherent dance.

Every now and then I glance over at the dog, who's likewise slowly losing her threatening aspect and becoming Wanda in my mind, an individual just like me or Jesse, by virtue of her stoic and unignorable presence. She has thick reddish-gold fur, with a white chest and paws. Her expression is intent, quizzical, and a little judgmental. Her ears stand up in triangles, and her eyes are cinnamon brown. Once in a while I find myself making eye contact with her, recognizing in her gaze an awareness of me, wordless, watchful. She's taking me in. I have no idea what conclusions she's drawing, but I know she's got them.

"Sorry about your mother," Jesse says from the next room. "That must be rough."

"It is rough," I say, "but not for the reasons you'd think."

"So is your dad still alive?"

"He's been dead since I was a kid."

"How'd he die?"

"Heroin overdose."

"What was his name?"

"Tommy Calloway."

"How'd he get hooked?"

"No idea."

"Where was he from?"

"Aroostook. A potato farm."

"The County," says Jesse. "I know it well."

As I dip my brush into primer and slide it along the seams of the ceiling, I find myself telling this stranger about my father, the parent who abandoned us because of his addiction, while my mother stayed in spite of hers. I have so few memories of him: a wayward, charming man, here and then gone again. All I know about him, really, was what Lucie chose to tell me. And being Lucie, she both romanticized and disparaged him. He was a deadbeat loser and a tragic figure, often both in the same sentence, because my mother had a gift for conflating opposite qualities, attributing contradictory traits to people. Probably because she was so ridiculously mercurial herself, she figured everyone else must be too.

Talking about my father gets me wondering about the Calloways, whose name I share—this clan, the other half of my DNA, the Irish half. My father had four siblings, but I only ever met one of them, his younger brother Ed, the father of my cousin Eileen, who was a little younger than Celeste and me. Uncle Ed and his wife, my Aunt Mary, were proper grown-ups, unlike my father and his other siblings, or so I had been led to understand by my mother. Uncle Ed managed to escape the Calloway curse by somehow getting into college, then law school, and then he passed the bar, and then he was a divorce lawyer. He married a woman from away, also a lawyer—they met in law school—who was as unlike any of the other Calloways as it was possible to be in our narrow socioeconomic circles. So my cousin Eileen's parents were actual grown-ups, in a family that had very few of them.

"Your mother sounds like she was quite the rig," Jesse offers.

I laugh. "You would probably have liked her. Most people did."

I remember that Uncle Ed and Aunt Mary also went to church, Catholic of course, and voted Republican, unlike my parents. Ed helped my mother, pro bono, through her second and third divorces, of course not the one from his brother, my father, but the one from Bill Johnson, the Vietnam vet, and then, twelve years later, the one from Malachi Michaud, the retired machinist who gave my mother this house in the divorce. Although, come to think of it, the fact that she kept this house was no doubt thanks to Uncle Ed, so I have him to credit indirectly for this unexpected bequeathment.

One summer, Uncle Ed and Aunt Mary came up to the Gautreau family camp for a few days and brought my cousin Eileen. She was an odd, annoying little girl of about nine with red hair and strong opinions and a big vocabulary. She bragged to Celeste and me that she was already growing boobs at age nine and knew all about where babies came from and wanted to show us a magazine she kept hidden, trying to impress us in a frantic bid to come with us to "town" for ice cream. My sister and I, much too old and busy for the likes of Eileen at ten and twelve, cruelly left her behind, sitting alone on the porch steps, as we rode our bikes off to the tiny village three miles down the rough road, whose primary attraction was a crude general store with a freezer full of ice cream novelties.

It dawns on me now that my sister and I were mean snots to our poor cousin because our mother poisoned us against half our living relatives by repeatedly bad-mouthing them. If my parents had stayed together, or if my father hadn't died, I might have had a whole group of relatives to claim me and maybe to love me. Of course this is an entirely pointless line of hypothesis, but ever since Suzanne mentioned Eileen a few days ago, her name has apparently rooted itself in my brain, spawning curiosity. So she's still in Maine. I wonder where she lives, how she is, what she's like, how much her childhood differed from mine. I wonder who the Calloways really are, now that my mother isn't around to tell me they're trash, to adamantly keep me away from them all.

The light starts to dim in the kitchen as the sun sets. I call to Jesse, "Are you hungry?"

"I could eat," he snaps back. My cousin would have said the same thing.

I get out my phone and order a large pizza while Jesse goes upstairs to take a shower. I have wine, and there's beer in the fridge if Jesse wants it. I'm hoping he has food for Wanda. If not, I hope she likes pizza.

When dinner arrives, I set the pizza box in the middle of the living room. Wanda watches me, her expression hopeful. There's a stubbornness in the set of her jaw that I like, a hint of willfulness.

"I'm sorry," I say to her, "I don't think this is for dogs. But of course that's up to your person."

She slides back on her haunches as if this makes perfect sense, her eyes on the pizza box.

Jesse comes downstairs with wet hair, carrying a bundle that looks like a hobo's bindlestiff without the stick. "Do you mind if I do some laundry?" he asks. I jerk my thumb at the washer and dryer in the pantry off the kitchen, but he's already headed there. As the washing machine fills with water, he takes Wanda outside to walk her around in the grass. I watch through the window as she deposits a turd and he bends down and swipes it with a plastic bag on his hand, then knots it, twists it neatly, and deposits it in the garbage bin. He busies himself in the kitchen, washing his hands and talking to his dog, seemingly in no rush to eat, which I can't help feeling curious about. Who knows when his last meal was? But for all I know, maybe he eats three square meals a day at the soup kitchen. Finally he comes in, sits on the floor across from me, reaches into the box, and palms a slice of pizza.

"You're not a vegetarian, are you?"

He laughs, sticks the pointed end of the sausage, pepper, and mushroom slice into his mouth, and bites off a piece big enough to make him unable to answer. When I go into the kitchen to fetch the beer and wine, I see that he's given Wanda a collapsible dish filled with kibble and another one of water. Her snout is buried in her dinner.

We work our way through the pizza, Jesse eating the lion's share, falling into that easy chatting of fellow tired laborers, comparing notes, planning tomorrow's work. Wanda comes in quietly and lies next to her owner, watching me.

"So this was your mother's house," he says, looking around.

"For a long time."

"You and she were close?"

"No," I say, "we were not at all close. We were estranged, in fact. It was a total surprise that she left it to me. I hadn't seen her in ten years."

"You'll get a fortune for it."

"I need the money." Since we're sitting here on the floor, nothing to do but talk, I figure I might as well tell him. "I just lost my job a few days ago. So it turns out to be a stroke of luck that I got this place."

"You lost your job, why?"

"Old and in the way. It's how things go these days."

He crinkles his nose with gratifying skepticism. "How old are you?"

"Fifty-three. What about you?"

"I'm thirty-six," he says, ducking his head. "I know, I look eighty. You would too if you had my lifestyle. Anyway, fifty-three isn't *that* old."

"It is in my business."

"What business is that?"

"Journalism. So where are you from?"

"Waterville," says Jesse. "My dad was a plumber, and my mother taught in the elementary school. I left and came down to Portland after high school, worked construction."

"Then you hurt your back." I'm talking with my old Maine accent. I haven't heard myself use it in years. The cadence of this conversation feels comfortable and familiar, the staccato recital of facts that passes for an exchange of deepest intimacies in this part of the world.

"And then I hurt my back," Jesse echoes. "So I guess we're both in the same boat now."

As if Wanda has decided something, she stands up and shakes herself. Her toenails click on the floor as she makes her way over to me. I sit very still as she sniffs my hair and face, and then I allow her to lick me on the chin three times with her soft, dry tongue. Following this, she subsides onto the floor right next to me and rests her head on my thigh. She sighs mightily and gazes up at me.

"So you like me now?" I ask her.

"You're not a threat to me," says Jesse. "She's made up her mind about that."

"Took her a while." I put out a tentative hand and rest it on the top of her head, which is bony and has a ridge that fits into my cupped palm. Her fur is soft under my hands, and I find myself making little circles with my fingertips, massaging between her ears. She seems to like this— she grunts, settles in even closer to me, and closes her eyes. Her trusting warmth gives me a sneaky biochemical rush of some strong emotion, a mix of tenderness and calm.

"Where did you get her?" I ask Jesse.

"Someone dumped her down on St. John Street. Tiny puppy, and it was January. She was half frozen, crying in the snow. I stuck her in my shirt right against my skin and bought some goat milk for her and fed it to her with an eyedropper. Didn't I, girl? I raised her. And make no mistake, she'd die for me. No one can get near me without getting her hackles up."

"You're lucky," I say, and I mean this.

"I earned her trust," he says. "No luck about it."

He plucks a third beer from the cardboard six-pack holder, cracking the bottle cap off with his teeth. I pour myself a second glass from the bottle of red wine. Jesse looks around at the fresh floors, the echoing front room, "So what did your mother die of?"

"Cancer."

"My dad died of liver cancer. What kind did she have?"

"Ovarian."

"Was she really bad at the end? My dad was in a world of shit."

"According to my sister, she was, but she had morphine in hospice."

He gives me a hard stare. "What do you mean, according to your sister?"

"I wasn't here."

"What do you mean?"

The back of my neck prickles with heat. "I was on deadline. And we were estranged. And she told me straight out she didn't want me here." Do I sound defensive? I feel defensive. Jesse is looking at me as if I murdered her. "She didn't like me. And I couldn't stand her."

"She was your mother."

"True." I don't want to get into my whole history with Lucie, and I don't owe this guy an explanation. "Anyway. That's how it went, and it's over now."

"When I heard my dad was sick, I hitched straight up to Waterville. Hadn't seen him in eight years, but I went. I helped my mom take care of him till the end. It's what you do, Rachel. You take care of your family."

"I took care of her since childhood, Danny. I didn't owe her anything."

"My name is Jesse."

I barely hear him. I realize I'm tipsy now, and to my shock and dismay, tears are welling in my eyes, hot and acidic. I slap them away. "She was mentally ill and an alcoholic. She was so needy, and I tried so hard to help her. But she finally broke me. She pushed me away so hard. Took me completely for granted and resented me. Tried to sleep with my boyfriend. Maybe she did sleep with him, I don't know. She broke my heart."

"She was your mother." His voice is brutal.

Tears are channeling down my cheeks and splashing onto the front of my shirt. Damn it, it's the wine. And the work. I'm exhausted, wrung out. And this conversation snuck up on me. "I know," I say.

"My dad could be a tyrannical dick. Seeing him weak and in pain was terrible. I sat up with him all night and sponged his face and put Vaseline on his dry lips. I wouldn't have missed that. We need family close by when we come into this world, and we need family when we leave it."

"I wasn't here," I say in a sharp voice. Goddamn this self-righteous hobo, who does he think he is? It's unbearable, this ache in my chest. "And now she's gone."

He stands up, groaning in the back of his throat and theatrically holding on to his lower back as if it's red-hot with stabbing pain. "I'm going to take Wanda out one last time before I head up," he tells me.

I start to gather wadded paper napkins, the greasy pizza box, our empty bottles. It's like the detritus after a college dorm party.

He pauses at the front door. "I just want to say, I'm sure I seem sketchy as shit, but I swear I'm harmless."

"Good to know," I say as he and Wanda head out into the night.

But I'm uneasy as I get ready for bed. I lock my mother's bedroom door and lie awake for a while. I hear Jesse and Wanda come back in, climb the stairs, and shut the guest room door. Then the house is silent except for the occasional wet shushing of tires on pavement outside. The aftermath of all that emotion is making me seasick. I'm in the grip of an immense and futile sadness. If only my mother had had the wherewithal to push her ego aside and acknowledge that I took care of her the best I could, understand that it wasn't easy for me, but I did it, because I was her daughter. She wouldn't even have had to be grateful necessarily, I just needed her to recognize the truth, that she needed me, and I came, and I wasn't a perfect nurse by any means, but I didn't mistreat her. But she was too vain to see herself that way. She had to see herself as the innocent victim of my blundering bossiness, so much better off without me.

So I stayed away, because that was what she wanted. I'm going to have to live with that for the rest of my life. Maybe the gods are punishing me, taking everything I hold dear, for letting my mother die without me: David, my job, my sister, Wallace, my home in DC. They're righting the balance by stripping me of my entire identity and purpose. And I have to live with that too.

Well, things could always be worse, as Aunt Jean used to say.

Sixteen

Two days later, Jesse and I loiter in a wide, bright aisle of Home Depot, looking at cabinet doors. Jesse has turned out to be highly opinionated in this matter, and I can't figure out why. He has no reason to care, but he dithers for a surprisingly long time, torn between Shaker and flat panel. They're almost identical. He's hung up on whether you want to see the seam, or whether you don't. I stand by, secretly rooting for Shaker, but letting him decide. There's no telling what people will fixate on.

My phone chimes. Priyanka has texted me a photoshop of Martin Gold's face transposed onto a bulldozer. We've been trading invective-laden insights into his evilness as he purges more writers and editors, we suspect with the ultimate aim of shutting down the whole magazine for good. Why, we have no idea, but that's the way everything is going. Meanwhile, Priyanka has been offered a promotion to my old position at a fraction of my salary. We're both angry about this. She's going to accept it, though, and I don't blame her.

"The thing is," Jesse is saying, "Shaker is classic, you can't lose. But this one just looks more contemporary. It's the same design, but updated. It feels fresh. It looks good."

He paces and flexes his hands and snaps his tape measure in the air. He's jumpy. I have no idea what his drug situation is. I imagine he needs a fix. For the past two days, he's been working with dogged zeal that borders on mania, from early in the morning until after dark. We've painted the whole place upstairs and down, including the ceilings, moldings, doors, trim, and windowsills. This morning, while I scrubbed the fridge and stove and cabinets inside and out, Jesse recaulked the shower tile and fixed the dripping kitchen sink faucet.

"Okay," he says finally, flicking the tape measure back into its shell. "Let's go with Shaker."

"Shaker it is," I say. Before he can change his mind, I start stacking flat boxes onto a trolley cart. It works. He instantly stops pacing and helps me, sifting through the stock to find the right ones.

He's champing at some invisible bit, hyperactive, already pushing the cart down the aisle. "We need cabinet hardware and paint."

"Yes," I say. "Basic knobs and blue-gray."

While we're looking at paint colors, my phone bleats its generic ring. My caller ID informs me that it's my brother-in-law. I take Neil's call, if only because I know he'll keep calling and leaving me voice-mail messages and calling again until he gets me in person on the line. He's a profoundly insistent person when he wants something.

"Hello, Rachel," his voice says loudly into my ear.

"Hi." I haven't heard a peep out of my sister's family since I laid into them. "What's up?"

We both wait through a short silence as he takes a running leap into what he's calling about. "I'm calling to thank you for saying those things you said the other day."

I'm genuinely impressed. He's managed to get an entire declarative sentence out without one scrap of what-ho jollity. He sounds like a changed, or at least chastened, man.

"I guess I needed to say them." I'm flicking through strips of paint chips: Water's Edge, Cloudy Sky, Smoke. Who names these colors? A frustrated poet.

"I never meant to be that husband and father. I slipped into it over the years. It's easy if no one checks you."

I allow another short silence to balloon between us.

Neil clears his throat. "Of course I'm not implying that it was anyone else's responsibility to call me out on it."

That is in fact pretty much what he's implying, but it's his turn to talk.

"Anyway, I haven't had a drink since that day you came over." He sounds as if he can't believe these words are coming out of his own mouth.

I show a chip of Providence Blue to Jesse, who nods his approval. Without my having to ask, he takes it to the young woman behind the paint counter and asks for a gallon of the stuff.

Neil's voice is tentative. "I'm really going to try to do this. I might try an AA meeting."

"I'm rooting for you, Neil."

"Much obliged, sister mine." So we're back to faux-arch hipster-dadspeak. I can't say I have a lot of confidence in Neil's ability to quit drinking for real. But it's a start.

I hang up and follow Jesse, who trundles our laden cart up to the cashier.

"So it's just the cabinet doors, then we're done?" he asks as we load it all into the car.

"That's right," I say. "Then I'll write you a check for the whole job."

Jesse rolls himself a cigarette and gets into the driver's seat. I've been asking him to drive, just to give him something to occupy himself with, because he's jumpy as hell. I sense that he's in pain, but he doesn't complain, and he's been working harder than I have. He's been nothing but humbly appreciative of everything—a safe, comfortable place for him and his dog to sleep, the opportunity to wash his body and his clothes, the food and coffee and beer I provide. As for me, I'm starting to like him, but even worse, to worry about him. Ever since our conversation about family, I've felt between us a growing, inevitable mutual investment in each other's troubles. But he's a stranger. I don't want this feeling of exposed vulnerability with him. I'm glad this job is almost over. I'll be relieved to pay him and say goodbye.

As we cross the bridge over to the peninsula on I-295, I look over at him. His window is open so he can blow smoke out of the car. His skin is pale and sweaty. He flicks his cigarette nub out the window into the rushing air. His thumbs twitch against the steering wheel. As we drive through Deering Oaks Park, I catch him glancing off to his right at the people hunched in the sudden rain squall that's just burst from the leaden sky. I imagine he's scanning the crowd for his dealer.

But he drives on, splashing through the green light, and aims the car at my mother's house. He parks and we carry everything in through the downpour.

Wanda lies crouched by the back door, thumping her tail slowly, staring at Jesse, unblinking. The instant he reaches for her leash on the counter, she's on her feet, her entire back end swinging in an arcing canine rhythm, stretching and vocalizing and panting gently, staring out the window. It's amazing to me how expressive a dog's body is, nonverbal language in articulate motion.

"I'll take her," I say. I don't want him to vanish back into his demimonde, his underworld, just yet, in case that's what he's planning to do. "I could use a walk."

He lets us go with a shrug and starts opening boxes, taking the new cabinet doors out.

I don't bother with a raincoat. The rain has let up for now. Outside, Wanda takes her time sniffing, crouching, and wandering over the sidewalk as if she's searching for something she's lost. I follow behind her, attached to her by the six-foot strap, trying to envision the world through her nose, the layers of sidewalk-level smells, footprints and other dogs' pee and shit and old funky food, the dirt coming to life after the rain, the carcasses of insects, acrid stink of cigarette butts, all the dust and detritus of a city. She seems enthralled with every square inch of cement and brick. I hear her snuffling air and expelling it through her nostrils.

I walk her briskly through the heavy, sodden air, along Baxter and over to Bayside. Now that it's not raining anymore, people are thronging the Preble Street shelter's little yard, crowding the wet picnic tables, perched on the water-darkened concrete levels. Their dogs lie at their feet, breath steaming in the raw stillness.

And there's the thin swarthy woman with her current dog—Trixie, I remember, the disappointing nonreplacement for her beloved long-dead Stella. She's standing with her back to the wall, watching everyone with a critical squint, which I now suspect is just her normal expression.

"Trixie," I tell her doleful elderly shepherd, lying in a state of perma-nent resignation at her feet, "this is Wanda."

Old Trixie and young Wanda exchange a moment of grave eye contact. It occurs to me that maybe they know each other already; maybe Jesse and this woman are acquainted, from the soup kitchen or just living on the streets. Trixie pushes herself up with some arthritic difficulty and touches her nose to Wanda's. Wanda rolls over on her back on the damp pavement. As the old dog shoves her snout into the young one's underbelly, the wom-an's eyes burn with fierce focus on a group of men at a nearby table who are squabbling with impressive energy among themselves. "Trixie, that's enough."

"Let's go, Wanda," I say, and Wanda allows herself to be tugged away. As we head back down the hill, we fall together into a satisfying rhythm, adjusting our paces to each other's, always aware of what the other is doing. Why have I never had a dog before? I could get used to this.

When I burst into my mother's house, shedding raindrops from a fresh squall, I see Jesse has made progress. Several of the new cabinet doors are painted and drying. I unleash Wanda and leave her to lap at her water bowl while I go and stand by the front window. The big panes are smeared and spattered with rain, headlights speeding through the afternoon downpour, reflecting in the wet pavement. The lawn just outside the win-dow is a blur of tender green.

"So your sister came by while you were gone." Jesse comes to stand next to me, looking out with me over the open cove at the brick baked-bean factory by the bridge, with its smokestacks that belch molasses-scented steam. "She was looking for something of your mom's."

I glance at him. "Celeste was here?"

"She acted like I'd broken in. I think I might have convinced her that I'm legit. But she's not happy about this whole . . ." He gestures around at the freshly painted walls and gleaming floor, dropcloths and tools every-where.

The thought of Celeste barging in unexpectedly on Jesse gives me a shudder of sympathy for both of them. "What was she looking for?"

"She said a shearling coat?"

"It's gone," I say. It was in fact one of our mother's nicest possessions. I had actually contemplated keeping it, but it reeked of her perfume, so it went in the bag with the rest of her stuff. "She could go and get it at Goodwill for ten bucks if no one's scooped it up yet."

"She looks like she can afford it."

"Yeah, she's super rich."

"So you come from money? So why . . ."

"Why am I busting my ass to fix up this dump? Because my sister's a multimillionaire, but I'm broke. Our family was working-class. Celeste married into money. You've heard of the Fish King, Matthew Baxter Bailey?"

"Sure," he says. "But he's been dead for a while."

I laugh. "She married his great-grandson."

"No shit. Sweet beans," he says, and we both get to work without another word.

Jesse does most of it. I'm distracted, thinking about meeting my cousin tonight. It occurred to me to google her name yesterday, and almost immediately I found an Eileen Calloway in Portland. Then I saw she was a certified public accountant, which couldn't be right, since CPAs are law-abiding and good with money, and in Lucie's version of things, the Calloways were a bunch of check-kiting meth-heads and petty lowlife grifters. But her profile photo showed a woman about my age with flaming red hair and an overbite and bright blue eyes and a cheeky, shit-eating grin, and I instantly recognized that odd little girl from all those decades ago up at the camp.

I emailed her, and she wrote back within minutes, friendly and matter-of-factly accepting of me, this cousin showing up out of nowhere, maybe because Suzanne had already greased the wheels for me. Just like that, we now have a date for a drink at a place down on Commercial Street.

"I have to go out soon," I tell Jesse, wiping a smudge of paint off my thumb. "I'm meeting a friend for drinks."

"Okay," he says over his shoulder, dipping his brush into the paint can. "I can get these done tonight, and I'll hang them tomorrow morning. Then I'll get out of your hair, me and Wanda will hit the road."

I don't like how melancholy this makes me feel. Objectively, I need Jesse to leave so I can call Suzanne and get this house listed as soon as possible. The job is finished. "Sounds good," I say, heading up the stairs. "We did it, huh?"

At quarter to five, I'm showered, wet hair brushed, dressed in the spiffiest clothes I brought from DC, a forest-green sweater dress and my motorcycle boots.

"Do you want me to bring you back some food?" I ask Jesse.

"I'll take the dog out and get something," he says. Without a word, I hand him fifty bucks in cash, which he takes, also without a word. He follows me into the living room to see me off, waves briefly as I head out the door. As I walk by the picture window, I see him standing motionless in the middle of the room, his hands by his sides, his face averted, looking at the floor. He looks forlorn, but maybe I'm projecting.

When I rap on the glass, he looks up sharply, startled. "I'll be back soon," I mouth. He salutes me with two fingers flying from his brow, a flash of a smile.

Fifteen minutes later, my cousin Eileen and I are perched on tall stools around a high round table in a place called Waves, whose enormous front window looks out at the harbor, kelp-shaggy lobster pots piled on the docks, choppy blue water. Eileen lives in the Old Port, and her condo is on a nearby wharf, just a couple of blocks away, so this is her local. The decor is Boston corporate, pastel accents and beige leather banquettes, trying hard to be authentic but contemporary and thus achieving an outdated, provincial soullessness meant to appeal to the tourist industry, chowhounds in search of the city's much-ballyhooed cuisine, cruise-ship passengers come ashore for the day.

But tonight, the first Friday in June, it feels like an after-work crowd of locals. "Listen," Eileen tells me when I first walk in and get a gander at the pink and baby-blue painting over the bar, a beach and lighthouse at dawn, with fake fishing net draped overhead, "I know, I know, but wait till you taste their food. It's the only reason to come here aside from the hah-bah views." I like her instantly. She hugs me warmly, without hesitation, as if we've been close all these years instead of strangers. We accept menus from the bleached-blond waitress and order lavishly, and soon our table is crowded with drinks and a vast platter of raw Damariscotta oysters on ice.

"Is it just me," Eileen says with a sharp grin, "or do girls their age make you glad to be our age?"

She nods at the next table over, where three women in their early twenties sit with their heads together in exuberant self-absorption, punchy and raucous, all of them as fresh and provincial as this bar, pretty young Maine girls, just like I used to be. They may not see me, but I see them, their innocent, arrogant power and youth, the joys of being glossy and fertile, all their major mistakes and disappointments and compromises and missed opportunities still to come, unimaginable to them now.

"Not just you," I say. "I hope they don't make any of the stupid mistakes I made."

"But that's how you earn your perspective and wisdom." Eileen squints at the oyster she's about to eat, which seems to quiver palely on its shell, wet and exposed. "Do you have kids?"

"Nope. What about you?"

"I do not," says Eileen. "Although I do have a cat who generally hates me."

That settled, we resume slurping oysters with abandon.

When all the shells are empty and upside down on the melting ice, Eileen fixes me with a bright stare. "So where have you been all these years? I like you. I wish we'd been in touch."

It's suddenly very loud in here, as if the volume of conversation has been cranked up all at once along with the music. I'm radiating heat. With the tips of my forefingers and thumbs, I fan my own chest with the front of my sweater dress. I decide on total blunt honesty. "My mother turned my sister and me against our father's family, all you Calloways. She made it into some kind of loyalty test."

"Surely not once you hit adulthood and came into possession of your free will."

"No," I say. "I don't know why she had to die for this to happen."

"She was complicated."

"That's one word for her."

"Her head always seemed like a hard place to live in," says Eileen.

"You thought that about her as a little kid?"

"I had an overactive brain."

Our plates arrive, and to my happy surprise, the food turns out to be plain seafood with traditional garnishes and sides. The decor has led me to expect trendy ingredients and froufrou bullshit, but it's exactly the opposite.

"You were right," I say to my cousin, my mouth full of perfectly broiled cod so fresh it's still rich with brine, "the food is good."

"Last time I saw you and Celeste was up at your mother's camp. My dad was helping her with her divorce."

I realize I've been staring at Eileen with curiosity, ogling her face for familiarity, resemblance. I see Celeste's expressive squint between words while she thinks, the set of my own mouth. My father is emerging in strong flashes, too, those blue eyes, that grin, that frank and staccato way of talking. I wonder if all the Calloways are like this.

"We were such bitches to you."

"I was such a little pest!"

"What can I say? We were prepubescent assholes."

"I'm embarrassed, the things I said."

We both laugh.

"Well," I say. "We're grown-ups now."

Eileen looks as if she's about to say something, then thinks better of it.

"Spit it out," I say. "Nothing is off-limits here."

"Okay," she says, then takes a deep breath. "I've always wondered, what happened to Celeste?"

"Married a Bailey, twin teenagers, West End mansion, does a lot of yoga."

"No," she says. "I mean, up at the camp, that time I was there?"

"I have no idea," I say. "What are you referring to?"

"Something happened with some fat guy from Boston, I thought."

I search my memory while she watches me closely. "I have no clue. Like what kind of thing?"

"Your mother was flirting heavily with him. Maybe they were hooking up. I heard Celeste telling Aunt Lucie something bad about him, and Aunt Lucie slapped her."

"Did he molest her?"

"That was what I gathered."

Cold horror. "It would be exactly like my mother to blame Celeste for stealing her man."

"Yes," says Eileen. "That was the conclusion I came to, thinking about it afterward."

"Celeste was ten years old that summer." My heart thuds in my ears.

"So she never told you?"

I shake my head. "So much went on throughout my childhood that no one ever talked about. You know, my mother liked to badmouth the Calloways. But really, we were the fucked-up ones." I shake my head again. "I can't believe I never knew this. Poor Celeste. My God."

Eileen slaps her own forehead. "I haven't even asked, have you moved back up to Maine now?"

"I'm not sure how to answer that."

"Really? Why?"

I tell her everything. My mother's death, losing my job, my iffy living situation.

"Jesus," she says, lifting a finger in the air as the waitress rushes by. "We need another drink."

After we order two more rye mules, she says, "Okay, this is a crazy idea and you'll probably hate it, but I know of a nonprofit that's looking for a grant writer and PR person. It's way beneath your skills, I'm sure, but they're a good outfit, just four women, they help recent immigrants apply for loans and navigate the bureaucratic system to start their own businesses. They're called Building Bridges. Please just tell me to shut up if you're not interested."

"I'm listening," I say sincerely, even though the very idea of this job is giving me a curdling dread, the do-goodiness of it, the bright-eyed boredom of worthy fundraising.

Eileen nods. "I'm involved with them professionally, but I'm also close friends with the director—Liz Duffy, she's excellent. She started Building Bridges a few years ago because nothing like it existed yet. It fills a real need."

"Liz Duffy? I've heard of her." I squint at the melting ice in my empty copper mug. "I think my friend Suzanne Brown mentioned her."

Eileen laughs. "Suzanne and Liz and I are in a book group together—we've all been friends forever. We read nonfiction only and drink like fish and argue and fall down laughing. If you stay up here, maybe you'd want to join?"

The idea of a book group makes me feel even more antsy and dismayed than a job writing grants for a nonprofit. I feel soft tentacles suctioning on to me and a knee-jerk urge to escape. But what am I so afraid of? There's nothing inherently scary about cultivating female friendships over wine and books. All women aren't dangerous and toxic to me, just because Lucie was.

"That sounds fun," I hear myself saying. To my surprise, I mean it. "Thank you."

When our next round arrives, Eileen holds up her glass. "I wish I'd known you all these years."

"I'm glad to know you, finally," I say, knocking my glass against my cousin's. And I mean this, too.

Seventeen

As I drive home through the fresh, clear spring night, I feel an ancient dam collapse somewhere, in my head or my heart or both. I'll sell the house, I'll seek out all the Calloways. And tomorrow, I remember suddenly, is the day Celeste and I are supposed to drive up to the Gautreau camp to spread our mother's ashes. I had completely forgotten. I'll have the entire ride, hours in the car, to ask Celeste about the guy from Boston. And I'll see Aunt Jean again. Uncle Frank and Aunt Debbie will be there, my mother's brother and his wife, Danny's parents. For the first time in my life, I'm actually hungry for family. My mother starved me of them, and I never realized it. I never questioned her, and that was my fault. Eileen was right—I was perfectly free all this time to seek them out.

As I drive along Baxter, a small, dark shape moves along the sidewalk to my right. In the light from my headlights, I can tell it's a dog. It looks like Wanda, and then I realize that it *is* Wanda. I pull over and open the passenger door, and an acrid smell hits my nostrils. "Wanda!" I call to her. "Get in! What are you doing on the street?" She recognizes my voice and leaps in next to me with a high sobbing bark and pushes her entire body against me, making juddering noises in my ear, licking my face over and over. Her leash is attached to her collar. It snags on the gearshift, so I have to untangle it and push her off me and hold her down firmly in the passenger seat with my right hand so I can drive.

Approaching my mother's house, I see flashing lights and hear the *whoop-whoop* of a siren as an ambulance pulls out and streaks past me, going the other way. Up on the lawn, billowing smoke drifts through flashing lights. Amid firefighters and emergency personnel, I see Jenny Baum, my mother's next-door neighbor, standing in front of her house, hugging a bathrobe to herself and staring at the scene, motionless and dumbstruck.

It takes me an extraordinarily long time to realize that my mother's house is on fire, and that most of it is in fact already a smoldering, burned-out black shell. Part of the roof has caved in, windows exploded. Shards of glass glitter on the lawn. The air is bitter, choking. The house has turned into a fuming hole, collapsing in on itself.

I park and stumble up the lawn, leaving Wanda safely in the car.

"I'm going to sue the pants off you," Jenny shouts when she sees me. "I saw that man you had in there. What did you expect? All this smoke. Now my house is full of smoke! It's a miracle it didn't burn to the ground. You endangered my life. It's all your fault."

I ignore her and walk up to the nearest police officer, a very young-looking snub-nosed kid whose name tag reads "Officer McDougal."

"Did you see a man named Jesse here?" I realize I'm almost shouting. "I was living there, and he was working for me. I just left to go out to dinner and came back . . . I have his dog in my car."

"They pulled a guy out a few minutes ago," he said. "Took him to the ER at Maine Med. Is this your place?"

"Yes."

"Was there anyone else living here? Anything of value?"

"No. There was no one else. And nothing of value. Just my clothes."

We stand side by side in silence for what feels like several minutes, watching the last section of my mother's roof collapse as black smoke billows upward. It's mesmerizing and beautiful in a horrible kind of way. I feel a light spray of water against my cheek from the hoses, carried on the breeze.

"Well, I hope you have good insurance," the young cop says out of nowhere. He's grinning stupidly at me, obviously pleased with his joke.

And I almost laugh too, because I'm numb, loopy with disbelief. I turn and walk back toward the safety of the car, ignoring Jenny's glare, and buckle myself in. Wanda is making anxious noises with her mouth, squeaking and yawning and gnashing her teeth. I stroke her with shushing soothing sounds until she goes quiet.

It's all unreal, a fresh spring night. The evening sky is a transitional clear violet tipping toward dark blue. The air smells of fresh dirt, new plants. As we speed through the quiet streets, Wanda sits upright next to me. Whenever I can, I turn to glance at her, but her eyes won't meet mine. She stares ahead through the windshield. "Sweet girl," I say in a crooning, soothing voice I've never used before. Talking to her is helping me more than it's helping her, I know. It's the only thing keeping me from banging my head against the steering wheel over and over, dissolving into crazy laughter. "I swear it's going to be okay, I'll protect you, it's all going to be okay." I hardly know what I'm promising. I just know that I need to say it.

At Maine Medical, a few blocks from Celeste's house and a universe away, I park in the visitors' lot, leave Wanda in the car, and run through the double sliding doors into the nearly empty, brightly lit waiting room of the ER.

"I'm looking for someone," I tell the attending nurse, panting hard. She's around my age, short salt-and-pepper hair, hooded eyes like an iguana's. "His name is Jesse Fecteau. He came in an ambulance."

"Can you spell that name for me?"

She clicks around on her computer and picks up her phone handset, talks to someone on the other end, so quietly I can't hear what she's saying. I'm itching to see Jesse, to tell him what a fucking shithead of a fuckup he is, although I imagine he's not in any shape for that yet, he's probably being bandaged for burns and treated for smoke inhalation.

She gives me a level, expressionless stare. "Are you a relative?"

"He's my cousin," I lie without a second thought. "He's been staying with me."

"One minute, someone will be right out."

I wait. Minutes tick by. I stare at the clock by the blank TV screen as if

I could will it to do my bidding. It's 8:57, then 8:58. The sky outside is dark. I hear nothing but my heartbeat galloping weirdly in my ears, the beeping of some medical monitor somewhere, a low hubbub of faraway voices, the air molecules rearranging themselves as the attending nurse and I breathe. My head buzzes with adrenaline. I keep catching myself exhaling loudly, hear myself muttering words under my breath: "I leave you alone for a few fucking hours and you burn it all down, you cretin, after all the work we did, you idiot, how could you, that house is all I have in the world and now I can't even pay you . . ."

A nurse appears through a doorway and motions to me. I follow her through a sealed door and down a linoleum hallway lined with empty gurneys, a nurses' station with its banks of computers behind a high countertop, several people clustered behind it.

"Is he okay?" I ask her retreating back.

"We're going to need you to identify him," she says.

The truth hits me. "No."

She turns to look at me, her neutral expression cracking, a little stricken. "They didn't tell you?"

"Where is he?"

She unlocks a door and brings me into a small, dim room that is instantly flooded with fluorescent light as soon as she hits the wall fixture. She indicates a gurney. The person lying on it has a sheet pulled over their face. She peels it back to show me. "Is this him?"

Jesse's eyes are closed, his face as alive as if he were sleeping. He smells acrid from the smoke that killed him. The nurse watches my face. She's young, as young as those girls at the next table at Waves earlier, but her eyes are tired. She's got other places to be, rounds of patients who need her.

"Yes," I say through a frog in my throat. I cough hard. "That is Jesse." Part of me believes he'll wake up in a little while. This can't be right. My eyes are shocked dry. "How long has he been here?"

"Not long. He was DOA. The EMS did everything they could in the ambulance. Shot of Naxolone, paddles, oxygen. It was too late. I'm sorry."

And then I see it, what happened. Jesse OD'd on something, fentanyl probably, and passed out with a lit cigarette in his mouth. There were all kinds of chemicals around the house, and the dropcloths were saturated with turpentine and polyurethane. How is he not as charred as the house? His face looks untouched by flames.

"He was a good guy," I tell the young nurse, irrationally and a little defensively, although she's shown no judgment.

They release his things to me, which are nothing more than the contents of his pockets, a wallet, a small baggie of treats for Wanda, and a dog tag on a chain embossed on one side with "Jesse Fecteau, A Pos, Catholic." The other side is covered with a striped sticker: red and green and black. I look in his wallet: Maine driver's license, Visa card, Veteran Health ID card, and a folded photo of an ordinary-looking middle-aged couple, probably his parents.

So Jesse was in the army, he fought in a war. I should have guessed there was more to his story than a roofing accident.

There's paperwork to fill out, arrangements to make. It seems fitting that I should do these administrative things. I said he was my cousin, so he belongs to me. And as long as I'm busily filling out forms, I don't have to face the enormity of what has just happened.

It's not until I walk out the doors of the hospital into the fragrant night that I remember Jesse's widowed mother up in Waterville. I'll have to call her and tell her. There's no one else to do it. I stand under the portico of the ER, wondering if he ever told me her name. How many Fecteaus could there be in that town? Maybe Jesse is related to them all.

I suddenly yearn to be sitting at Celeste's kitchen counter with a glass of wine or chamomile tea, comfortingly surrounded by her family's evening routine. She'll be ripshit when I tell her what happened, but so be it. It wasn't my fault, not really.

I send her a text: "You there?"

She texts back within seconds, "What's up?"

When I call her, she picks up right away. Tersely, without drama, I tell her what happened and where I am.

"I have nowhere to sleep," I tell her. "Everything's burned."

"Oh my God, Rach," says my sister. "Come over here. Of course you can stay with me."

"I have a dog with me."

"That's fine. Just come."

I collect my car from the lot and drive the few short blocks to the prom, thinking Wanda might need a walk before we go to Celeste's. As I get out and lead Wanda across the grass with the leash wrapped around my wrist, my mind suddenly conjures up an image of all those Red Rose figurines, melting or exploding on the shelf inside the door, gone forever now.

I stand on the broad clifftop that overlooks the Fore River estuary, its industrial warehouses lit up below me, and, beyond it, the wooded glacial floodplain that stretches west toward the faint black shape of the White Mountains on the horizon. I don't know whether to laugh or to cry at the desperate absurdity of this world and my place in it.

My phone rings again: a local number I don't recognize. Thinking it has to do with the fire, with Jesse, I answer. "Hello?"

"Is this Rachel Calloway?"

"Speaking."

"My name is Liz Duffy. I'm a close friend of Suzanne Brown and Eileen Calloway's. Is this an okay time to talk?"

I shrug at no one. "Sure," I say. "How are you, Liz?"

"Well, I'm great. Suzanne and Eileen both told me to call you, independently of each other—I guess the word is 'commanded.' They said you might be looking for a new job. I googled you after Eileen called me just now, and you're far too qualified, my God, what an impressive career you've had. Apparently you're . . . between positions at the moment?"

"I just got laid off." I sit on a bench, breathing hard. Wanda looks up at me, surprised, then sits on the grass and waits.

"Well, that sucks. I'm sorry." Liz's voice is velvety, self-assured, flecked with grains of laughter. "Obviously you have all sorts of possibilities in terms of where to go next, but I wonder if you'd be willing to come in to the office next week to meet with me and my staff, see what we're about, in case we can entice you to join us in any capacity you'd be comfortable with."

"Okay," I say in frank disbelief. "Text me the address and a good time for me to come in on Tuesday or Wednesday."

I stay on the bench for a moment after I hang up.

Wanda sets her chin on my thigh, and I massage the top of her skull, that pointy ridge under her soft fur that fits the curve of my palm so perfectly.

Part V

Eighteen

Celeste and I set off at nine o'clock the next morning. I figure I might as well leave town, because it's Saturday, so there's nothing for me to do about the house, no insurance claims to file or police reports to confirm until Monday. Dogs aren't allowed at the camp, so I've left Wanda in the care of Mallory, who has promised to lavish walks and attention on her while I'm gone.

Lucie's urn is swaddled in a beach towel in the back seat. In the way-back sits Celeste's enormous, jam-packed green suitcase, which holds enough clothes for at least three months for fifteen people, let alone two days in the woods for two. I don't bother pointing out to my sister that we won't need all that stuff. I know her well enough by now. And since all my local possessions were burned in the fire, I can't be choosy or critical.

As Celeste drives up I-95 through inland rural Maine, we don't say much. We're both gobsmacked at the fact that I invited a drug-addicted stranger into our mother's house and he burned it down. I can't defend myself. What would I say? The truth: I couldn't find anyone else to hire, and he reminded me of our cousin Danny.

Foremost in my mind, distracting me, are two pressing facts: my mother's next-door neighbor Jenny threatened to sue me for recklessly damaging her property and endangering her life, which means I'd better get my ducks in a row fast with my DC condo in case she tries to come after it. And I need to find another place to live, fast. I can't believe I'm considering this, but I remember that Fred, Celeste's one-night stand, was looking to rent the extra room in his Bayside house for eight hundred a month. My mind has seized on this fact and is clinging to it as if it were a life raft. I can't go back to DC, not to live, although I will visit Wallace as often as he'll allow me to until the end. And I definitely can't stay with Celeste. Neither one of us could tolerate that.

I come up with a rough plan to address both these problems. When I get back to Portland I'll file an insurance claim on my mother's house and get the deed to the condo put into Declan's name, relinquishing all ownership so the court can't seize the property as collateral. I have to protect Wallace. And when Declan buys me out of my share with some of Wallace's life insurance money and keeps the condo, which he clearly wants to do, maybe the amount he gives me, along with the insurance payout, will be enough to cut a deal with Jenny, who will no doubt carry out her threat to sue me to avenge my mother in some misguided final act of loyal friendship. A court case would be prohibitively expensive and painful, so I'll just offer her everything I've got.

And then I'll be left with nothing, but that's okay, that's just how things are now.

I turn to Celeste. "Remember Fred, the guy from the other night? Did you learn his last name?"

"Brower," she tells me without missing a beat or asking why I want to know. Her tone is dismissive. She doesn't want to talk about Fred.

I thumb around on my phone until I've found his Instagram profile, which informs me that he's a musician and a proud native of Biddeford, and his pronouns are he/him. I fire off a message: "Hi, Fred, it's Rachel, Celeste's sister from the other night. Do you still have that room for rent? I'm looking for a place for my dog and me."

I slide my phone into my jacket pocket. "I'm sorry Neil and the kids aren't coming with us."

My sister diddles her thumbs on the steering wheel. "Mom said she wanted just you and me to spread her ashes in the lake. She was specific about that. She said, and I quote, 'You and your sister do it, my daughters, just the two of you, put me in the middle of the lake.' So why should I drag them all the way up to the camp?"

"Really? I would think she'd want a big audience."

"I don't know, maybe she was embarrassed to have anyone else see her that way."

I look sideways at her. "Which way?"

"Ashes," Celeste says with a half smile. "But I guess it's all ashes now, right? Her body, her house. Ashes to ashes and more ashes."

"At least her clothes and furniture are safe at the Goodwill," I say. "And I still have her car."

"She hated that car. She wanted a red convertible."

"By the way," I say, remembering, "Neil called me yesterday to tell me he's quit drinking, ever since I went ripshit on your family."

"Yeah," she says, smiling. "Thank you for doing that. I guess I over-reacted."

"Which wouldn't be like you at all."

To my immense pleasure, she laughs.

I pounce on the opening, take a breath, and dive in. "While the house was burning down, I was out having drinks with our cousin Eileen Callo-way. She's great, you should meet her."

"Okay," says Celeste without much interest.

"She was up at the camp when we were younger, remember?"

Celeste is quiet.

"She said something happened that summer when she was there. She asked me about it, but I had no idea what she meant. Something to do with you and Mom? Some guy Mom was flirting with?"

"You knew exactly what happened, Rachel."

"I didn't, I swear."

"Of course you did. You were right there. You didn't defend me. You let Mom just walk all over me."

"I had no clue, Cellie, I swear. I wish you would just tell me."

"You saw the whole thing. You just don't want to admit it."

"Saw what whole thing? Admit what?"

She huffs.

Silenced by a deep stalemate, we exit the highway and drive due north along a cracked, bumpy two-lane road, past miles of scruffy woods punctuated with double-wide mobile homes and run-down capes set in small clearings, yards littered with old machinery and junked cars and tarp-covered woodpiles and rusty swing sets. We round a curve up a small hill past a woman hanging up laundry at the side of the house and kids playing in the front yard.

"*Maine*," says Celeste with a dry burr in the back of her throat.

I glance over at her and catch her eye roll, which I guess is a reference to an ancient shared joke about our home state and its native people, although for once I'm not in on it. I'm remembering the grinding loneliness of poverty in Maine, being aware as a kid of how we must have been perceived by other people, how we looked from the outside, how we even *smelled* poor. I remember the dark little apartment in Biddeford that reeked of mold and cat pee where we lived all through our junior high and high school years. And the freezing-cold double-wide on a rural road near Gorham with newspapers stuffed into the walls for insulation where we lived for three years when Celeste was in elementary and I was in middle school.

She snorts. "I can smell the meth from here. Or I guess fentanyl is the new white trash drug now."

"Sadly, yes."

"Mallory would slap me for saying white trash. She said it's the N-word for white people."

"Who cares about white people's feelings anymore?"

"I'm allowed to say it, though, because that's what we used to be, right? Growing up." She sounds defensive, as if Mallory has put her on trial. We're driving along a cracked blacktop through a small town, jouncing over frost heaves past a ratty little post office, a boarded-up former automotive shop, a run-down strip mall with a nail salon and a pet groomer, crabgrass growing in the cracks in the asphalt of its little parking lot. "That," she says, pointing out the window at a frame house covered in cheap maroon siding. "*That* is who we are. Right there."

"True," I say. "But we got ourselves out."

"No one helped us," says Celeste.

"We had some really good teachers. Thank God for the public schools of Maine. Remember Mrs. Marengo? You had her, too."

"She was such a hardass," says Celeste. "She didn't like me because I failed to live up to your standards. But really, we did it ourselves. No one helped us."

I refrain from pointing out that her entire luxurious financially solid adult life is courtesy of the Canned Fish King's millions of dollars, her husband's fortune. "I'm sorry about Mom's shearling coat," I say instead. "Jesse told me you came by looking for it. I donated it to Goodwill."

To my surprise, she gives me a sidelong shrug. "I snoozed, I lost," she says. "You gave me plenty of time to say I wanted it, but I forgot about it until all of a sudden I wanted it." She hesitates. "The house looked beautiful, Rachel. You worked so hard on it. Goddamn that hobo."

My chest warms with gratitude that she's actually taking my side. Even so, in spite of everything, I feel an odd urge to defend Jesse, to tell Celeste that he did me a favor, erasing the past like that, freeing me from having to deal with the hassle of selling it. But I can't afford one second of magnanimous philosophical detachment. Thanks to him, I'm totally screwed.

My phone buzzes with an answer from Fred: "Hey, Rachel, it's still available if you want to check it out. Dog is fine."

I write back, "Out of town this weekend, can I come by on Tuesday?"

He responds immediately with the address. Okay then. I can't believe I'm actively contemplating moving in with a thirtysomething kid who slept with my sister, but there it is.

"Who are you texting with?" Celeste asks.

"Fred," I tell her. "Your one-night stand. I'm thinking about renting his room."

"What? That's ridiculous. You're staying with me until this is all cleared up and you get back on your feet."

"I need my own space, no matter how bare-bones it may be," I say. "But thank you."

She smirks at me, shaking her head. "Fred, ha!"

Now we're bouncing along a narrow road that runs through wooded wilderness, with occasional numbered logging and fire roads leading off into the heavy underbrush. If you looked down at Maine's Great North Woods from a plane or Google Earth, you would see a rough, disturbed landscape of young, weak trees, interrupted at intervals by patchwork swaths of clear-cutting that look like pillaged scar tissue in the exposed, rucked-up earth, violently raw: cut stumps like broken yellow-brown teeth, lumps of tumbling granite, open water flashing pale, frigid lakes and ponds interlaced with streams and rivers like veins of silver.

There is nothing serene or restful in this landscape. We're leaving civilization behind, heading straight up into dense, savage, ruined country where logging roads become overgrown again after just a few years of neglect, but the man-made industrial damage goes much deeper. The rivers are still full of old tree trunks, waterlogged sunken treasure from the early days of heedless full-bore ravaging, the glut of cutting and chopping that took away all the huge old trees, back when stacks of massive fresh-cut logs waited all winter for the ice to melt before the lumbermen floated them downstream to the mills. Most of those old-growth tree trunks were made into masts for warships for the British and sunk in battle and now lie at the bottom of the ocean.

As we come around a wide bend, Celeste slows and flicks on her turn signal, even though we haven't seen another car in ages. I know exactly where we are. At a hand-lettered board sign that reads "Gautreau Camps," we turn onto an even narrower dirt road and the car pushes through a low tangle of overhanging branches and leaves, with the occasional fallen branch or rock to steer around.

Grandpa's camp is at the very end of the dirt road, on top of a granite-studded rise overlooking the lake. We drive past a cluster of cabins and park in a big bare dirt parking area by a rough-looking two-story log house with a porch that wraps all the way around the front and one of the sides, screened in and full of places to sit. The lodge looks every bit as haunted and rustic as it did when I was little, as if it had grown out of the forest like a fungus or hemlock tree.

"I'll go find out where we're staying," I say.

"I'll wait here," says my sister.

I head up the wide porch steps, open the heavy front door, and step into the main room of the lodge. My scalp prickles as I inhale the familiar air with its underlay of old sweat embedded in the upholstery, the sour tang of ancient wood smoke. Nothing has changed here in decades, or ever. There's a feeling of inevitability in the battered couches lining the walls, the tweedy armchairs slouching around the braided rug in front of the stone fireplace. The floor-to-ceiling plank bookshelf is full of old maps and nature guides, bird-watching books, and possibly every book about Maine ever published before 1979, most of which I read as a kid, lying on this same slouchy couch.

At the far end of the main room is the side hall leading to the staircase and the room that used to be Grandpa's office and is now, I assume, Aunt Jean's. I pause at the foot of the plank stairs that lead up to the bedroom where Grandpa always slept and where, I further assume, Aunt Jean does now. I run my hand along the banister, inhaling the yellow-tinged smells. The varnish has eroded off the treads, the wainscoting is cracked, the runner threadbare. When I was little, I used to hide in the crawl space under the stairs between the rubber boots and fishing gear, eavesdropping on anyone who was talking nearby. For some reason it creeps me out now, that dark little closet smelling of damp rubber and musty canvas and dry rot. I walk by its odd-shaped door, moving fast.

The long wooden table by the swinging doors to the kitchen still has the same dozen tall-backed chairs around it. The huge sideboard hutch is as monolithic as an Easter Island head, with deep drawers on the bottom and two conjoined sets of glass-fronted cabinets above. An assortment of teapots and pitchers sits on its recessed marble countertop, along with a bunch of upside-down mugs, one right side up, bristling with coffee spoons. The sight of those spoons, dull with tarnish, waiting to impart a bitter, metallic taste to hot drinks, gives me an unpleasant back-and-forth temporal emotion, slippery, unmoored from the present. I'm nine again, or eleven, or thirteen, always an odd year. An odd child in an odd year.

Hearing voices, I gear myself up to be polite and friendly as I push through the swinging double doors into the kitchen. Aunt Jean is pawing through one of several paper grocery bags on the floor. "Well, you paid too much for this," she's saying to a jug of maple syrup. "Michaud's is cheaper and better, too."

"They ran out," says Willie. "Nothing to do."

Aunt Jean turns to look at me. We haven't seen each other in twelve years or more. Her pixie haircut is now pure white. Her face has shrunk. But her spine is as straight as ever, and she moves around with that aggressively self-righteous energy that implicates everyone else as a lazy good-for-nothing. She must be ninety by now.

"Rachel," she says. This woman fed me my bottles when I was a baby and held me and changed my diapers when my mother was too drunk, the first months of my life, maybe even a year or more. Even so, she makes no move to hug me. "You and your sister are in the second cabin. There's sheets and blankets in the wardrobe down there." She turns back to the groceries, rattling a big bottle of Advil. "Willie, you think I'm a millionaire, generic is the same thing but half the price."

Willie winks at me. "Hello, kid," he says to me.

Willie Bacquet is a lean little man with a beaky deep-tanned face, a thin-lipped grin, and flickering eyes that see everything. For decades he has been the camp's jack-of-all-trades and groundskeeper as well as wilderness guide and outdoor sportsman, Grandpa's right-hand man. I remember once being in a canoe with him, when I was young. He reached over the side and pulled up a dripping trout with his bare hand, held it aloft as if to give it a brief glimpse of the world, and slipped it back into the water a second later. Looking back, I realize it was probably on a hook and line. But at the time I thought he had magic powers. And he let me think it.

Outside, Celeste and I are quickly swarmed by a cloud of blackflies as we trudge along the soft pine-needle-covered path between the lodge porch and the safety of our cabin. A few of them land on my scalp. I loathe these creatures, the way they get tangled in your hair, bomb your eye sockets, invading every pore and orifice they can. Off to our right, the algae-choked lake is amber, rippling under an overcast sky clotted with thin, dirty clouds. Gooseneck Lake is shaped like a bulbous elongated head, on whose forehead the camp sits, a long curved neck dangling from it, more like an embryo or a tadpole than a goose. The woods press thickly all around the shore. The close air smells like dirt and rot and bark and decay. I know this smell as well as I know the smell of my own skin.

Celeste lugs her green suitcase behind me as I step up into our two-bed cabin, a tiny woodshed with a tacked-on front porch, rough board walls, and one screened window. It contains a table and chair, two single iron bedsteads with spongy ticking-covered mattresses, and a wooden cupboard. I set Lucie's urn on the windowsill and look around. Celeste deposits the suitcase on the sloping floor and goes out again without a word.

I take two sets of sheets out of the cupboard. These are worn and patched but clean. I spread the fitted bottom sheets on the thin mattresses, unfolding over them the top sheets and then two dense wool blankets for each bed. It gets cold up here at night, I remember, even in early June.

Through the low windows I see my sister down on the dock, sitting with her feet in the water. I check my phone. There is no signal up here, not one bar. No access to anyone but the people here, no possibility of email or messages for two days. But who's going to need me? No one. I'll survive. The tightly hinged screen door gives that old familiar slap behind me as I traipse back up to the lodge, hoping Jean might give me a chore to do, anything at all.

I find my aunt in the kitchen, chopping onions at the counter. She stares at me without expression when I come in. Her head looks as small and hard as a coconut. Her stringy little biceps are flexed, as if she's gearing up to fight me.

"Can I help you with anything, Aunt Jean?"

She ignores this. "How long are you here for? Celeste said the weekend."

There's never any point trying to ingratiate myself with Jean. When I was little, I learned to stay out of her way unless I had a specific chore to do. "Two nights, I think," I say. "We brought our mother's ashes."

"Lucie," says Jean skeptically, as if she has any other sister, or we any other mother. "This is really what she wanted?"

"Apparently," I say. "It's what she told Celeste."

Aunt Jean makes a sound in the back of her throat whose meaning is completely mysterious to me. "Dinner's just fried onions and canned corned beef and egg noodles," she says. "Nothing fancy. I don't cook any-more like I used to. But there's plenty of it." She shoots me a look as if she were assessing my worth. "Get yourself a beer if you want one."

I open the refrigerator and look inside. The old-fashioned metal freezer is paved with ribbons of ice, aluminum ice trays wedged into the narrow cavern. The fridge's two deep shelves are crammed with haphazard piles of food. A large box of cheap no-brand canned beer sits on the right side.

"Shut the door as fast as you open it," she snaps at me. "Propane isn't cheap."

Back in the olden days, this place was called rustic. The big cookstove is propane. Another propane tank fuels the generator that runs the refriger-ator and water heater. Kerosene lights the lamps. The woodstove and fire-place in the main room heat the lodge itself, and the cabins aren't heated at all, since the place is uninhabited from October through May.

I crack open a can and take a swig. It's sour and bubbly and so good. "What's it like here all winter?'

"Cold and dark. No one's here. I'm in Bangor."

The beer is simultaneously cold and warm in my chest, such a pleasure. "I bet it's very peaceful," I say, surprising myself.

Jean turns on the burner under a cast-iron skillet and spoons a lump of hard white grease from a tin can into it. A moment later, when it starts to spit and smell like bacon, she dumps the chopped onions in and pokes at them with a wooden spoon.

"It's the darkest and loneliest place in the world," she says.

"My mother loved it here."

"First I heard of it."

"Well, she wants her ashes in the lake, anyway."

"Funny place for Lucie to want to end up. I would have thought a plot with a view and the fanciest gravestone in Portland. Shows what I knew of your mother."

Jean goes to the pantry and fetches three cans. She hands them to me, then an opener, then a large saucepan. While she tends her onions, I get to work, dumping the corned beef into the pot. It looks lurid and greasy.

"Are there a lot of guests coming up this year?"

"A fair amount." Jean clears her throat. "Business is pretty good."

I take this to mean that there aren't, and it's not.

"The usual folks are starting to die off." She looks up from her onions and cocks her head at me.

I set the pot full of corned beef on a stove burner. "You could advertise the place as an off-grid retreat," I say. "Attract the urban hipsters. They'd love it."

Our eyes meet for a split second. I could swear she almost grins. "Well, if city kids want to come and look at the damn trees, any paying customer is welcome."

Car doors slam outside, and I hear loud voices, Uncle Frank's, Aunt Debbie's. In they traipse a few minutes later, Frank with his crafty gap-toothed grin, beady dark eyes, and soft-bellied, bowlegged, skinny-limbed body, Debbie with her pneumatic boobs, plush moles, and tiny gymnast's hips. They look much older and sadder than the last time I saw them, beaten down by their only child's suicide.

"Hey!" Uncle Frank shouts at Aunt Jean, sweeping her into a bear hug. She submits to it like a stoic wild animal, her arms dangling at her sides. I remember now that Frank has always liked to make big gestures, florid and dramatic, as if he were a big-time Jersey mob boss instead of a legitimate small-town Maine businessman.

"Just in time for dinner," says Jean.

"It smells delicious," says Debbie, her nose crinkling in a way that suggests otherwise. "Hello, Celeste dear. It's been years."

"I'm Rachel," I say.

"Of course you're Rachel," she replies, as if she knew who I was all along and was just mocking me. The Gautreau family tradition seems to be that even if we don't recognize one another, we still know we're related. This is only heartwarming if you care about family, which I suddenly seem to.

We all take our seats around the kitchen table as Jean begins dishing out food. Willie sits at the head, Frank at the foot. Celeste wanders in and slides into a vacant seat across from me, next to Debbie.

"A toast," says Frank sharply.

Celeste palms me a can of beer, and I crack it open without thinking.

"My little sister would be damn glad to see us all sitting around the old family table like this, in her honor." Frank holds up his can of beer, clearly relishing being the man of the family. Willie Bacquet watches him steadily, dark eyes unblinking. "And you know if there's one thing Lucie loved more than anything, it was attention."

Celeste and I exchange a look. "And to Tante Jean," says Celeste. "Thank you for hosting us."

I give a small cough at "Tante." Celeste ignores me.

Jean looks up briefly from dishing out more hash to Frank, then goes back to it without a word. She's not exactly hosting us. I'm aware of the fact that we're all paying for our two nights here; we're guests like anyone else. Only Willie and Jean belong here. They both look as if they emerged from this place, were formed of the same rough planks, have become molecularly inseparable from it.

Because I'm hungry, and because this is a family meal and I am related to these people, I eat my entire plateful of food and pour the cold, frothy, deliciously bitter IPA down my throat. Wallace's voice in my head has gone totally quiet. I'm back in Maine, among my people again, eating and drinking like a native, because that's what I am.

Nineteen

I wake in heart-pounding panic, disoriented, convinced I'm in my bedroom in DC. But the air smells like pine needles and cold metal. The
bedsprings make a rusty sound when I turn over. I don't have to launch
myself toward the coffee maker and drive to Annapolis. I don't have to go
to work ever again. They're all there without me, carrying on.

I lie on my back in the calm quiet, saturated in sweat, my body molten
with almost painful heat, like an internal burning rash radiating outward from my sternum to my hands, the back of my neck, my scalp, my
toes. Out of the corner of my mind's eye, I glimpse the fleeing outlines of
an intense dream whose general contours reveal an image of my dying
mother's body—I was washing it, feeding it, giving it medicine, it isn't
clear—whatever it was, I couldn't escape.

I peer over at Celeste in the other bed. She's lying with her eyes open
in the dim predawn light.

"What are you doing awake?"

"I don't know," she says. "I slept like shit. Should we just do it now and
get it over with?"

"I need coffee first."

"I'll go make us some," she says, getting out of bed. "Meet me at the
dock. Bring the urn."

I lie still for a few minutes, listening to a loud splashing on the lake, followed by the high, echoing call of a loon. I get up, dress quickly in Celeste's cargo pants and hoodie. It feels wrong to cradle my mother's ashes in my arms, so I hold the urn stiffly out in front of me with two hands. The air is heavy and raw. Leaves from last fall lie in sodden heaps around the tree trunks, their colors dulled to mulch on the ground. The dark, jagged silhouettes of pine tops bristle against the whitening sky. I feel a chill on my sleep-heated skin as I walk down the path to the lake and out to the end of the dock.

A canoe bobs in the water, tied to a cleat. I don't remember seeing it there yesterday evening; Willie must have put it out for us at some point last night or early this morning. Strange thing to do in the dark. I sit on the edge of the dock and dangle my legs into the canoe. A breeze ruffles the surface of the lake. I feel Celeste's footsteps on the boards before she appears with two mugs and hands one to me. "Are you ready to do this?"

We slug our coffee and set our mugs on the dock. Celeste places the urn in the center of the canoe and takes up her old position at the bow while I untie, clamber into the stern, and push off. It has been decades since I was in a canoe, but it instantly comes back—the sweep of the paddle, the flick of the wrist to steer. The water slides by under the hull as our paddles plunge and pull and rise. Neither of us says a word.

I guide us toward Egg Island, the little hummock of land in the middle of the lake where we used to camp when we were little, just the two of us, with a bag of cookies and sandwiches, two flannel-lined canvas sleeping bags that got a little wet on the way over. They had a pattern of ducks on the lining. Celeste was scared of bears, so I made a pile of rocks to throw at them in case they attacked us. I conjure an image of her sound-asleep little face in the early dawn, her mouth slightly open, her breath fluttering the ducks on the flannel while I lay in my sleeping bag beside her, my arm muscles tensed, half wishing a bear would attack us just so I could be her heroine and savior. I was nine, eleven, a malnourished neglected little string bean myself, but I was itching to defend my sister, no doubt displacing my own deep need for someone older to protect me.

The shore is a dense wall of bristling pines and hemlocks thronged up to the very edge of the water and stretching back for hundreds of miles in every direction, interrupted only by clear-cuts. And here we are, two tiny fleas on a teardrop in the middle of it all with our dead mother's inciner-ated flesh and bones.

"This feels like the middle," I say, laying my paddle across my knees.

Celeste reaches back and hoists the urn, unscrews the lid, and pulls out the compact weight of ashes tightly wrapped in a plastic bag. She looks at me, stricken. "I can't."

I turn the canoe so our backs are to the stiff little breeze that's risen as the sun's rays poked through the tops of the trees. "Yes, you can," I say. "Face away from the wind."

Celeste takes a deep breath. She hefts the open bag carefully in both hands, shaking it with slow precision as she dumps the remains of our mother's body into the water. It takes a while. The finest particles are caught by the moving air, borne over the surface like a cloud of gnats.

"Into this water we consecrate you, our mother," she says, trying to rise to the occasion with solemnity that doesn't come naturally to either of us, but then her breath catches on a panicky giggle. "Oh my God, Rach, there's so *much* of her."

We watch pieces of bone sink and disappear below the ashes, which bloom through the water with a milky density, like a cloud mass moving through the sky. Then the bag is empty. The ash ceremony is over. That's it, Lucie's in the lake. My cruel, drunk, wayward, beautiful, intelligent, crazy mother is gone. What a strange life she had, what a strange person she was.

"I feel a little bruised still," my sister says after a short silence. "I'll get over it. But that was rough. She wasn't okay with being old and dying. She saw herself as young. Right up to the end."

"Lucky her," I say. "She always had her ideas about herself to protect her."

The silence between us is full of all the things my sister can't or won't say to me. I can feel them knocking around her skull, clamoring to be free.

"It's good," she says, letting the moment pass, as always. "This is good. We did what she wanted. She's at peace now."

"Please tell me, Celeste. Tell me what happened when Eileen was here. I swear on my life, I have no idea. I'm not in denial. I truly do not know."

She's quiet for a moment, then says in a low, flat, hurried voice, "The man from Boston. The one Mom liked. You were reading on the porch. I was in the living room and he pulled me on the couch with him. I thought you heard me—I was calling for you, I called your name, and you didn't come. Then when I told her what happened, Mom was so mad at me, she actually slapped me. She said I was a little slut and I should watch myself or I'd get in even worse trouble."

"Oh, Celeste."

"Like I was stealing her man."

"What did he do to you?"

"You know, the usual creepy molester stuff. Pinned me on his lap and pushed his fat fingers everywhere and told me to be quiet and he'd buy me a present."

"How did Eileen know this, and I didn't?"

"Because she was listening like a little sneak when I talked to Mom about it. So I got her alone and socked her in the shoulder and told her to stay away from me forever."

"Oh, my God, Celeste. No wonder you've been so pissed at me all these years."

"I haven't been pissed at you."

"I wish I had known. I would have told Mom she was a monster, because she was. She was a monster to say that to you. I'm so sorry that happened."

"Oh, come on—it's all in the past, it's ancient history, whatever. You didn't know. I just thought you did."

"I wish I had. My God. I'm so sorry."

"It's okay," she says. "It's really okay."

As we paddle back to shore, I stare at the empty urn tipped over on the canoe's bottom, lying on its side like a bottle without its genie. I remember that sense of urgent disgust for my mother's body I felt in my dream. In one motion, I lean down, grab the urn, and toss it over the side of the canoe. It lands with a splash, fills, and sinks.

Celeste glances back at me. "Why did you do that? You know that urn cost hundreds of dollars, right?"

"What were you planning to do, serve soup in it?" We both laugh. "I'll pay you back."

"Forget it," she says.

The morning air is keen and fresh. The sun warms the back of my head as we scud over the water.

Out of nowhere, Celeste laughs again. "Remember that time she took us to Puerto Rico?"

The entire trip comes back to me in an instant. "She rented a stick shift."

"With no idea how to use a clutch."

We both picture Lucie jerking the car along the rutted road, shouting at it, slamming her feet on the pedals, shaking the steering wheel.

"We got so lost."

"Didn't she just stop the car at one point and set off on foot without even waiting for us?"

Together, as one, we remember our mother parading around San Juan like a batty, demented duchess. She asked directions to the beach in loud, slow English with a fake Spanish accent, since she didn't speak Spanish, while the polite natives tried to keep straight faces. "Why were they laughing at me?" she asked us back in the car, furious, as we lurched and choked our way in a direction that turned out to be inland, away from the beach into blinding sun and heat and traffic.

"And then hours later, when we finally got to the beach—"

"She swam."

I see her in her orange one-piece suit and white bathing cap, doing a stately crawl parallel to the shore for exactly half an hour, while Celeste and I were left to wander the beach with a pack of mangy, skinny homeless dogs, none of whom, by the grace of God, infected us with rabies.

We were mortified by our mother back then. We did not appreciate her idiosyncratic dignity, her preening flamboyance, her dogged zest to experience life to the fullest. We resented her total disregard of our wishes. We agreed that she was insane, and we weren't wrong, but we were also cruel pubescent girls, and in retrospect I see her brash heroism, mired as she was in her own swirling internal storms.

Pulling up at the dock, we climb out and tie up the canoe.

Celeste yawns and stretches. "I'm going back to sleep. Will you come wake me up when it's time for lunch?"

I follow the smell of bacon and coffee into the kitchen. Jean is at her post at the stove. Uncle Frank, Aunt Debbie, and Willie Bacquet stand around with thick white mugs of coffee, not allowed to help, just getting in the way. I wander over to look out the window, yawning.

A vise grips my shoulder, and I turn to behold Aunt Jean's beady little eyes.

"Get yourself some breakfast," she snaps, "and come with me."

I palm a few strips of bacon and a biscuit and munch on them as I follow Aunt Jean out through the main room, through the front door, and down the path toward the cabins.

Twenty

Jean's small and rickety, but she's speedy. She hops up the stairs onto the small front porch of the closest cabin, the one where the most important guests always stay. Celeste and I used to call this place the Fancy Cabin. We weren't allowed in here, but we used to sneak in for thrills and rush out shrieking.

"Got people coming tonight," Jean says over her shoulder as she pushes on the door. I follow her in, batting at cobwebs. She sets her workbasket on the floor with a thump. We stand looking around, our hands on our hips. The air smells simultaneously of mildew and dry rot.

As Jean throws open the windows to air it out, I take legitimate stock of the place from my adult perspective. It's nothing special, just a plain square room with an unfinished wood floor and rafters overhead, but it's a lot bigger than the other cabins, with a higher ceiling, so it feels airier. It has a real mattress on a cast-iron bedstead. Two comfy armchairs flank a small table and the most prized object in the entire camp: my grandmother's brass standing oil lamp, which has a fluted glass chimney and fringed, painted shade. It stands tall and elegant on three legs, incongruously refined in this rough place. As kids, we were under serious threat of death if we so much as breathed on it.

I find it interesting that not one person in my own family has ever, to my knowledge, stayed here, this unspoken agreement we all share as a family that none of us is any more deserving of the Fancy Cabin than anyone else, or rather, none of us deserves it at all.

Framed by the cabin's screens and windowpanes, through the shadowy woods, are glinting patches of sunny open lake. Something about looking at these bits of lake through the screens and wavy old glass, the way the breeze makes the pine boughs shift and sigh in moving shadows on the pine-needled ground, the way the water shines, bright as metal, I feel a thud in my chest, the dread of the past, inescapable.

Aunt Jean opens the little closet. "You take down the bedding. I've got to check the bathroom."

I shake out a stiff, clean bottom sheet, let it get a belly full of air and settle slowly over the mattress. I tuck in hospital corners, remembering the day Jean taught me to do this, make the bedding all tight and square. I still do it every time I change my sheets at home, and every time, I think of Aunt Jean without even fully knowing I'm thinking of her.

It has never actually occurred to me before, maybe because I've always been working too hard to think about it, that my own work ethic must have been handed down from my Acadian forebears, who drove themselves doggedly, dauntingly hard, without stopping or taking a breath, until they dropped dead. Here's Jean, my tough little aunt, still working as hard as ever at ninety. And Uncle Frank, still toiling away, running his store.

Of course my mother never worked, but she was an aberration, like a tumor or a freak accident.

I hear a clang in the bathroom, a squeak of air. "Crap on a cracker," says Aunt Jean.

I stand in the bathroom doorway, holding the top sheet. "What's wrong?"

She whaps a skinny pipe with a wrench and the pipe groans in response. Finally a thread of ochre water emerges from the tap and gradually turns into a clear gush. She turns it off, stows the wrench back in her workbasket, pulls out a sponge and a can of Comet cleanser, and gets back to work.

While I finish making the bed, smoothing the thick quilt over wool blankets, plumping up the pillows in their cases, Jean swashbuckles around the cabin with a broom, attacking dust and cobwebs and sweeping them out the door. Her ropy arms wield the broom like an extension of willpower. I notice a slight hitch in her step, as if she's favoring a bum hip, or an arthritic knee, or both. She's gritting her teeth and letting the pain just be, her face resolute, with a tough unconscious sweetness. Watching her, I realize that Aunt Jean is the most decent person I have ever known. Decency, the fundamental trustworthy drive to do what's needed, what's right and good for the world, a quality so ordinary and dull that it's taken for granted, even mocked, until it's in short supply. Like oxygen or water.

"There's a dust rag in the basket," she says. "You can do the lamp, but don't break it."

I fetch a rag and begin dusting the precious lamp. Its painted shade has a scene of grazing deer on it, the brushwork delicate, each antler precise, each flower a deftly rendered starburst.

"Careful with that!"

"Of course," I say, loving this uncharacteristic feeling of dutiful obedience Jean inspires in me. I can't suppress an upwelling in my chest that rises like a sneeze. I say before I can stop myself, "Thank you for saving my life when I was a baby, Aunt Jean."

She doesn't stop sweeping. "What are you talking about?"

"You fed me and changed my diapers because my mother was too drunk to take care of me."

She's silent. I have no idea what she's thinking, but I can hear her harrumphing softly to herself, clicking her tongue against her top teeth. Of course she's shoving away any unwelcome feelings this ill-mannered outburst of mine might have invoked in her.

"Well," she says, giving the broom a hard thump on the welcome mat on the front porch, "someone had to."

"My mother's house burned down last night. I hired a homeless guy to help me fix it up to sell it. He reminded me of Danny. He died in the fire. Her house is gone."

Aunt Jean leans on the broom. Her little walnut face is bunched up, squinting at me. "Is that so."

"It's my own damn fault, I guess." I'm done dusting the lamp. The cabin is clean. We're finished here, but I'm not ready to leave. I look back at my aunt, who is still looking at me, standing very still. "But I just lost my job. That house was all I had in the world. Maybe I deserve all this bad luck. I didn't visit my mother for ten years."

Aunt Jean gives me a curt nod as her bright eyes rake my face. "Well, she wasn't an easy mother for you, I know that much."

We give each other that searching, silent look, the one I know from growing up in Maine. It's that back-and-forth that says, on one side, "I know what you're thinking, and yes, it's true," and on the other side, "Well, I'm imagining the worst right now."

"I wasn't there when she died," I say. "She told me to stay away, but I could have come, and I didn't."

"Well, I didn't either." She cackles. "So there. We're both terrible people." She's gleeful. I see her in a flash: the plain, taken-for-granted first-born daughter, unmarried, childless, hardworking, watching her gorgeous, charming, crazy little sister flit through life, needy and drunk, divorcing husbands, neglecting her daughters, playing the victim. My grandmother died young, when her kids were all little. And my grandfather spoiled Lucie, I know that much.

"You raised her after your mother died, then you took care of her baby when she couldn't," I say. "You didn't owe her a damn thing."

"Well, you took care of her all your life," she snaps back. "So neither did you."

She shoos me out of the cabin and we walk up the path to the lodge, Jean's workbasket slung over her sinewy forearm. She takes the lead, and we frog-march ourselves back to the lodge kitchen. Jean busies herself at the sink, washing breakfast dishes.

"Can I help you with anything else?" I ask.

Her silence is all the answer I get. Much as I would love to hang around my aunt all day, absorbing her ability to adapt and survive and persist in the face of things, I absolutely do not want to get in her way. My mother's ashes are dispersed. Celeste is asleep. There's nothing to do now. But I can't sit still. The memory of Jesse's face on the gurney is haunting me. The shattered glass on the lawn. The smoldering, charred front of the house.

I look out the window with intense restlessness.

"I think I'll take a walk," I say.

My aunt doesn't answer, maybe because she can't hear me over the noise of crockery and silverware in sudsy water.

I walk down the long, sloping meadow past Jean's kitchen garden, straight rows of raised beds packed with straw, bright with the new green of shoots. I wave my hands around my head to ward off blackflies dive-bombing my ears. Other insects, dragonflies and butterflies, dart in and out of tall stalks of grass.

At the bottom of the meadow, I find the path along the lake. I plunge into the woods and am instantly in a different world, a cohesive world of greens and browns, trees shifting and rustling in the hazy sunlight that filters down through the leaves. The ground is damp and spongy under-foot with pine needles and thick green lichen, rotted fallen logs covered in moss. The rippling sunlit lake to my left reflects sideways so the tree trunks seem to be the narrow screens for a watery, out-of-focus movie.

I jump across a shallow stream whose slowly turning pools are studded with pine needles and leaves. A chipmunk flies across the path just ahead of my feet, a kinetic flash of elongated reddish fur and it's gone. War-blers call from bough to bough, an advance warning system informing the woods of my arrival, although I'm sure every animal within a mile-wide radius can hear me.

I stomp along over gnarled roots and embedded lumps of rock, feeling scratchy, unsettled. So much about last night is not adding up. First of all, why was Wanda out on the sidewalk all by herself? Why did she have her leash on? Why wasn't she in the house with Jesse when it burned down? How did she escape?

After hugging the lakeshore through sheltered, boggy undergrowth, the trail abruptly climbs a steep hill off to the right to run flat along a ridge past smooth granite outcroppings. The trees are still dense overhead, but the ground is drier, harder, and instead of moss and lichen and wet earth, the air now smells of pine. Sunlight burns through the leaves and warms the top of my head. The flies aren't so bad up here, away from the streams and bogs. I can't see the lake anymore. It's very quiet.

I should go back now, but I can't bear the thought of sitting around the main room like a lummox, rereading those old books all day. I keep going, plunging forward with dogged determination. After a while—I have no idea how long; I've lost track of time—the path runs into an open meadow full of wildflowers, purple and pink, yellow and orange. The bright air is perfumed with floral smells so strong they're trippy, almost three-dimensional. Bees trundle through the flower heads, which rock in the breeze with so much motion that I feel like I'm in the middle of a knee-high miniature fireworks display.

As I pass through the center of the clearing, I spot the square granite foundation of a cabin that must have burned down long ago. I stand on the old foundation for a while, watching the bees at work. They remind me of Aunt Jean. The sun warms the top of my head. I fall into a daydream, old memories and anxiety about the future. Everything runs together, coalesces in this one moment.

Or maybe it wasn't an accident. Of course. Maybe Jesse meant to do it. It was a spectacular fuck-you to me. He flipped me the bird. He died, and he took my house with him. But he saved his dog. Who is my dog now. Did he mean for me to take her? Like, sorry I burned the house down, but here's a dog for you instead? What a twisted, fucked-up thing.

Agitated, I look for the continuation of the trail on the other side of the meadow. I spot an opening in the trees and plunge back into the woods. The path seems less sure here, but I follow it anyway down a long, sloping hill through a cluster of firs into a dense copse of smaller pine trees. I walk into this gloomy thicket and out the other side, up a short hill and back down into more boggy woods, waving my hands around my head to ward off flies. I jump from rock to rock across a swift, shallow stream, the water glowing amber as if from rust, and then I lose the path entirely.

I look back at the trail. It now appears to be naturally formed byways between the trees, a game path beaten by deer and bear.

When I look off to where I imagine the lake must be, there's no reassuring glint of water. I see only more trees, leading to more trees. And everywhere I look are fainter paths and trails that I now realize aren't actual paths or trails at all.

It's been more than an hour since I left the camp, I would guess. I'm deep in the woods now. I've always known how easy it is to get lost in these woods. There was a recent news story about a hiker who went off the trail into these same northern woods just briefly, to pee, and couldn't find her way back, and that was it—one slip, and she was gone. She eventually died of exposure and starvation, less than two miles from the trail.

How stupid and careless of me. I haven't paid attention, I'm too distracted. The sun is high overhead, burning dully white behind a thick bank of clouds that's moved in while I've been walking, giving me no sense of direction. My instinct is all I have now. It tells me to go back the way I came, back to the flowery meadow.

As I walk, the air cools, the woods darken. The first raindrops hit my head just as I emerge back into the clearing. Standing on the vanished cabin's old foundation, I survey the trees on the opposite side, hugging myself to keep warm as the clouds burst open. I cross the meadow and peer into the woods, walk one way around the meadow and then back the other way, scouring the edge of the trees for an opening, finally standing under the protective low bough of a wide pine tree.

I can't believe it. I'm lost in the woods.

Twenty-One

The rain drives down in blowing sheets. As I watch little rivulets of water slide down the sheltering pine bough above me and drain neatly out at its tip, like a natural gutter spout, I tell myself that streams eventually empty into lakes. If I go back to the stream I most recently crossed and follow it downhill, it will probably lead to the lake, and from there, I can follow the shoreline back to the camp.

I skirt the meadow until I find the last place I entered it, marked by an odd branch of rust-colored pine needles at eye level that I happened to notice when I passed it the first time. I duck into the woods. Immediately the heavy rainfall turns into discrete drops here and there, with a loud patter overhead. The ground underfoot is almost dry still. I descend a slight slope and continue, hoping to find the stream. When I don't find it, I keep going anyway, on and on.

The dull light has slanted into afternoon. All the colors are darker now, and a new smell rises from the forest floor like a fog, deep and funky, emanating from the earth and plant matter underfoot. Walking through the darkened, dripping woods, I'm aware that I'm alone. There's no one around but the trees, and they don't care; they just stand there, blank and still.

I wonder now exactly what Celeste said to Jesse when she came looking for the shearling coat and found all our mother's things gone, her house empty, a sketchy-looking dude painting the walls. I can imagine her playing the grieving younger daughter, shocked at her older sister's selfishness and coldness, her chest heaving: "All her things are gone? I can't believe Rachel would do this to me!" She must have told Jesse that she took care of our dying mother while I stayed away—he already knew that, I'd told him myself. But hearing it from Celeste must have clinched his harsh judgment, made him see me through her eyes. This bothers me, and the fact that it bothers me bothers me even more.

After what feels like another hour of humping myself through bogs and climbing hills, I stop and turn in a slow circle, looking outward for any glimmer of direction through the trees. But I find only a terrifying uniformity. It strikes me that you could not devise a better environment in which to trap a lost animal. It's as if the trees themselves planned it, luring me in with the careful intelligence of a spider, their network of roots underneath my feet a kind of web, waiting to absorb the minerals from my organs, the carbon from my bones as I decompose.

I wonder what's going on back at the camp. Celeste is no doubt pissed that I didn't wake her up for lunch. I wonder if Jean will send Willie out to look for me when it starts getting dark. But no doubt the rain has washed away any signs of my passage, so even a keen old tracker like Willie might be stymied.

A white orb burns through the clouds straight ahead of me; the sun, lowering. That means that I'm heading west now, which I decide to believe is the right direction. But if I can't find my way back to camp by sundown, I'll have to spend a night in these woods. I set off again, limping a little. A blister has formed on my right heel from the chafing of my damp sock. My left knee has a crick in it.

I imagine my sister's reaction to Jesse's unexpected presence in her mother's house, her high-handed outrage at his audacity, a duchess catching a commoner in her boudoir. Poor guy—his only crime was working for the too-low wage I offered him. She must have made him feel like a turd on the bottom of her shoe. He probably also thought I didn't deserve to inherit that house. There I was, selling it as fast as I could, right after my mother died. I wasn't sentimental about it, or her, at all. He could just as easily have killed himself outside on the lawn, if that's what he needed to do. But instead he probably thought, Fuck this whole family, I'm burning this place down first chance I get.

Along with being pissed at him, I'm hurt. I can't fathom his hatred of me. He knew my situation, he knew I was shit out of luck, and he knew I used to be a poor Maine kid like him. I thought I treated him well. I fed and housed him and walked his dog and confided in him and worried about him. I let him choose Shaker cabinet fronts. I trusted him. Oh well. Big mistake.

And maybe it wasn't just me and my family he hated, but the house itself, everything it represented to him. He chose to live rough. Maybe he couldn't stomach the thought of the futile stupid lives of the entire human race, living in shitty little boxes, waiting to die. Maybe burning the house down along with his overdose was also an act of intentional sabotage, a kind of protest, like climate activists who set themselves on fire, public deaths to call attention to all the things they can't change any other way.

Okay, this last scenario seems unlikely; Jesse didn't strike me as someone given to grand gestures. But how the hell do I know who he was? Everyone contains all manner of secret selves.

The real truth is that I will never know why Jesse burned my mother's house down.

I hear the stream before I see it. Its banks are thickly grown with ferns, and it seems wider than the stream I crossed before. As I follow it downstream on its meandering way through the bottom of the forest, slopes rise on either side. For an instant, I think I see open lake water glinting through the trees. But it's just a patch of wet lichen on a granite outcropping catching the watery sun through the underbrush, a shimmering mirage.

I peer ahead into more woods that look exactly the same as those I've been walking through all day. Soon the sun will set. I think about climbing a tree to get my bearings, but these trees all look impossible to climb, too weak and spindly to bear my weight, not high enough to reward the risk. All I could see from the top would be more trees.

I'm so thirsty. A trickle of sweat runs down the small of my back, and won't evaporate or absorb into the cloth of my shirt. It just sits there like a puddle. My empty stomach shrieks. My legs are blocks of lead. I see myself only a few hours ago, traipsing through the meadow like a chow-derhead, setting off on what I idiotically assumed would be a nice little walk in the woods.

High above the forest's leafy ceiling, the early-evening sky is now clear and blue. I peer ahead into the trees and see more trees, more forest, more undergrowth, and the occasional hulking gray boulder. The air is struck through by low sunlight, shafts shooting sideways through the trees, making a striped pattern with the dark, solid tree trunks.

There's a good chance I'm walking straight into the deep wilderness. And even if I'm not, this place is so wild, the trees so dense, I could pass within a hundred yards of the camp or the lake and never know how close I came. Maybe I'll die out here. That seems as likely an outcome as any right now.

At this thought, I feel my mood soar into optimistic expansiveness. There's probably a sound neurochemical explanation for this. I chalk it up to the stress of being lost and afraid, which has apparently made me go happily insane. This reminds me of my entire childhood, which I survived by manufacturing this same sanguine, irrational buoyancy in the face of grim hopelessness. The woods are a gilded living kingdom. The lumps of granite look like friendly gnomes; powdery bark curls off the birches' trunks, heavy rich paper engraved with rust-colored lines like a wedding invitation; the ferns are comical, elegant hairdos on invisible heads. So I'm lost in the woods, oh well. I might die sooner instead of later. No one living being in this place is any more or less important than any other. A fern, a hawk, a bit of lichen, a tree—they're all equals, they all have their place. Everything dies, a transfer of energy, a passing of matter into a new phase. Time will pass, and things will change. I am not stuck in stasis, because nothing is. And that's the deepest truth of all. If I die here, my body will become useful as food and mulch. It can feed the insects, the worms, and then I'll be part of all of this, too. Okay then.

After the sun sets, the woods are plunged into a lingering half-light, a deepening gloom. I estimate I have about half an hour before it's too dark to see. I stop again, rubbing the small of my back, yawning, flexing my aching knees, doing squats. I'm looking for a hollow to bed myself down in, padded with pine needles and safely far from any game trails. I've been walking for so long, the sound of my own footsteps crunching loudly in my ears. The quietude of the woods beats in on me, oppressively inhuman. There's the low murmur of moving water, sleepy bedtime discussions among the birds, a rustling as nocturnal animals emerge, the warm low-lying daytime air lifting with a great collective sough through branches into the cooling sky. I feel a chill on the back of my neck.

Off to my right there's a sound that I think at first is human, a huffing exhalation, branches crackling, a grunt. I almost call out, thinking it's Willie come to find me. Then I catch a whiff of rank organic filth, and I realize it's an animal, a large one, probably a black bear, and it knows I'm here, too. I can't see it, but I can hear it make its slow way in a semicircle around where I'm standing, as if it's curious about me, sussing me out.

I pick up the biggest stick I can find and hoist it as I move to the stream and cross it, walking as fast as I can without running, staying by the water, hoping to mask my tracks, my noises and scent. Across the stream, through the underbrush, I glimpse movement in the dim light. I can hear branches cracking under the bear's massive weight. Every now and then, I catch a whiff of reeking fur. It's keeping pace with me, stalking me.

I know that unprovoked bear attacks on people are extremely rare. I also know that black bears are shy and unlikely to kill humans. Neither of these facts is comforting right now. I'm so scared I'm keening in the back of my throat. It's one thing to think about dying of exposure, starvation, or hypothermia. It's another thing entirely to contemplate being eaten alive, fully conscious while my stomach is ripped open, my skull crushed, my limbs torn off, listening to the sound of my own body being consumed while I bleed out. This strikes me as the absolute worst of all possible deaths, that violent proximate intimacy with my own predator while it uses my living body as food.

My body is alight with adrenaline. I'm reduced to the state of all prey, a rabbit, a field mouse, jogging now, tripping and stumbling, catching myself, my breaths short and jagged. Every nerve in my body is sparking.

Looking down at a rushing stretch of water, I see a large rectangular metal box, half submerged in the stream and secured to a tree on the opposite bank with a metal wire looped through one of its handles. I squat down to get a closer look. When I unhook the metal loop and open it, I see several cans of beer floating there.

Up on the opposite bank looms a large, dark structure, rough and square. It takes a moment, a second glance: it's an old hunting cabin with a sloping moss-covered roof and a small shed off the back, stacked high with firewood.

Just like that, I know where I am. It's my grandfather's hunting cabin, eight or so miles from the camp on foot, and directly across the lake. I've looped around the lake, completely out of sight of it but instinctively keeping it on my left the entire time. Crouching on the bank, I go very still, listening. There's only the rush of the stream now, nothing else. The bear, if it was actually a bear, has melted back into the woods. My heart skitters with relief. I hop across the stream and find the half-hidden path leading up toward the cabin.

The ambient sounds of the woods fade away as I enter the clearing, back in human territory. I go up the steps and into a small dark room with rough pine flooring, bare rafters overhead, a plank table built into one wall, a small old woodstove next to it, a kindling basket next to a short woodpile. Two primitive wooden bunks, top and bottom, are built into a wall. Boxy hand-hewn cupboards line the wall by the latched door.

It's disorienting to be suddenly inside, almost like walking into another person's head, after being alone out in the wild woods all day. I've only ever been here once before, more than forty years ago, the year I turned twelve. As the oldest grandkid, I was invited along with Willie and Grandpa on a fishing trip as a sort of coming-of-age ritual. They fried the trout they caught for breakfast and dinner. I caught nothing and spent two miserable nights in a sleeping bag on the floor. Celeste was invited, or rather forced, to repeat this experience when she turned twelve. And of course Danny, the only boy of us three grandkids, was taken fishing and hunting with the men as soon as he was old enough to paddle a canoe, and every year afterward from then on. He spent a lot of time here.

And this was where he was living when he shot himself, out on the porch. He put his handgun in his mouth and blasted the back of his head off. And then he was free.

Quaking with thirst, I find a semi-clean-looking tin mug and fill it from a large plastic container of "spring water" sitting on a shelf. I drink it in one gulp, then fill another, and a third. I fish a can of baked beans out of a wooden box of ancient provisions in the corner, prying it open with a rusty can opener that looks like it predates my birth by a decade. I'm so hungry I want to swing open my torso on hinges and dump the canful directly into my stomach. Instead, I shove the baked beans from the can into my mouth with an old tin fork as fast as I can, barely chewing.

When I've eaten the whole thing, I take a few deep breaths to steady myself, looking around at my cousin Danny's life. No one seems to have been able to come and deal with it all. Everything appears to be untouched, just as it was right before he shot himself. The cabin is organized, in that everything has its place, but it's messy, too, my cousin's unwashed socks and underwear stowed under the bunk beds, a haphazard pile of clean dishes on the table, fishing gear jumbled together in the corner, as if Danny preferred to exist in ordered chaos, indecipherable and adolescent. He was in the army and a war veteran, so he had both the mindset of a trained soldier and the fucked-up traumatic aftermath of combat. The cabin holds the negative imprint of his presence, exactly the way my mother's house did hers. I can feel his afterglow, dissipated through the air of the place.

My stomach full, thirst slaked, I go down to the stream and palm a can of beer from the cold box, then saunter back up to sit on the bench, my back against the cabin's outer wall. I rest my feet on the railing, looking out at the darkening clearing. I wonder if I'm sitting in the exact spot where Danny killed himself. There's no visible trace on the rough weathered boards, no sign of his death at all. But I feel it. While I drink the beer, Danny's beer, I stare up at the darkening sky, watch stars pop out in pinlights. The funny bent tip-tops of hemlocks are silhouetted against the sky like shaggy wizard hats. The night air smells of fresh raw pumpkin, a sweet vegetable funk. I can hear various nocturnal creatures rustling. None of them sounds bigger than a raccoon.

I'm chilled in the night air, but for some reason I don't want to build a fire, either in the wood stove in the cabin or in the ring of rocks in the scruffy yard in front of it. It just feels like too much trouble. So I pull up the hood of my hoodie and hunker into its long sleeves, glad to be here instead of shivering in a pile of pine needles somewhere out in the night.

When I heard that my cousin had shot himself, I felt real regret. I feel it again now. I wish I had spent more time talking to Danny. But what I also feel, tempered by Jesse's death, is a respectful and odd sort of envy. Danny and Jesse couldn't take it anymore, so they chose to exit. They must have known too much to bear, both of them, after going to war. I don't blame either one of them for bugging out. They had every reason to escape the intolerable tedium and stress of lives with no reward, no hope that anything would ever be better.

Craning my neck back, I look up at the stars, the splashy arc of the Milky Way, and feel a detachment so profound it's like I'm untethered, floating. If I wanted to, I could choose to stay here and die like Danny did, remove my own wasteful body from the general global overload of human life, an act of conscious generosity. Literally no one needs me. All I do is take up space, consume resources, spew waste, contribute to the problem.

I wonder if I have the guts to do it. I can imagine the moment of putting the gun in my mouth, swallowing the pills, putting the plastic bag over my head, and then my imagination balks. I have no idea what happens after death, but based on accounts of people who've come back from near-death experiences, which is the only information we have, I've always vaguely and hopefully pictured floating up, up, and away to dissipate gradually into the ether. I'm not afraid of death, in fact I'm curious about it, but suicide boggles me. Almost every living thing actively resists its own death until the last gasp. Trapped animals gnaw off limbs; fish thrash in the net. Even houseflies run away from the swatter. Life wants itself. Taking the matter into your own hands goes radically against the natural way of things.

But what even is the natural way of things now? We've made our planet inhospitable to the life it sustains. It's likely that we've wiped ourselves out, and most other living things along with us—it's just a matter of time.

If that's not mass suicide, I don't know what is. So why not determine the manner and time of our own individual extinction? It's the only real control we have.

At this thought, a heavy wave of sleepiness rolls over me. I lurch to my feet and drag myself into the cabin. Plunking myself down on the lower bunk, I kick off my shoes and pull the scratchy wool blanket over me. The air in here is frigid, the mattress lumpy and hard, but I barely notice before I'm pulled down deep.

I wake at first light and put my shoes back on. The air snaps with cold as I step out the door, head out to the far edge of the clearing, pull down my pants, and hang my ass over a log, trying not to shiver. Wiping myself with a fern, I pull my pants back up, scrub my hands on a clump of moss, and walk back toward the cabin. When I put on my hoodie, it smells of yesterday's flop sweat and dirt. Breakfast is four heaping spoonfuls of instant coffee mixed with cold water in a cup, then a crusty old jar of Skippy that I carry out to the porch, where I sit on the planks in the warming sunlight and spoon peanut butter into my mouth.

Here I am, still attending to this body I live in, dragging it forth into yet another day.

I set off in silence. My dream-soaked brain is still turning over slowly, sputtering, a cold engine. My legs and back are stiff from yesterday's hours of walking and the long night on the hard bunk. My joints have been aching on and off in general, a sign that I'm not young anymore, as if I needed another one. Even so, I find myself relaxing into the walk, now that I know where I'm going. The trees and stream and spongy ground blur into benign familiarity as the woods slide harmlessly, featurelessly by.

As I follow the stream downhill over pine needles and moss, I fall into a rhythm of motion, occasionally tripping over rocks and roots but lulled into a half-conscious stupor, as if I'm sleepwalking. The mist burns off as the sunlight reaches the hollows, leaking through the trees and dancing on the moving stream, glinting on the rocks. Somewhere not far off, a woodpecker machine-guns its bill against a tree trunk, fast hollow pocks.

All at once, the enfolded, textured safety of the woods opens out into the enormous flat sunlit lake. And there's the Gautreau camp, straight across from where I stand. I wonder what Aunt Jean is doing right now. She's probably cooking breakfast, wondering where the hell I am. I can hear her snort at me for galumphing along on game paths, getting myself lost, stumbling with idiot luck on Grandpa's cabin. It makes me grin to think of my tough, cheeky old aunt, keeping it all going, stubbornly alive. She'll never give up. She'll die when she's absolutely forced to, not one second sooner. To do otherwise would be unseemly.

I look up and down the shoreline, but there's no canoe hidden in the underbrush. I strip and tie my clothes tightly into my zipped hoodie, tie the bundle around my neck, and stride barefoot into the water, clenching my teeth against the cold. I stumble on the rocks, which are smooth and slippery and hairy with algae. When the bottom turns sandy and smooth, I plunge in all the way, come up gasping to breathe. The cold is insane, irrational. I want to race out of the lake straight back into the woods. I strike out in a furious breaststroke, a scream bubbling in the back of my throat, then pull into a rhythmic crawl and head out into the sunny, empty lake. Slowly my body adjusts to the temperature as my muscles wake up.

Halfway across, I take a break and lie on my back, making slow snow-angel patterns with my arms and legs in the water to stay afloat, looking up at the clouds. The sky is pure intense blue, with little fleecy puffs of white floating through it. The smell of the water, alive with animal and plant and mineral matter, bacteria and microbes and algae and decomposed life, penetrates deep into the most ancient folds of my brain. I'm part of it, and it's part of me.

My mother is in this lake. Her ashes have dispersed throughout, tiny bits of her burned body suspended in the water. She's the literal lady in the lake. She lives here now, Lucie; this is where she is.

I turn myself around and around in the water, feeling heady with expansion, like I'm stretching far out of my own head, beyond my limited self, inhabiting the whole world. I catch my breath on the surprised joy of being outside myself and fully embodied at the same time. My young body is gone forever, has turned into this infertile older one with joints that twinge and muscles that aren't as strong as they used to be. But it houses a brain as sharp as glass.

I tread water, looking back at the shore I just came from, a nondescript spit of land choked with pine and fir and spruce, interrupted by a stand of birch flashing bone white in the sunlight. It's all silent over there, dark scraggly forest growing to the banks, low hills rising uninterrupted to the sky. Beyond that shore, the lake folds itself into a series of coves and inlets meeting forested fingers of land and disappears. I can't see the end of it.

I turn again to look at the familiar silvered boards of the boathouse and dock of Gautreau Camps. What's waiting for me over there is the rest of my life. An inherited dog. A rented room in Bayside. A job I may or may not be suited for. A tipsy, opinionated book group. My mother's old car. The only family I'll ever have.

Whole lives have been built on much less.

I pull myself into a crawl again and launch myself toward all of it, swimming as hard as I can.

About the Author

KATE CHRISTENSEN is the author of seven novels, most recently *The Last Cruise*. Her fourth novel, *The Great Man*, won the 2008 PEN/Faulkner Award for Fiction. She has also published two food-centric memoirs, *Blue Plate Special* and *How to Cook a Moose*, which won the 2016 Maine Literary Award for Memoir. Her essays, reviews, and short pieces have appeared in a wide variety of publications and anthologies. She lives with her husband and their two dogs in Taos, New Mexico.